The Opposite Sides of a Coin

Dominic Wong

First edition May 2021

Book design by Karen Lloyd
Author photography by Owen Vachell

ISBN: 979-8-73-207310-2

www.DominicWongBooks.co.uk

For Mum and Dad

The Opposite Sides of a Coin

Boys are devils who become angels.
Girls are angels who become devils.

Parenting proverb, Anon

Part One

'Lucy'

It was the blood running down her face that woke her. It was in her eyes. In her hair. In her mouth. She could taste it. She could even hear it, throbbing and pulsing from her head. She could hear something else too.

Footsteps. Downstairs. Pacing.

Lucy tried to open her eyes. A sliver of sunlight burned her retina, adding to the pain coursing through her body. She winced and turned her face, her cheek nestling deeper into the soft fibres of the carpet. The other cheek was burning from the pain. Through a half-squint she could see the white window frame, the skies darkened outside, the white wooden cross in the middle of the pane. Her red curls, fallen down over her eyes, dangled lifelessly, swaying to the soft breeze of her breath. Another wet stream inched slowly down her head and onto her neck. She closed her eyes and willed the throbbing to stop. Of course, she'd been beaten before – her father, the bullies at school, random strangers in the street.

This was different.

The plastic cutting into her wrists and ankles for one. Being tied to a tipped-over chair that was restricting her every movement another. The closed door left little chance for a hero to rescue her. There was always someone – a passer-by, a good Samaritan, a policeman – that would warn her attackers off. No chance of that. She needed her wits and for that she needed to focus.

Lucy replayed the events of the last few days, the preceding months, the 'lost' years between university and moving to London. It was supposed to have been different, a chance for a new life, make new friends. Perhaps even find love to alleviate her lonely existence. But she had always been on her guard. And now this. She took in a lungful of air and held it as long as she could, feeling the throbbing subside. She straightened her back as much as she could against the back of the fallen chair, pushed back her shoulders and worked her neck. Confidence started to build in her, strength from deep within seemed to course through her veins. Her body was ridged – poised – and now her brain started scrambling. She knew his secret. But he didn't know hers.

Well, the other one. The one he hadn't worked out.

He was in a funk about that rhyme, the one that had popped into her head when she had seen the photographs. It had given her time to think and a morsel of satisfaction whilst her wrists were tied behind her back.

With a nick nack paddy whack.

The rhyme gave her courage. It had touched a nerve.

The footsteps got louder. Heavy and deliberate. Up the wooden stairs and then muted on the thick carpet. The door flung open as he entered the room. BANG! She closed her eyes again and tensed her muscles, ready for a casual blow – a kick to the head or torso – but it didn't come. She heard the door click shut and the padding shoes stopped at her head. He cupped her chin in his hands. The corners of her mouth curled into a smile.

Showtime.

Chapter One

"Hey! HEY!"

Lucy heard the booming voice behind her but chose to ignore it. Amongst the throng of commuters, he could have been shouting at anyone. She kept her head down and quickened her pace.

"Excuse me!"

She felt a hard tap on her shoulder and braced herself.

"Oh," he muttered as she turned and faced him. He quickly averted his eyes down to a pink glove in his outstretched hand.

"Erm. You dropped this." A blush arose on his face and his ears.

It was her glove. A frilly hem around the cuff.

"Oh," she said and took it off him. "Thanks."

His eyes shot back up to her face. Staring.

"Do I have something on my face?" she said. "It's my lipstick, isn't it? I've smudged it again."

"No, no," he stammered and hurried past her without another word.

She tucked the glove into the handbag hanging off her shoulder, gripped the straps and ducked into the dreary, drizzly day. She hurried along the Hungerford Bridge, keeping her head down and eyes on the ground in front of her, thinking about the man wondering what thoughts had been running through his mind, what assumptions he had made. She wanted to take them from her brain and throw them into the brown sludge of water below her. Normally, she enjoyed the respite of the bridge after being pushed up against the glass of the train doors by the sardined commuters on their daily migration from the suburbs to the centre of London. But now she was in a bad mood. She slowed her pace and let commuters dance around her, their heads down or lost in a world within their headphones.

Disconnected from the humans around them. If she had screamed, it wouldn't have made any difference. A glance or two perhaps. A side-step.

Just another weirdo.

So much for moving to the Big City to meet people.

She reached the middle of the bridge and stepped into an alcove that jutted out over the river. The view from the Eastern side was her favourite view of London, opening up the panorama to reveal the mix of the old and the new, St. Paul's Cathedral dwarfed by the imposing financial skyscrapers of the 21st Century. Each year, the façade changed, but underneath – in the bowels of the capital's soul – nothing changed at all.

She took several deep breaths in, filling her lungs and exhaling with force, determined to change her mindset into the positive. Breathing in a calm colour, expelling the angry colour. How many times had she done that standing on a precipice looking down? Familiar feelings ran over every inch of her being and then dissipated with every outbreath. Therapy had helped her a lot. A horn from a pleasure boat honked bringing her conscious back and scaring the pigeons that roosted in the girders. A few zealous tourists raced to look down at the near-empty vessel. The red lettering on its side was faded and cracked, peeling off.

That could do with a lick of paint.

The sky darkened and a light drizzle began. People around her hitched up their collars, some putting their newspapers on their heads. The steps down were slippery from the new rain, so she trod carefully in her pumps (she had never got used to heels) and turned into the tube station, a brief break from the rain. She patted her head to feel the damage – water was never good for curly hair. She hurried through the station and out the other side, into a narrow street that bustled with people and deliveries. The streets were dirty with grime from centuries of rubbish and dust blown along this slender street. Dampened cardboard and strewn paper stuck to the ground by the rain.

Charing Cross station's courtyard teemed with delivery vans and taxis, dropping suited men with long black umbrellas at the station entrance. They looked up to the sky as they exited the back of their black taxis, slamming the doors shut and hurrying inside. Umbrellas were not needed for the short hop to the dry insides of the station, nor the rain threatening enough to get their masculine tailor-made suits too wet. Towering above them, stone sculptures of Queen Eleanor and angels looked down on them – and on Lucy. The monument used to mark the spot where all distances to and from London were measured, and here she was – right at the centre of it all. She had traversed this spot many times whilst criss-crossing London, head down in a travel guide, getting her bearings. Lucy had visited so many times over the past few years – changing her clothes in the train's toilets away from the accusing eyes of her father – blending into the scene and the scenery, getting used to it, before making the big move south.

The drizzle intensified, a possibility that a downpour was due. She zigzagged through the increasingly busy street, past workmen in dirty yellow overalls and women in high heels and knee-length skirts, their calves toned and tanned. She crossed the road, dodged past stationary red buses, tooting scooters and black taxis. It felt as if their dirt and grease attached themselves to her nostrils. She got to the heavy door of Starbucks as a woman left and squeezed in before it shut out the rest of the world. A whiff of coffee hit her nose and a sense of warmth, familiarity and safety enveloped her. Her bad mood was lightening. She checked her hair – nearly thirty years of having a mop of red curls on her head meant she knew how uncontrollable it was. Only now it was longer, down to her shoulders, much more difficult to manage. She self-consciously smoothed the back of her hair down and joined the queue of people waiting to order their coffee.

Al greeted her like an old friend as she got to the counter.

"Ah, Miss Lucy! A flat white with an extra shot as usual?" he grinned.

His green apron was spotless, and his infectious smile showed off his white teeth against his brown bristly moustache.

He was the type of employee that faceless chains loved to recruit and were lucky to have. He was genuinely happy to see you; made you smile and got you what you ordered efficiently and effectively. Whilst it gave Lucy a warm feeling inside – someone familiar, who knew her and remembered her order – she knew that it was an act. He didn't really *know* her of course, just recognised her face and what she liked to drink. It was a little bit of fake happiness in an otherwise depressingly lonely city of 10 million inhabitants.

"As always please, Al," Lucy replied with a dry smile.

"Anything I can tempt you with to go with your beverage?" he asked, his hand splayed across the plastic-wrapped calories along the counter and his eyes darting to the croissants and muffins. This small part of the act of faux friendliness ruined the illusion. A script.

"No, thanks," she said as she did every morning.

He tapped on his screen.

"Please, Miss Lucy, when you are ready."

He gestured to the card machine on the counter and she glided her credit card across it. Even paying for stuff was contactless.

"Thanks Al," she said as he handed over the receipt.

He was already looking at the next customer as she shuffled along the counter to the pick-up point. Lucy thought about getting her phone out of her pocket as she waited for the shushing and the popping of the coffee machines to deposit her morning drink. Anything to avoid making eye-contact with someone gawping at her. She resisted the urge. Emails could wait a few more minutes until she got into the office, and she couldn't be bothered to scroll through the mind-numbing social media updates of people having wonderful, exciting lives. She stood with her back to the wall and sighed. Almost all the tables were full of young people, some with their laptops out and some with their shoulders hunched over their phone, as if protecting it. Teenagers sat opposite each other with one earphone in their ear, the other lifelessly dangling, staring at their own devices, checking Instagram posts of other people socialising and having fun, rather than chatting to the person opposite them. She felt her eyes glaze over.

"Lucy! LUCY!!"

She snapped out of her trance and wrapped her fingers around the oversized mug that sat on the counter. A small bit of warmth came through to her fingers. She looked up and tried to spot a spare seat. There were no empty tables so she would have to awkwardly sit with someone else. A small dread arose in her chest. A middle-aged man with his back to the wall stared at her, his arms folded across his chest, his head cocked to one side. His eyebrows suggested a hint of recognition.

Not you.

She scanned the other tables, customers, bags and trays and spotted a chair haphazardly poking out, as if someone had been in a hurry to leave and hadn't pushed it back in. A man, about her age she reckoned, sat opposite it, his head bent over a silver laptop furiously tapping on the keys. She walked over, zigzagging past the higgledy-piggledy tables and bags that littered the floor and stood by the empty chair. He seemed to be in the zone of whatever he was doing, oblivious to the to-ing and fro-ing's of the customers going in and out. She considered clearing her throat to get his attention but stood awkwardly instead, hoping her presence would make him glance up.

He was what Lucy would call a classic, good-looking guy. His dark hair was cut short at the back and sides and a small quiff protruded at his fringe. His face was symmetrical, giving him a handsome clean-cut look. He had kind, brown eyes, and it seemed to her that the small dimple on his left cheek gave him a schoolboy innocence. He wore a white, American style button-down shirt with the sleeves rolled up, like the ones worn by frat boys. A dark blue bird logo sat on his breast, matching a dark blue t-shirt underneath. It accentuated his muscles touching the cotton fabric.

Nice.

Bright blue trainers tapped quickly under the table. His skin looked smooth and healthy. A sign he looked after himself. He seemed familiar and she thought about all the 90s romcom Hollywood movies she had seen and the guys she had had crushes on. Crumpled next to him was a grey hoodie, the JW of Jack Wills just visible. She unconsciously tucked a stray lock of her red curly hair behind her ear. A crash of crockery and cutlery behind the counter caused him to look up suddenly. Lucy stood stock still. His brown eyes locked on to hers, the corner of his mouth upturned slightly.

"Hey," he said, revealing a line of perfect teeth.

"Hi."

She waited for the rejection. Instead, the void between them narrowed.

"Erm, can I help you?" he drawled in an East Coast accent.

"Um, oh. Er, can I sit here?" Lucy felt her face redden. "Please?"

"Oh, yeah, sure," he replied, half standing.

"Thanks," she said softly.

"Let me just get this stuff cleared away for ya." Lucy flushed; his American accent made her giddy. He adjusted the position of his laptop to give her more room to put her mug down.

"Sorry, er, thanks," she said back, sheepishly, feeling her ears burn.

He moved his laptop so it was square in front of him and hovered his fingers over the keyboard. She averted her eyes and placed her white mug on the table, away from the spill zone of his laptop. She pretended to be busy, her way of not having to make small talk, although she really wanted to. She decided not to get her mobile phone out. Instead, she fussed in her bag and looked around the room, occasionally glancing to see if he was looking at her. The noises from the café seemed to disappear, the customers blurred away in her peripheral. She stole a glance at him, noticing the beginnings of crow's feet on the side of his eyes and the tiny freckles on the bridge of his nose. When their eyes met, he darted his away. Then he looked back and she held his eyes. She stared into his light brown eyes, the ones you could sink yourself into for hours and hours. He gazed deeply at her too, penetrating her eyes and then looking around her entire face. Her eyes, her lips, her cheeks, her hair.

There was an intensity. A feeling that he was not just looking *at* her but *into* her, deep within her soul – how she felt, how she viewed the world, what her future might be. Perhaps. There were not many men she had met that could understand her.

The bang of the till shutting snapped him out of his trance, his brow unfurled and looked at her as if in amazement, as if she was a celebrity he had only seen on screen and who was now sat in front of him in real life. She was mesmerized too. There was an intangible charm, a boyish look of a lad next door, one of familiarity, innocence and safety. He was the type of man Lucy could take to see her mum, who would squeeze her hand as if she'd made a good choice.

A gust of wind blew in through the door as a heavy-set woman backed into the café wrestling an umbrella, trying to fold it away. He rolled his eyes and pursed his lips. She smiled an embarrassed smile.

It seemed neither were sure what to say or who should speak next. Lucy unconsciously tucked a curl back behind her ear, looking down at the table. He watched, mesmerised, as if he had never seen anyone do that before.

She took a deep breath, her shoulders rose, her chest puffed out. She was going for it.

"Er, sorry to have disturbed you, you looked busy," she offered, finally, glancing down to his laptop. The ice had been broken.

"Oh, no, not at all," he dismissed, shaking his head. "Not. At. All. Just working on a coupla of things, ya know." His consonants slurred into one. He shut the laptop lid down immediately, giving her his full attention.

"You're not from around here, are you?"

As the words came out of her mouth, she immediately cringed at the crassness of the line. She felt like a right idiot. Still, it was a question which warranted an answer.

"No, I'm not." He smiled a cute smile. The lines around his eyes creased, confirming the thought that he was older than she had suspected, perhaps even a little more than she had first thought.

"I guess you can call it a vacation, I'm here for a few days, maybe longer, hoping to get some inspiration." His eyes darted back to his computer and immediately back up again.

"Let me guess, east coast?" Lucy said.

"You guessed right! New York State originally, then I moved out to Colorado Springs, by the mountains."

"Oh, very nice!" She felt herself slipping into his charms like a melt-in-the-mouth biscuit oozing over your tongue. She had always had a thing for the New York accent, it must be her brother's addiction to Robert de Niro and Joe Pesci films when they were growing up. But probably more Ross Geller.

"And what are you trying to be inspired about?"

He wasn't forthcoming with the conversation, so she tried to fill the gaps. He was still gazing deeply within her eyes, and when she spoke his eyes moved to her lips, watching every word that came out, like a deaf person lipreading. She tried to remember what she had had for breakfast, hoping he wasn't staring at a stray bit of food stuck between her teeth.

"Um, well. I know it's going to sound kinda odd and dumb but I'm trying to write a book."

He looked sheepishly at her waiting for some kind of approval.

"Oh, no, that's not dumb at all. We all want to try and do something like that but never have the time, do we?"

"Yeah, I guess so. Well, I've got some time now, so I thought I'd give it a go. I doubt it will go anywhere except this Mac though."

"You don't know till you try, right? What's it about?"

"Yeah. Sure," he hesitated. "Erm, well, it's about this American guy who comes to London after his wife dies, and er, meets this girl." He looked nervous, "And, um, falls in love."

"Classic," she responded nodding her head, "Love at first sight? How does it end? Guessing it's a 'happy ever after'?"

He chuckled, a deep laugh from within.

"Well, no, she, erm, dies in the end," he said, and Lucy gave a mock-sad face.

A glint shone in his eye.

"Well, if I told you, I'd ruin the ending, right? And then you wouldn't buy the book, then I wouldn't get world famous and rich!"

She joined him in his fantasy with a giggle. They looked at each other again, in silence. The air between them charged and comfortable. The lonely outside world disappeared from her mind. He snapped out of it first.

"Erm, I guess you're from around here then," he asked.

"Yes, yes I am," she blinked. "Well, originally from Nottingham. You know, where Robin Hood lived."

"Oh, that's so cool!"

His eyes lit up.

"*I'd die for you, walk the world for you, uh-oh*," he sang out tunelessly. Lucy grinned at him, her mouth askew, warming to him every second.

"Yeah, something like that!"

Silence enveloped them again.

"So, what do you do then?" he asked, picking up his mug.

"Oh, I, erm, work in PR. Boring. Oh dammit! What time is it?!"

She stood slightly to get her phone out of her pocket and the screen came to life. *9:17.*

"I'm late for work!"

She jumped onto her feet and looked about the table and the chair to gather her things. He stood up and tried to speak. It seemed he wanted to say something, but the words got stuck in his throat.

"Well, it was nice to meet you…" The words hung in his mouth.

"Lucy," she responded, "Lucy." Her hand automatically reached out. He took it, firm and assured, and gave it a gentle shake. An electric charge seemed to go through her fingers.

"Joe," he countered confidently. "My name is Joe." Their hands didn't leave each other as quickly as they should for two strangers who had just met. Lucy bit down on her lip as she considered walking out of the coffee shop to her dull office.

"Joe. It was nice to meet you, Joe. Good luck with your romance." She removed her hand and shot her eyes to his laptop.

"Oh, yes. It's not a romance actually. More of a thriller. Thank you, though." His eyebrows furled again, as if he was about to say something painful.

"I'd love you to read it sometime. Get an honest opinion." He looked up and into her eyes – that penetrating gaze again.

"Erm, look, I don't know anyone here. It sure would be nice to get a bit of local knowledge. You know, research for my book. I like to be meticulous in my planning." That cheeky smile came back. Lucy couldn't help but smile in return.

"Yes," she said confidently, straightening her spine. "Yes, I can be your tour guide."

The words came out a bit too fast and excitedly as her lips cracked into a wide grin. She felt the colour rise in her cheeks, making her light freckles disappear.

"Awesome, that's just what I need. When do you finish work?"

"Uh, um, just after 5. I can meet you here if you like."

"Sounds like a, uh, plan." She wondered if the word 'date' fluttered in his mind like it did in hers. "I'll be waiting outside. Promise."

With that he sat back down and she turned to walk out of the door. An elderly chap held the door open for her; his hand curled around his takeaway cup. He bowed his head as she thanked him as she turned back and saw Joe watching her leave. His face neutral, a wry smile etched on his face.

Outside, the sky had dried up but the black clouds sat low. She hitched up the collar of her coat as traffic and noise filled her ears. She headed through the throng of the crowd to the office, a spring in her step, her heart beating wildly. Maybe her decision to move to London for a new life wasn't so bad after all.

Chapter Two

Lucy rushed to the big, transparent frontage of the PR agency where she worked. An account manager in his suit and tie arrived at the door at the same time. Kieran, she thought his name was.

"Sorry mate," said a skinny guy with a long pole cleaning the glass, as he moved a light blue bucket full of shammies and cloths out of the way with his foot. Kieran hurried in through the door before her. The window-cleaner shook his head at Lucy and gave an exaggerated rolling of his eyes. The dark hair on his chin and top lip reminded her of her dad's moustache: the times he used to kiss her mum full on the lips, as she fell into a fit of giggles; how he had nonchalantly stroked it as he watched the television; the way it used to twitch when he was shouting, the only thing that stood out on his angry face when her eyes were blurry with tears.

Who would want to have a moustache? And who would want to kiss a man with one, all tickly and itchy?

Lucy rolled her eyes back in response and stepped inside the vast void of the reception area. Her footsteps echoing on the tiled floor. A quadrant of awkward-looking chairs, a glass table with that day's newspapers placed lopsided on it and a curving lampshade looking like an island in a sea of space decorated the huge space. A distance away an imposing reception desk stood like a pantheon, ready to welcome the company's visitors. Behind it, Johnny, an unambitious school dropout, spun side-to-side on a small black chair, his thin black tie slightly askew on his shirt which had the top button undone. Lucy waved a greeting as per usual and he nodded back, his eyes closing and opening in perfect rhythm to his head going down and up. Behind him stood the company's logo, in huge 6-foot lettering, a Latin name with no relevance to PR, but full of values and corporate bullshit.

Lucy beeped her pass through the heavy wooden doors and stepped into a light and carpeted open-plan office. The only sounds that greeted her were the tapping of keys and people talking loudly on phones. Jess raised her head above her computer screen like a dome from the depths. Her straight bleached-blonde hair with a perfect centre-parting showed first, then her curled fake eyelashes fluttered up and down, framing bright blue eyes, as she saw Lucy walk towards her. She raised a hand and waved. Lucy self-consciously waved back looking around to see who else had seen her arrive late. No-one seemed to notice. She walked past the foosball table, the staple piece of furniture in today's trendy workplace, as Kieran joined a couple of account managers by the coffee machine in the kitchen. They glanced up at Lucy as she quickly walked past. Bright green, shiny apples sat in a wooden bowl by the sink.

"Hiya! Trains running late again, huh," Jess said as Lucy reached out to switch on her PC. It wasn't a question as she wasn't expecting an answer.

"I had a nightmare this morning," she continued, oblivious to any response that might come her way. "I was sitting on this train and this guy sits down next to me and he STINKS. Then he opens a packet of cheese and onion crisps and stinks the whole carriage out even more. I mean, he's a scoffer, he just shoves the crisps in his mouth and bits just like fall on me. And the noise! Like, shut your mouth when you eat, man! Then, THEN, he wipes his hands on his jeans. Ew!"

She said the last word like an American high-schooler, immediately pulling Lucy back to Joe, the thought of him growing up with perfectly formed, cheerleader-type girls like Jess, flirting and pouting in the school hallways.

"That's disgusting," Lucy retorted to confirm her approval, screwing up her face.

"Yeah, it was. And first thing in the morning too. Why do guys do that?" Again, it wasn't a question that warranted an answer.

"And he was ugly," she said to herself as if that closed the case. She twirled the end of her hair with her index fingers, rolling it over and over again. Lucy turned back to her machine and fired up her emails.

"So, how was last night?" she asked swivelling back to give Jess the attention she craved.

"OMG, it was amazing!" As Jess crossed her legs, her miniskirt rode up her thigh and more firm, tanned skin showed, just enough to get the guys, and her male clients, excited.

"My bestie Kaz came over. She's flying off somewhere tonight, so we opened a bottle of white. O. M. G. I haven't laughed so much in ages. We were trolling this weirdo on Insta, he's been liking all of Kaz's posts and writing seriously raunchy comments. You wouldn't believe the things he put."

She turned and bent down to her handbag to find her phone, whipped it out and furiously typed in the passcode in a flurry like a swordfighter giving a final blow. Instagram opened up.

"You got to see them Luce."

Lucy recoiled. She hated the word. It was Lucy. Not Luce. How many times did she have to tell her?

"It's ok, I believe you Jess."

"I know I know but you got to see them." Her perfectly filed thumbnail with crimson polish pushed the screen upwards. Images and photos of people, with blue skies and food, flew up.

"Here, check this one out, we were crying over this one!"

Lucy smiled deliberately and gave the 'oh what!' cry to hasten the conversation on.

"So you were, what, just saying nasty things back to this guy?"

"Yeah, I mean look at the things he was writing on her posts, he deserved them, right?" She showed her another comment, with language that would make your mother-in-law blush.

"Sounds like a fun night Jess," Lucy said emotionless, turning her attention to her inbox. She wasn't interested in the name-calling and bullying; she had had enough of that for a lifetime.

"Totally was Luce!"

Jess became absorbed in her phone and her Insta feed, giggling every now and then with memories of the previous night's debauchery. Jess's life seemed so much more exciting to Lucy than her own. A bubbly blonde versus a frizzly redhead. She knew who would win that one in a head-to-head contest with the guys. Last night she had curled up on the sofa with a trashy novel and her cat sat on her feet. Perhaps Joe could be the one to break her out of her shell, and be more like Jess – full of stories, excitement and confidence.

Lucy clicked through the unread emails and quickly became distracted by social media. She scrolled through the dross of Facebook. Scrolling and scrolling. Pictures of people having a better time than her. The false veneer of ego. The desirable front stage hiding the messy backstage. It was a never-ending feed of showing how wonderful other people's lives were compared to your own. She remembered Joe and thought about searching for him. Did he have a girlfriend? What did his exes look like? What was he doing today? She started to type "Joe" into the search box but quickly deleted it. How stupid. She didn't even know his surname. Or anything about him for that matter. She heard footsteps come up behind her and closed down Facebook to look busy.

"Luce," a stern voice behind her said. She recoiled at that word again. "Luce, a quick word please."

It was Emma, her manager, who turned back to her office before Lucy got the chance to reply.

"Sure," she said anyway, to no-one in particular. Jess shot her a look as Lucy got up from her chair, picking up a notepad and pen before raising her eyebrows in a conspiracy nod.

She followed Emma into her office; a glass fronted box that could have easily made a goldfish feel at home. A transparent glass desk with a plush green plant and her laptop sat on top. Otherwise, it was completely devoid of anything else – not even a pen.

"Take a seat." She gestured to a round glass table with four black chairs around it. Emma sat in the one right next to her and crossed her legs. A sign of being warm and cosy; a friendly chat.

Well, at least it's not going to be bad news.

"Good night last night?" Emma asked, pushing her black-rimmed glasses up her nose. The warm words did not match her expression which read *I couldn't care less.*

"Yeah, it was alright, thank you. I didn't do much," Lucy replied, waiting for Emma to get to the point.

"How are you settling in here Luce? You've just moved down to London, and I know it can be a bit daunting. Are you making friends, going out … easily?"

"Yeah, it's fine" she said, her back straightening, thinking it had been almost a year since moving. "I'm settling in fine."

"I just want to make sure you're alright, you know? The guys in the office treating you ok." She looked over her glasses.

"Er, yeah. Why?" Lucy furrowed her brow at the remark.

"Oh nothing."

A silence snuck in between them. Emma shuffled in her seat.

"Um. Did you sort out that issue with your cat with your landlord?" She patted her hand on Lucy's knee and smiled awkwardly. Lucy looked down at the hand, a huge diamond on the ring finger. She had sorted out that 'issue' months ago.

"Thanks for asking Emma." She got the feeling that her boss needed a bit of sycophancy. "That's really kind of you to ask. Yes, it's all sorted. Bit of a pain but all done now. I like being here. It's a really nice company and everyone is so friendly."

"Yes, we try really hard. We are friendly here. That's the culture I wanted when I was brought in. I just want you to, you know…"

Ok, here we go.

"Well, we're a PR family and want our staff to embrace the culture of what PR means. And that family means our internal family and our external family."

She swept her hands over to create an arc with her fingers on 'internal' and spread them out on 'external'.

"We work hard but we also play hard. Get to know the team, come out for a few drinks. Mingle with our clients. Have some champers darling!"

An awkward silence filled the office. Lucy felt her face redden.

"Well, you know," Emma faltered. "Get involved a bit more. Let your hair down." There was again a touch of a patronising tone to her voice as she pushed up her glasses again. It was like she wasn't comfortable in Lucy's presence.

"Yeah, I know I should," she said. "It's just that I've tried to maintain a boundary between work life, and you know, home life." The emails on her iPhone already blurred the lines, and the office WhatsApp group constantly pulled her into work mode.

"Luce, as I said, we work hard here but we play hard. We are one big happy family."

Her mind flashed to Sophie; a senior account manager who had been made redundant a few weeks ago when they lost a big client. She had liked Sophie.

"I'm quite happy to play the weird aunt that sits in the corner."

Emma snort-laughed at the surprise of the comment.

"Just take my advice Luce. Reach out to our clients, invite them for a drink. Come down to the pub with us. You've got what it takes Luce, I'm sure you'll go far in PR." She surprised herself with a knowing nod and the corners of her mouth dropped down at the rhyme of the last sentence. Lucy was sure it would be on the next away day presentation.

"OK, thanks Emma. I really appreciate it."

"No problem," she said, patting her knee as she got up and moved back to her desk. As Lucy left her office, she called back.

"Oh, and one more thing Luce. Call me Em, yeah?"

"Yeah, alright. Em," she said leaving "Em" encapsulated in her glass cell.

Lucy ambled back to her desk. Jess was brimming with excitement, an expectation of gossip, unable to contain herself. She eventually gave in.

"Weeeelllll?" she asked. Lucy looked at her, blankly.

"Oh, nothing Jess. She just wanted to make sure I was settling in. Asked me to get involved a bit more, you know, with the clients."

"Damn good advice Luce. Get stuck in. Have some champagne whilst the company are paying. I went to this amazing bar the other week with Matt. You know Matt from P&G? OMG you should have seen the chandelier, and it was all decked out in red and gold plush seats. We were knocking back the shots. He got a bit handsy but nothing I couldn't handle." She dismissed it with a wave of her hand.

"Anyway, the next day he signed the extension to the contract. Boom!" She raised a hand and pretended to drop a microphone to the ground. Boom indeed.

"Yeah, not really my scene though," Lucy replied.

"Sod your scene, just go out and have a good time. Live your life and be a bit, less, you know, *stuffy*. Come on, Em's paying after all. She wants you to wine and dine the clients. Just a bit of flirting, let your gorgeous hair down, keep the champers flowing. What have you got to lose?"

Lucy blushed. She shrugged her shoulders, nodded and looked back at her screen.

"Yeah, I suppose." Perhaps she could try to be a bit less *stuffy* later with Joe – she could give it a try.

"Happy to give you tips if you want Luce," she said as she swirled back to her screen, finger twirling in her hair. All that was missing was a pop of bubble-gum to punctuate the end of the conversation.

The morning dragged on. A few emails came in from clients and Lucy wrote a couple of reports and made a smattering of calls to journalists. She wrote down everything she did ready for the end-of-week report, justifying the ridiculous hourly rates. She called a client and asked if they wanted to meet for a lunch or a few drinks, attempting to be flirty on the line.

She got a non-committal reply from her half-hearted try. Well, at least she tried.

At lunch, she went out along the Strand to get overpriced sushi from a hyped-up chain which was as tasteless as the cardboard it came in. She kept looking over her shoulder in case Joe was still around. She even peered through the window of Starbucks to see if he was still at the same table. Of course he wasn't. He was probably on an open-top bus tour, soaking in the sights of the capital, or traipsing the streets hoping to get a glimpse of the Queen.

She picked an empty bench looking out to the river, the dark slop making its pilgrimage to the sea, on its own journey. She settled down and looked across the water, reaching up to her neck where the scars used to be. Running her finger along her jawline her mind went back to her past, remembering her father's vice-like grip as he had forced her to the ground. *You ain't no child of mine,* he had spat in his clipped midlands accent, her mum screaming in the background to let go, the musty smell of sawdust prickling her nostrils. She could still feel the indents of each individual finger pushing into her neck, unable to move her head as the tips of his moustache tickled her ear as he roared into it. The sound of the door slamming and the comforting embrace of her mother, tears streaming down both of their faces. That was the first time, but there were many more to come.

The years after that blended into one: the struggles, the thoughts, the hurt and the violence. It was London that became her salvation. The tall buildings and alleyways that enabled her to hide in the shadows, away from the looks and recovering from the pain. She could keep to herself on the frequent visits, staying in featureless hostels and B&Bs, until confidence came to her. Her mother said it would take a while for the scars to heal, but in reality, they would be etched inside her forever.

No amount of counselling or time would allow her to forget her past.

Chapter Three

"Are you sure love?" she had said as she ran a finger along the mantle-piece and screwed up her face.

"Yeah mum, I'm sure. There's loads of jobs and loads of opportunities in London."

It was almost a year since Lucy decided that London was to be her home. New York had been a close contender but that felt just too alien and too far away. Her English accent would cause her too much attention and she didn't want to stand out. She wanted to blend in where nobody knew her.

"No, not that. I meant living on your own."

"We're not having this conversation again."

"I know, but London is just so-" She peered out of the first-floor flat window at the rows of terraced houses across the road. "-big." She bit her tongue. She wanted to say *lonely* too.

"It's fine. I want my own bathroom. I don't want to fight over whose turn it is to clean the fridge or who drank all the milk. Been there, done that." She could keep the place as messy or as tidy as she wanted to. Not that she could deal with mess though.

It's so tidy it's almost clinical, a previous flatmate once sneered at her.

"Well, I've asked Vicki to keep an eye on you. She's been very generous letting you have this flat for free. I know she's done alright for herself and all but it's just until you find your feet mind. Don't overstay your welcome." She paced over to the sofa and whacked it with an open hand.

"OK mum, I'll check up on her too. And I'll call you, you know I will."

"Yeah, I know love. Look, just get to know people, friendly people, and you'll be fine."

"Easier said than done though."

"Nah, a great looking girl like you?" She ran a hand over Lucy's cheek, gently caressing it as if touching it for the first time. "And you never know, you might find a decent fella!"

"Mum! Not likely!"

"How hard is it, eh? In a place full of people, places to go. What's that thing called? Tinder. You'll forget about your old mum in no time. When I met your father..."

"I know, I know. And look how that turned out."

"Yeah, well. You never know do you. By the way, do you remember when we moved down here? When was it?

"Yeah mum, I remember."

Only too well she wanted to add.

"Gosh, it must be twelve years. No, more. You were in the third year of, what was the name of that school again?"

"St. David's."

"Oh yes. St. David's." She reached up to the lightshade and plucked at a stray cobweb trail. They had moved to London in her early teens when her Dad got a job – a new school meant new bullies. She had lost her confidence. Again. But managed to make a few friends before being yanked out of that school a year later when her Dad was sacked and moved back up to the Midlands. Again. Where the depression set in. Again.

"Thanks mum," Lucy said. "You know, for everything."

"Oh, shush you. I'd do anything for you, you know I would." She padded over and gave Lucy a tight squeeze. "But I've got to get going. The train won't wait for me. Look, here's a couple of hundred quid. Get some clothes and some treats."

"Mum! You don't need to do that!"

"I know but I want to." She pushed the money into her hand. "London is bloody expensive! When I get back, I'll order a hoover off Amazon." She looked around the place as she left, the top of her nose crinkled.

Lucy watched her mum from the window disappear into the distance. She could hear the hum of traffic moving, people shouting and sirens wailing. A loft of pigeons fluttered onto the sloping roof of a house opposite. She wondered who lived in that house. And the one next door. And the one next door to that. What their lives were like. Their journeys. Their dreams.

She imagined what it must feel like for someone to spend the first night in prison. Couped up in their cell, wondering about their neighbours, if they would survive in their new surroundings or if they would get conned and taken for a ride. She was too scared to go outside and explore, being her first day and night in the big smoke with her 'new' self, so she switched on the TV and watched nonsense reality shows. Eventually she went to bed, turned off the light and cried herself to sleep, wishing morning would hurry up.

The next day she slouched in bed with her laptop on her knees, searching for jobs and ringing recruitment agencies. Everyone said she needed to email or submit an online form. *No personal contact please*, they seemed to say. After several instant autoreplies decrying the large volume of applicants and *you'd be lucky to even get a reply*, she decided to venture out. The flat was the upstairs of an Edwardian terrace, identical to the rows and rows of houses stretching off in all directions. Cars parked bumper to bumper: Land Rovers, SUVs, people carriers. Huge cars for little people. Each tree dotted along the pavement displayed a smattering of little flowers at its base, the residents attempting to brighten up their little patch of concrete with a bit of colour. She glanced into people's homes, net curtains and frosted glass covering the majority of windows. Bikes and bins squeezed into tiny front gardens that would be hard to fit a human in to get to them. She thought of her family home in Nottingham, with a bit of space, greenery and half the price of a small, terraced house in London. To get a bearing on her location, she tried to memorize the road names but they all started to jumble up. She came across a little row of shops, all independent except for a Tesco Express on the corner. A hairdresser, an estate agent, a computer repair shop, another estate agent and a convenience store, which looked in need of some TLC. A few women with pushchairs hurried past, their little bundles wrapped up tightly and sleeping softly. She walked around in circles for a couple of hours, getting familiar with her new neighbourhood before ending up back at the flat. She turned on her laptop, but no new emails had arrived. Her mum had sent one this morning asking how she was, but she decided to ignore it until another time. She typed Facebook into the internet browser and updated a status:

FINALLY moved to London, absolutely loving it!

And clicked on POST.

A bit of guilt washed over her, but hey, who cares. She had taken a big step and moved to the big bad city. Her friends would be green with envy. A notification popped up. Mum liked the post with a red heart. She was typing in the comments box.

"Glad you've settled in so quickly love! Hoover on its way!"

I'll deal with her email tomorrow, she thought.

She laid down on her bed, closed her eyes and drifted off to sleep.

She woke up with a start 20 minutes later, a drilling noise reverberated through the walls. Dazed and confused at the new surroundings, she looked around the empty room. A solitary desk and wooden chair sat in the corner, the laptop askew, a few metres from the end of her bed. She fished her phone out of her pocket and fired up the Facebook app to find 6 likes of her post and 3 comments: a couple of friends from her self-help group who she hadn't seen in years liked her post, her aunt and a friend of her mum's. Jemma, an old uni friend had written *enjoy* in the comments, and Claire, a pretty girl in her support group wrote *good luck!* A red notification popped up on the Messenger icon. She opened it up and it was a guy who was a friend of a friend of hers at uni who she thought she had met a couple of times.

Hey Lucy, it's Josh (Tom's mate). I'm also in London, let me know if you want to hook up. Always good to have a familiar face in London! Let me know.

She clicked on his profile and glanced through his posts: His status updates showed he was a popular guy, going to bars and restaurants, always posting pictures with other people his age. She vaguely recognised him but didn't really remember too much of who he was. His post showed he was 'in a relationship'.

Hey Josh, thanks for getting in touch

Immediately his tiny profile pic appeared next to her post, indicating he had read the message. Why not? She thought and typed in:

That would be great, thanks!

Again, his little face popped up next to the post. The three pulsating circles came up, showing he was typing.

Cool. I'm going out with some mates tonight at some new trendy bar, by the river. Tag along if you like. Don't worry if it's too short notice [smiley emoji].

Tonight! It was a little bit too soon for her to be going out, especially in Central London. But then she thought *I've got to do it. Carpe Diem! Why look a gift horse in the mouth?* She had a feeling he was waiting for a reply. Her miniature profile pic would have come up on his message, showing she had read it. Perhaps he was already sifting through her profile photos, remembering. She started to type.

Ok, sounds great. Thanks for the invite.

She hit enter and the three circles reappeared.

Awesome!

The reply was instant.
More pulsating circles. A link popped up in the next box. It was the bar he was referring to.

This is the place. Meet you there around 8. OK? Here's my number too.

The next box showed his number which she put into her phone.

See you there!

The three pulsing dots reappeared.

You look great BTW. I'm pleased for you.

She replied with a thumbs-up icon. A mixture of emotions coursed through: he remembered her from uni *and* he knew. Was he one of the good ones?

A few new likes appeared on her post. Within a few minutes of a post, she had suddenly got a social life.

Go with an open mind, she told herself. *Let your hair down. Don't be so* stuffy. *Enjoy it!*

She closed the laptop lid and eyed her unpacked suitcase. She let out a sigh, sat down next to the bag, unzipped it and started to make her flat a home.

Chapter Four

Four thirty finally came along and only half an hour to go until her meeting with Joe. Too late to start anything new and too early to knock off for the day. The office had quietened down and people had their heads down scurrying to finish their last bits of work to enable them to leave on time. The last thirty minutes dragged by, not helped by Lucy constantly looking at the clock in the bottom right-hand corner of her screen. She got up and made herself a coffee to waste a few minutes. As she stood in the kitchen a couple of guys came over and threw a plastic football into the foosball table. The pinging of it made a racket, punctuated by the occasional 'ohs', 'ahs' and laughter. She sauntered over and stood at the end of the table. They didn't acknowledge her but knew she was there as their backs stiffened slightly and they gripped the handles tighter to flex their muscles. With Em's 'advice' in her head, she braved it when there was gap in play.

"Can I join in?" she said tentatively. They both looked up at her and then looked at each other. They clearly didn't want anyone interrupting their game but gave each other a resigned look.

"Sure," said the taller one. "Come over to my side."

He moved along to make room for her, taking up the defensive rods. She gripped the handles and the other guy threw the ball in. His head was down, full of concentration. He didn't want to lose this one. It reminded her of when she was forced to play football at school – the others taking it far too seriously when she really couldn't have cared less. The ball pinged around, the guys actually passing it to each of the players rather than spinning the men as Lucy did. Her plastic men stuck on a pole didn't react quick enough to the speed of the ball. Eventually it hit the back of one of her players and the ball stopped, she gave a flick of her wrist and it flew backwards into their goal. The other guy cheered and they both laughed.

"It's tricky to get hold of! Takes a bit of practice" her teammate said. They played a bit more and she could tell they were frustrated. They wanted to play by themselves, not have this amateur ruining their playtime. After a few more goals went in, she made her excuses, grabbed her mug and headed back to her desk.

16:54. Jess was not there; she had gone off to lunch at around 12 and hadn't returned, her screen was alight and prompting her for her password.

Lucy looked around. Emma was in her goldfish bowl talking seriously with a couple of trendy-looking media types. She was showing them a presentation adorned with the company's brand colours and logo. At the other end of the office, Lucy saw a few scalps poking up from behind screens. Waiting for the clock to tick to 17:00, she fired up Facebook and scrolled through. 16:58. She started to close down her computer and silently slipped on her jacket. When she thought two minutes had passed, she got up, walked through the heavy doors and nodded a goodbye to Jonny on reception.

It was only a couple of minutes' walk to Starbucks and her heart was racing the whole time. This was the first time she had met someone she fancied who didn't know anything about her or her past. She tried to decide what to say, how to greet him. Was it a handshake, a hug, a kiss on the cheek?

No, way too soon.

As she turned the corner onto the Strand, she saw him standing outside the café, holding a white Starbucks takeaway cup in either hand. He was looking left and right, seeking her out among the growing number of commuters. She waved to him, a bit too enthusiastically, and he attempted to wave back, forgetting his hands were full. He smiled brightly instead.

"Hiya," she said, a big smile on her face relieved that he was there.

"Hi," he said and extended the coffee cup over to her.

"Flat white right?" The cup acted as a physical greeting and she was pleased that any awkwardness was avoided.

"Oh, lovely, thanks. How did you know?"

"Well, the only thing I do know about you is your name and what coffee you drink." He glanced quickly over to Starbucks.

"Oh yeah, right," she laughed, took the drink and politely had a sip. It didn't have an extra shot; he wouldn't have known that.

"Nice day?" he asked in a way that servers in American cafes ask.

"Rubbish but that's what you get for doing a job you don't enjoy," she replied.

"Ah that sucks. Life's too short to be doing something you don't enjoy, particularly if it is eating 9 hours into your 24 hours a day."

"Yeah, but for now it pays the bills," she said with a shrug.

"Yeah. Sorry. Erm, I don't really know what you do. I know you said PR before you had to rush off but I don't really know what that is. In fact, I don't know you at all."

It was the truth. She was meeting a complete stranger whom she had only met that morning for a few minutes. True, a cute stranger, but a stranger that was new to this city, on their own. Just like her.

"Oh yeah. I've only been there a few months. It's alright," she said, shrugging her shoulders.

"Well, that sounds pretty awesome. You've got a job in London. That's pretty cool," he countered.

"Yeah, I suppose so. It's just a means to an end." She gave another slight shrug. "So, what do you want to do?" she said.

"I'm in your hands, Londoner," he replied with a smirk, looking around the vistas of the Strand.

"Ok, what have you done so far?"

"Well today, after I met you, I walked up to Covent Garden". He said *Covent* as Co-vent, rather than the British Cov-ent.

"Watched a pretty funny guy doing some juggling, then walked along to Lie-cess-ter square"

Lucy smiled at the Americanism of his speech.

"*Less*-ster square" she corrected with a smile.

"Oh yeah, right. *Less*-ster" he said slowly and sarcastically. Lucy warmed to him.

"Then I walked right up to Piccadilly Circus and then to Trafalgar Square. I've got this real useful map." He went to his back pocket and got a worn and dog-eared map of London.

"I saw Buck-ing-ham Palace and those weird guys with the furry hats. They were awesome." He pronounced each syllable of Buckingham carefully and considerately, like she always imagined Americans doing.

"Sounds like you've had a more productive day than me. I thought we could have a walk along the Thames, see some of the sights." She had already mentally planned a route along the southern part of the Thames, googling a few facts that she could spout out to impress him with her knowledge of London.

"That sounds cool. And thanks," he said in a softer, apologetic tone.

"No problem at all, my pleasure," and it really was. She would have been sitting in her flat on her own with just the television for company otherwise.

She nodded in the direction of Charing Cross and they set off, each carrying their coffee. They crossed the road; he was furiously looking left and right, unsure which way the traffic was coming.

"Not used to this driving on the left thang you got going here." Lucy smiled and they strolled along the narrow street down to the river, walking towards Embankment station down the dreary, dirty street she had walked up earlier that day; the rain now dried up. They talked briefly about the weather, the classic common ground all humans on earth had and she suddenly became self-conscious of her hair. It could be a frizzy bomb, or it could be behaving itself. She tucked a curl behind her ear, a girly play that she had seen in countless films. She looked over to him to see if he noticed. He was looking up and around as they walked along the street. She kept looking at him, with a smile on her lips.

Just before Embankment station they turned right under Charing Cross station. It was darker here with a smattering of shops under the train tracks: a Subway, a Costa, a newsagent and a closed-down bike shop. The air became dank and dark before they emerged into bright sunshine, took a left and walked up the steps of Hungerford Bridge, the west side that looked out to the London Eye and the Houses of Parliament.

"Now that's what I'm talking about," Joe said excitedly, whipping out his mobile phone for a picture. It was a beautiful sight. The wide river with sightseeing boats chugging along, the majestic wheel towering above, Big Ben and its history looking over London. Joe took a few snaps and Lucy offered to take one of him.

"Sure, yes please," he said like an excited schoolboy. She took his phone and he posed in front of the view, a sultry pose, his eyebrows slightly furrowed. He took it seriously as if this would be posted immediately on social media.

"And now one with the two of us. I need to capture this moment that you've showed me with the person that showed it to me!" He took the camera and she stood next to him. He extended his arm out, camera in hand, and they posed next to each other, squeezing their heads in, their cheeks very gently brushing up against each other. Or maybe that was the breeze that she was imagining. She didn't smell any cologne on him. He didn't touch her or put his arm around her which he could have done to take advantage of the moment. She felt safe with him.

"That's an awesome picture Lucy," he commented, looking down at the phone. She reacted to hearing her name from his soft American accent, her heart seemed to skip a beat and felt a warmth flush her cheeks. He looked at her, as if reading her mind. Those deep eyes again, the deer-in-the-headlights look of seeing someone familiar in real life. The intensity. It seemed to last longer than it probably did. They snapped out of it, blinking.

"I love it Lucy, you are lucky to live in this city. I live near the mountains, hardly any tall buildings."

"Colorado, wasn't it?"

"Yeah, Colorado Springs actually, but it's in the state of Colorado. Have you been?"

"No, I've only been to New York. I love America, would love to explore it more."

"Well, when you come over, look me up, I'll return the favour of tour guide." He said this genuinely, as if she really would come over to Colorado.

"So, tour guide, tell me something interesting."

"Ah ok. Well. The River Thames was built in the year 2000 to celebrate the Millennium. It was opened in 2001, a year late due to a combination of going over budget and low rainfall." She'd been practising this in the office. She looked at him waiting for a response, his head was nodding. Then he looked over to her.

"What?" a smile crept on his face, the small dimple appearing in his cheek. Lucy smiled a big smile, a cheeky grin, with her white teeth showing.

"Haha! You almost had me," he chuckled and pushed her gently on the arm. The first bit of physical contact between them. He continued to chortle in a natural way.

"I'm gonna have to watch out for you!" They continued walking along the bridge, the dark swirling mass of water beneath. She pointed over to the London Eye.

"Seriously though, there are 32 pods on the London Eye and there are 32 boroughs in London. One pod for each borough. But the pods are numbered one to 33. That's because there is no pod number thirteen." This was true, she found it on Google that afternoon.

"Is that right? Which borough do you live in?"

"Wandsworth, it's kind of south and west London" she said pointing in the general direction.

"Where are you staying?" she countered.

"Oh, some budget hotel in Paddington, I think. It was at the end of the train line from the airport so I figured it would be easy. It's ok, nothing special," he glanced at her like he had offended her.

"I don't really know that area," she said, which was true. She hadn't really explored all the areas of London. She did know the Grand Union was around there.

"It's near the canal isn't it," she offered, trying to show her knowledge of London.

"I'm not too sure about that. It's pretty grimy and I just jumped on the tube downtown." He said tube, *toobe*, accenting the 't'.

They reached the end of the bridge and took a look back. The Houses of Parliament glistened, the evening sun going down behind it. A few airplanes made their way to Heathrow disrupting the vastness of the sky. A few whispery clouds started to turn pink. They stood looking out.

"It's going to be a nice evening," Lucy said, in a trance.

"Yep," he turned and looked at her, those deep brown eyes once again seemed to bore into her. "Beautiful."

Lucy daydreamed that it would have been entirely natural for Joe to have leaned in, their lips connecting, the sun setting, London in the background. She would have allowed it too. But she snapped out of it.

Too soon.

She turned to bound down the stairs, leading to a gold fairground carousel. Joe jogged to catch up. They went down the steps and took a quick left back on themselves, away from the London Eye and underneath the bridge they had just come across. The imposing grey Royal Festival Hall appeared on their right, the bustling chain restaurants underneath having a busy evening. Lucy moved over towards the river, away from the bustling concourse and slowed down their pace. Human statues drew a crowd and a few young dancers gathered people into a circle, encouraging them to clap in sync with the music. To the side of them she noticed a thin older woman urging the reluctant crowd to join in, dressed in similar baggy clothes as the dancers. She was part of the group but stood out, her age and haggard face in contradiction to the clothes and her crew. Lucy was used to spotting those who stood out from the norm. She carried on walking, leading Joe along the path, the river to their left, grand buildings on the other side of the brown liquid flowing to the sea.

"Over there is the Embankment," she pointed over the river, breaking the comfortable silence.

"The river used to be much wider here and in the Victorian days they built the embankment to make it narrower." Joe turned to look out over the river.

"In those days the river was full of all sorts of smelly nasties, so a slow-moving river made it stink. The narrower river squeezed the water and made it move faster through the city to the sea." She gestured in the generation direction of the sea. He nodded, taking it in. He looked at her and cocked his eyebrow. Those brown eyes again.

"Is that the truth this time?"

"Swear on my life, I read it on the internet," she smiled.

"Well, it must be true then. Imagine those guys that had to build it, wading through all that crap to build the thing."

"I hadn't really thought of that." They stopped and looked out.

"A little change makes a big difference, huh?" he seemed to ask himself.

She quickly glanced at him. His eyes had a faraway look to them that seemed to be gazing further than the other side of the river. He took a deep sigh and looked at Lucy who was staring at him with her mouth slightly ajar.

"What?" he asked, the side of his mouth curling up to a smile.

"Oh, nothing," she replied and mirrored his smile. As she turned her body, she playfully kept her eyes fixed on his. It felt relaxed. Nothing felt forced or awkward, as if they had known each other for years.

They came to the graffiti covered walls under the National Theatre, where several young, tattooed guys were skating. The clang of their skateboards echoed as they slipped off and the dull roll of wheels skidded on concrete. The pair stood and watched for a few minutes, lost in their own thoughts. She occasionally glanced over at him, noticing his smooth, tanned skin, a wisp of stubble coming through. She caught a whiff of cologne and wondered if it was Joe's. Once, she turned back and his eyes were scanning her face, as if devouring every detail. Again, she interrupted his gaze.

"Shall we?" she said, indicating to keep going. They walked along the promenade of the South Bank, looking down at the pavement in front of them.

"So why London then Joe?" she purposely used his name, letting it roll in her mouth.

"Well Lucy, it's kinda hard for me to say," his eyes furrowed, and she looked over at him.

"I had some pretty bad luck so wanted to get away. I've always wanted to come to London, so I thought, heck, just do it. Kinda find myself again. Write some things down." He looked over the flowing Thames.

"It sounds a bit 'new age' you know but I just needed to get away from the States," he used air-quotes when he said, 'new age'.

"Not at all," she replied, empathising. It was obviously hard for him to find the words. "Sometimes you need some headspace to clear the mind."

"Yeah, I suppose so. So, it happened and I thought get away, do something I've always wanted to do and see what occurs". The word 'it' hung in the air.

Curiosity got the better of her.

"What happened? I mean, you don't have to tell me if you don't want to, its fine, you know." She spluttered it out.

"No, no it's fine. I haven't really spoken about it. Better to say it to a stranger who doesn't know me than someone I know."

They stopped at a corner of the promenade, a right angle of fencing forcing pedestrians to turn to the right where a mix of cafes in a courtyard were starting to fill up. Beneath them a sculptor fashioned a mermaid out of the washed-up sand that made a small beach. Joe stood with his back to the river, St. Paul's Cathedral rose over his left shoulder, the tall skyscrapers' flickering lights starting their nightshift over his right. He took a deep breath, prepared himself whilst his eyes developed a film of water.

"My wife and kids died in a car accident, just over a year ago." He breathed out heavily, like a weight of the world finally came off his shoulders. He blinked and a small drop of water fell down his cheek.

"Oh my goodness," Lucy exclaimed, covering her mouth with her hand.

"They would have loved it here," he turned and looked out to the river.

"I'm so sorry to hear that Joe," she considered putting her hand on the small of his back. He turned around, using the back of hand to wipe away the tear on his cheek.

"Everything happens for a reason, right?" He tried to joke to lighten the mood but they both knew it wasn't needed. Lucy smiled sympathetically.

"How old were the kids?" she asked.

"Young. Four and two. They didn't know what hit them, the officer said. I was at work and a couple of cops came in and told me to sit. Some drunk trucker was texting on his cell on Interstate 25 and mowed them down. They didn't stand a chance." He looked back out to the river, eyes turned away from her. There's nothing she could say.

"Yeah, my life ended just like that. The guy appeared in court a couple of months ago and that gave me the closure I needed. I thought I'm not going to let that asshole keep ruining my life, so I packed up and came over here."

"What did he get? I mean, prison sentence?" she said, hoping in some weird way to make him feel better, that the guy got what he deserved.

"I have no idea. I didn't go to the courtroom. I couldn't give a damn what he got. Whatever it was, it was way too short and whatever happens to him is not going to bring them back. I don't forgive him, and I don't want to give any more thought to him or what he does. Apparently, he's stone-cold sober now so that's one good thing. Hopefully it will never happen again." He paused. Lucy felt the void again.

"I'm so sorry Joe," she said again, trying to make him feel better. He wiped at his eye again and looked at her.

"Thanks Lucy, I appreciate it. It's not your fault. Sorry to dump it on you."

"No, no its fine. I'm glad you could tell me." She felt like she needed to hug him but she wasn't sure it was right. His honesty was endearing, trustworthy.

"Can we carry on Lucy? Your tour guiding isn't up to scratch," he smiled a sweet but sad smile. She mock-punched him in the arm, glad that the awkward atmosphere had passed. They carried on along the river, past the red-bricked Oxo Tower and array of independent shops and art galleries underneath it. They walked in silence for a while, Joe deep in his thoughts, Lucy appreciating the comfortable quiet, both in the contemplation of companionship in a heaving, lonely city. Her mind wandered back in comparison to her school days and the confusing issues that she had faced, her choices and being bullied. But no-one had died in her story. It put things in perspective.

They squeezed through the tunnel of Blackfriars Bridge, joggers with big headphones jostled past them and a lone saxophonist playing the blues, sound bouncing off the tiles. As they emerged from the metallic train bridge, St. Paul's Cathedral loomed large and the Millennium Bridge sparkled in the setting sun's fading light.

Lucy broke the silence.

"Just over there," she pointed to the other side of the river, where St. Paul's sat. "Can you see the two gold things on top of the two towers, just to the left of the dome of St. Paul's?" The gold glistened, surveying the sun.

"Yes, I see them. Look sparkly," he observed.

"Yeah. They are gold pineapples," she said.

"Oh, something to do with hospitality, right?"

"Yes, they do symbolise that, but back in the day they were a sign of wealth and status. You had to be rich to be able to afford to buy a pineapple. You could even rent one in Victorian times for your dinner party. To show off to your friends." She said this with an air of authority.

"Is that so?" he said, visibly impressed. "Internet?"

"No, overheard a tour guide." They both burst out laughing.

"They are everywhere in London. Pineapples I mean. Once you know, you see them everywhere. Usually in front of people's houses or big stately homes. Once I found out that fact, I couldn't stop seeing them. On fences, on top of monuments, on old pubs. I was taken to the Pineapple Pub in North London by one of my clients and I told the same story. He was less impressed by my facts and more impressed by my short skirt."

"Well, I'll need to look out for them then. I mean the pineapples, not the short skirts." He smirked at her, and Lucy grinned again, playfully punching his arm. Physical contact seemed to be more natural and forthcoming now, like a magnet pulling them together. They approached the expansive courtyard of the Tate Modern, its tall brick chimney elegant yet dominating the skyline. Commuters filed across the Millennium Bridge like the worker ants that they were. Lucy gestured over to it.

"That's the wobbly bridge. Now that really was built to mark the Millennium."

"Oh yeah I've heard of that. What a disaster huh! Research is everything." He looked indifferently up at the bridge. As they walked closer, they could see the twisted metal-like structure stretching out over the Thames to St. Paul's, the skyscrapers stood tall behind, like their chests were puffed out. People were on the walkway taking photos, the orange hue of the sun reflecting off the silver metal of the bridge. Lucy turned right to enter the Tate and Joe followed. They went in and made a beeline for the Turbine Hall. They walked right into the giant space and Lucy turned to gauge his reaction. He looked up, left, right and took a deep breath in. It was hard not to be impressed by the cavernous space for the first time. The silence was deafening for such a large area. A few people were milling around, a murmur of conversation getting lost in the tall hall, the black metal beams framing the white walls.

Lucy set her bag down in the middle of the floor and sat down. He followed suit, looking around trying to take in the enormity of the place. Lucy lay down on her back and encouraged him to do the same. They laid next to each other, head to tail, tail to head and looked up. Listening to the silence, in their own thoughts, having a rest, just being. The ceiling seemed to go on forever. Lucy took a long, deep breath and held it in. She closed her eyes and opened them again. She felt safe and comfortable, as she always did when she laid there. But for the first time she had someone to share it with.

Chapter Five

Lucy got to the bar by the river to meet Josh, her Facebook invitation, just after eight. She still couldn't believe it. She had only moved to London a couple days ago and was already at the launch of a swanky new bar. A pretty tall woman in a black pencil skirt and white airy blouse checked her name on a clipboard under Josh's name. She walked in and was immediately offered a champagne flute, balanced on a silver tray with half a dozen others, by a young man with a nose ring wearing a white shirt and a black tie. She took one and walked around the bar, trying to spot Josh.

The bar was full and buzzing with lots of people chatting in small circles. She didn't remember his face too well so she had a look on his Facebook for photos so she could try to recognise him. She was wearing a sensible, conservative black dress that wasn't too overly pretentious but was dressier than jeans and a top. A few men glanced over at her direction, smirked and nudged each other, and then looked away again. Her red hair had always gotten attention, probably due to the stark contrast to her pale skin. It must be the Irish side of her, although she had no idea where that stemmed from. The tightknit groups made it harder for her to see faces, only their backs were visible. The bar was full of open shirts and blazers for the men, and trendy black, tight-fitting dresses and heels for the ladies. A few had bright pashminas draped over their shoulders. Occasionally a howl of laughter emerged from a circle and heads flung backwards. Louder music started to kick in, a heavy beat and a strong bass. Voice levels rose to compensate for the increased volume. The atmosphere changed when the music blared. It became more relaxed; the bar seemed to get busier and a few people swayed or nodded their head in time with the beats.

Lucy had walked around the whole bar twice and hadn't spotted Josh. She considered pulling her phone out to check Facebook again to remind herself of his face or if there was a text from him. Instead, she decided to go on one more sweep and swapped her now-empty flute for a full one from a passing waitress. She thought she saw him in the corner of a group of six people, three women and three men. She casually walked over, hoping to catch his eye. She got closer and made full eye contact. It wasn't him. Embarrassed she turned away, her face reddened and headed towards the toilet.

God, I hate this.

Sitting in a cubicle, she pulled out her phone. No text and nothing new on his Facebook feed. A few extra likes and hearts appeared on her earlier post but none since she had left the flat. She opened up Messenger and typed a message.

Hey, I'm at the bar, are you here yet? she pressed send and sat back. The dull throbbing of the bass came through the toilets. The bathroom door opened and a couple of women burst in, the music filling the room, and then dulled when the door shut. The women were giggling and laughing. Lucy sat in absolute silence in her cubicle, willing a message to come through.

The phone lit up. It was Josh.

Just arriving Lucy, sorry a bit late. Two minutes away.

She got up and opened the door. The two women shot her a glance through the mirror as they applied their lipstick. They were wearing short skirts and crop tops, the upper half of their breasts making a perfect M over the top of them. She stared at them whilst they diverted their attention back to the mirror as she observed their slender bodies and lean legs. She went over to the basin, washed her hands and looked at her reflection. She glanced over at the two women and compared bodies.

At least my hair was behaving itself, she thought.

She had a small dusting of make-up on, blusher, not foundation. It had never really been her thing. In comparison the two women had thick, perfect make-up, their foundation line blending seamlessly into their healthy-looking skin. Their eyeliner accentuated their eyes flawlessly. Feeling inferior, Lucy tucked her curls behind her ear and headed out, the bass blasting in her face as she went through the door.

Lucy stood awkwardly by the Ladies, flute in hand, standing on her toes to look over toward the door. A few minutes went past and she saw Josh through the windows, laughing and joking with three other men. He was leading the pack, his back straight, the wings of his blazer flowed behind him. They came in and helped themselves to the flutes of champagne offered by the host. Josh looked around, like a meerkat, over the sea of heads. She waved but he didn't see her. It felt important that she waved in case anyone who had been watching her thought she was a loner.

Look, I've got friends!

She made her way through the small groups and Josh spotted her. He waved an enthusiastic hand over in her direction and walked directly toward her, gently pushing people out of the way. His cohorts followed in a line like rats following the pied piper.

"Lucy! You made it!" He immediately hugged her which took her by surprise, meaning she accepted the hug in an uncomfortable position, her arms pinned to her side, holding her champagne flute with the tips of her fingers.

"Nice to see you! You look great!" He pulled away and shot a look down her body. "Lucy, these are the guys, guys this is Lucy." They each nodded and smiled, but were quickly looking around the room, feeling uncomfortable, eyeing up the other women. They seemed disappointed with her after the description Josh had already filled them in on. They closed into a circle.

"So, Lucy, you made it to the Big Smoke, huh?! What you up to?" Josh shouted over the music, giving her his full attention, his pupils fully dilated, whilst his friends started to converse amongst themselves, eyes darting around the room.

"Well, I just got here so looking for some work really. I just decided to do it and come down."

"Excellent, that's just the way it should be. What kind of work you looking for? Something Englishy? I mean, you did English at uni right?"

"Yeah, I did. Anything really. I can write so thought I'd start there."

"I've got a friend who works in this PR agency, somewhere around Covent Garden. I'll put you in touch if you like." He took a big sip from his flute. "if that's the kind of thing you might want."

"Yeah. Yeah, that would be great. Thank you."

"No problem Lucy, we look out for each here. If you ever need anything, just give me a call. You've got my number now."

"Ok cool. And what about you? What do you do?"

"Me? I'm a copper with the Met. Bobby on the beat at the moment but hoping to move up the ranks."

"Blimey. That must be exciting."

"Yeah, yeah. Long hours and all that. I've seen some stuff. But we work hard and play hard, eh boys?" He raised his voice again, hoping to get his mates involved in the conversation. The guys looked over quickly, engrossed in their own discussions of hot women at the bar. Whenever Lucy spied a hostess coming towards her with a tray of glasses, she polished off her drink and grabbed another one, putting down the empty. Josh did the same, trying to keep up.

The buzz of the bar was getting to heightened levels now. People were shouting to be heard and she struggled to hear Josh talking in her ear. He talked constantly, telling anecdotes about some of the incidents he'd attended, as she nodded and reacted politely at the right moments: murders (*oohh!*), stalkers (*ew!*), busting drug deals (*flipping 'eck!*). His mates had left to find another area, leaving the two of them together. They had had a few glasses now and his words started to slur. His eyes went in and out of focus, and sometimes she caught him sneaking a peek down the top of her dress. His hands kept getting closer and closer to her, occasionally brushing her arm, causing her to flinch. When they squeezed in to let someone pass, he took the opportunity to press his body against hers, and sometimes his hand landed on the small of her back. They shouted in each other's ears, naming a few people they both knew and what they were up to. The music went up a decibel and Lucy screwed up her face at the impact on her ears.

Feeling nauseous, she made up an excuse and headed to the ladies. Inside, the beating bass muffled to a dull thudding but her ears were still ringing. She sat in a cubicle with her head in her hands. She heard women come in and out, the stall became fuzzy and started to spin. Long sniffing and taps running came through from the other side of the door. Her head throbbed in time with the bass. As she stood up, the blood rushed out of her head, so she sat right back down again, landing with a bump on the closed toilet seat. She felt like she was going to be sick but couldn't seem to muster up anything in her stomach to eject. She sat for a while longer and eventually stood up again.

Reaching for the handle, she used the cool metal to steady herself, blood returning to her head. As she left the cubicle a blast of bass came into the bathroom as two slim women in tight black dresses left. She followed them out as the door almost closed. She looked around and spotted Josh reunited with his mates. They looked blurry but it was clear they were laughing. She sidled up to Josh and he gave her a full champagne flute, the bubbles making lines in the glass. She thanked him but said she had to go. He leant back and gave a hearty groan.

"Oh no, not yet the night is just starting!" he said with genuine sorrow.

"I know but I want to get back. Thanks so much for the invite, I've had a great time."

"No worries Lucy, so nice to see you and you look great. I'll send you the name of my friend tomorrow. Drop me a text if you want to meet up again." He gave her a hug. Two of his watching friends sniggered and shared a private joke.

"And don't forget. If you ever need me, call me." He made a phone signal with his hand with a genuine look of concern on his face.

"Thanks Josh, see you soon," and turned to meander through the circles of people into the cool night air, the sound muffled as if earplugs had suddenly been inserted in her ears.

Around the corner she hailed a taxi. She gave her address and the taxi driver whisked her away, past endless buses, houses and tower blocks with their lights blinding, her eyes closing and opening, trying to fight the impending sleep. Finally, she collapsed into her bed and closed her eyes as the room swirled around. She didn't wake until the sun dappled through a gap in the heavy curtains.

Chapter Six

In the quiet of the Tate Modern, Lucy felt herself start to drift off to sleep, lying on her back in the uber-silent vacuum of the Turbine Hall. She heard Joe rustling next to her and looked up. He was resting on his elbows, surveying the expanse.

"Wow Lucy. I would never have thought to come in here, and never thought to lie down. It's stunning." She was now on her elbows too and they were looking directly at each other, down the length of their respective bodies. Their eyes seemed to go deeper than the surface, like they were seeking each other's souls. His eyes moved around her face again: her hair, her ears, her neck, her mouth. It was sensual without touching. A tingle radiated throughout her body. They stayed in that position, enveloped in silence, until a buzzer jolted them out of their daze. A Tannoy announced the place was about to close. Joe jumped up and reached out his hand to help her up. She felt his soft skin for the first time, their fingertips momentarily touching.

The sky was darker now, the faint orange and pink clouds to the West and the darker blue to the East. St. Paul's Cathedral was directly in front of them, the famous dome lit from beneath. They turned right and made their way back to the river. As they crossed the courtyard of the Tate, towards the Millennium Bridge, Lucy spoke first.

"So, you said you moved from New York to Colorado."

"Yeah, that's right."

"I've never been. I'd like to. I went to New York a couple of years ago. I loved it."

"Yeah, New York is kinda cool. A bit like London but busier." A helicopter buzzed overhead as they strolled under the Millennium bridge. The commuters had dispersed, leaving a few couples and tourists exploring the sights in the darkening skies.

"Not many tourists venture out to Colorado, unless they are skiing or visiting folks. I moved out after meeting my wife. We met at college; her family were there so I followed. Had a couple of kids and then…." He trailed off. His life story told in one sentence.

"What did you do there? I mean, it must have been hard to fit into someone else's life."

"You just do really. She was religious so we got married quickly. Probably too quickly and then her family are like, 'so when are the kids coming' and then the kids came. I didn't find it hard. I got a job pretty quickly at an immigration facility, helping aliens, that's what we call them, settle into American life."

"Wow, that's amazing. How did that go down? I imagine it's pretty rednecky in that area, 'Make America Great Again' and all that. Probably doesn't go down well with you helping the enemy."

He looked at her and smiled.

"Colorado is actually pretty liberal but yeah there are some rednecks, as you call them, areas. So, there's a bit of that but it's ok. These people need us. You can't imagine what goes on over in the Middle East and South America. The stories I heard make you rethink everything in your life. How people are treated, what they've been through, what they've done to get themselves and their family to safety." She didn't say anything; she didn't want to query anything. She just wanted to let him speak.

"The things I heard. I mean, women were raped. Raped, man, by men who were supposed to be freeing them. Bombs and mortars coming down and wiping out whole communities. Oh, wow, what's that?"

He snapped out of his sentence and she followed his gaze to a white circular building, jutting out from the modernity either side of it.

"It's Shakespeare's Globe. Well, it's a replica. It's the only thatched roof building in London."

"Oh, now that is cool. Shakespeare, huh. Read about him in school." He looked at her and grinned.

"Romeo oh Romeo, where are thee Romeo?" he recited, putting on an English accent, a really rather good English accent.

"Haha, I think it's 'O Romeo, Romeo, wherefore art thou Romeo?'" She overtly dramatized the 'Romeo' part and he looked at her impressed.

"English at university, I know it inside out."

"Oh, a Shakespearean scholar!" he said, again in a faux-English accent, "how very civilised!"

They laughed and turned back to the path running along the river. He didn't seem willing to continue talking about his job. They came to a couple of chain restaurants and Lucy's stomach started to growl. She pointed to the first one.

"Um, are you hungry, shall we grab something to eat?"

"Yeah, definitely!" He moved quickly to the first restaurant door and opened it sweeping his other hand for her to follow.

"Oh, thank you dear gentleman," she replied, giving a theatrical curtsey.

"It is but a pleasure ma'am." He pronounced ma'am as in jam, not marm as in arm. The correct way. They giggled and settled down at a table by the window, Lucy with her back to the river. The waiter brought the menu and enquired what they would like to drink. Lucy ordered a white wine and he ordered 'just a coke'.

"Do you not fancy something a bit stronger?" she asked, expecting alcohol as standard when on a date. Or maybe this wasn't a date.

"Erm, no thanks. I haven't touched a drop since the accident. You know, alcohol bad." Lucy gulped, realising what he was saying.

"Oh god, I'm sorry. I'll change," she hurriedly picked up the drinks menu.

"No, no. Don't be silly. It's fine. Have whatever you want. I really don't mind." He seemed to slip into that English accent with his quick words. It barely registered.

"I'm so sorry," she blurted out. She placed the menu back down in front of her and studied the food choices.

"Well, I know what I'm going to have." He pointed down at the menu. "Ham and pineapple." He looked up expecting a reaction. She clicked at the joke, relieved at the passing awkwardness and giggled.

"Haha, yeah, me too! Although I doubt wealth and stature are anything to do with it."

"It's celebrating the great hospitality of the British. It's a thank you to you for showing me around. I'm getting this, please don't worry."

"That's very kind of you Joe." The waiter appeared and placed their drinks on the table. The place was full and buzzing with couples and families. It filled with noise and clattering of plates, cutlery and wine glasses.

"Cheers," he said, and she clinked her glass on his.

They chatted easily; conversation flowed. He was attentive to her when she spoke and did that thing of occasionally looking at her mouth when she talked. Growing up in a suburban middle-class family in upstate New York, his father liked a drink, like Lucy's, and his mother was a traditional American wife – baked cookies and took him to soccer practice – and they lived in a white picket-fenced home. He had a sister who he hadn't seen for a while. On the account of the braces he had had to wear, bullies had made his life hell at high school. He spoke loosely about college and then meeting his wife, never mentioning her name, or going into details of his kids, which she didn't push. He said he had never liked football so hadn't got involved in the jock lifestyle which was so in tune with her image of an American High School from so many Hollywood movies. In fact, it sounded rather like the school she had gone to: unassuming, normal and boring; teachers, homework and bullying. Whenever she asked a slightly probing question, he went shy, looked away and said he'd rather not talk about it. She imagined the memories were still raw and painful. He was trying to get his feelings out by writing, which was what he had been doing when she first met him in Starbucks earlier that day. It felt like she'd known him so much longer.

Whilst moving away from his normality to Colorado had been hard, he had had to "man up" and look after the family.

His in-laws demanded it – get a decent, hard-working job and provide. He said again that he got married too young, but he didn't have any regrets. He had worked with migrants from South and Central America, places he had never been to, getting snippets here and there of what life would have been like from CNN and the tortuous first-person stories of rape, violence and robbery.

The accident had hit him like a punch to the gut, he said. Lucy couldn't imagine what Joe must have gone through. He had had a pretty terrible day of listening to war-torn tales when the police officers had come into his workplace. He said he felt weak the moment he saw them. His wife had been driving home from school when a truck careered across the lanes and slammed into their SUV, toppling over and crushing it like a pancake. The police said the car hadn't stood a chance against an 18-wheeler. And nor did the passengers: the children's bodies had to be identified by dental records.

The driver was unhurt and failed the breathalyser test. The police said they could smell the alcohol before they even got the kit out. Joe looked down at the table as he recounted the story, never meeting her eyes. The funeral happened like a blur, he said. He couldn't remember much except an empty house. Not long after, he threw everything away. All the clothes went to an immigrant charity and all his possessions were just chucked in the garbage. He went back to New York to be with his family and hung around for a while, letting his mother and dad look after him. It was almost like he was the one that needed help and didn't feel like giving his energy to help others. He couldn't care less about what happened to the driver. The damage had been done. If he got ten years or twenty years it wouldn't have made a difference. Lucy thought the fact the driver was now sober meant more than a jail term. She really felt for Joe, his honesty and raw emotion, as he was recounting this personal story. Perhaps she could tell him her story. How would he react? They both had emotional baggage, two peas in a pod. She instinctively wanted to reach out, hug him and tell him it was all ok.

Their pizza plates had long been taken and dessert brushed aside. After they had ordered a couple more drinks, he asked about her. Compared to his traumatic life story hers was as dull as the décor in the restaurant. Well, the bits she wanted to tell. She avoided his questions, physically like swatting a fly and emotionally by steering the conversation in another direction. He persisted and she said she too had been brought up in a fairly middle-class house, in a place where not a lot happened. She had been bullied, her dad was a prick and the lasting memory she had from her teenage years was the desire to escape from it all. She had moved to London briefly when she was a teenager when her dad got a job down there, but then was made redundant a year later. She was glad as she hadn't fitted into the school, said she got bullied for being different. She pointed up to her head and he chuckled, looking at the curly red hair.

She told him how for a few years after uni she meandered about, dead-end job after another, coming to London every now and then and a short trip to New York. Finally, she moved to get away from the staid life up North, hoping to find excitement and happiness, and maybe even love. He didn't take his eyes off her the entire time she was reliving her short and boring past. He sipped at his coke seemingly in awe of her, drinking in every word, not moving his gaze from her, which she found strangely foreign and comforting in equal measure. She didn't think she had ever received that look of admiration before, except from her parents – well her mum certainly, a long time ago. And she enjoyed it and appreciated being the centre of attention.

He asked her about her favourite movies, her song choices when she was happy and when she was down. He asked her where she'd been and where she wanted to go. Mostly all the latter were places in the States – the Grand Canyon, Chicago, the Deep South and the Mississippi River, Seattle, Vegas and Washington DC, Yellowstone and Big Sur. In fact, all the places made famous in the Hollywood glamour and TV shows. She had loved New York with its tall skyscrapers reaching for the sky and steam coming out of the ground; the hotdog sellers on every corner and the high-end shops of 5th Avenue; the sadness of Ground Zero and the optimism of the UN, all the flags of the world fluttering as one in the wind; the greenness of Central Park and the blue of the Yankees.

She had visited alone in order to spend time thinking and figuring out what to do with her life, a short holiday paid for by a small inheritance. But in hindsight, her only regret was that she hadn't had someone to share the sights and discoveries with her; a local, or someone close. The nights were short as she went to Times Square to look at the lights and bustle, and then headed back to the hostel, scared of the crime stories that radiated from all the hit television dramas. Joe listened intently, nodding when he heard something familiar from his home state, agreeing with every word she said. He said he wished he had been there with her, to keep her company. She said she would have liked that.

He motioned to her glass to see if she wanted a refill. Lucy checked the time and couldn't believe it. Ten o'clock. She looked behind her out of the window and the sky was dark and the lights of the nearby buildings were bright. London didn't sleep and even though it was late, London was still alive. She declined the drink, already feeling tipsy, and said they ought to get the bill. His frown deepened as he looked slightly disappointed that the evening was coming to an end.

"We need to finish the tour," she said optimistically. A wide smile spread across his face and called for the bill. He also asked to see the menu again. The waiter duly brought them over and Joe folded up the paper menu into a quarter and put it in his back pocket.

"Souvenir," he said, as an answer to her quizzical look. The restaurant had emptied out considerably but she hadn't even noticed.

Stepping out into the cool air, the wine suddenly hit her senses. How much had she drunk? They looked out over the wall to the river and saw a smattering of boats still chugging up and down the Thames. Music was emanating from one of them and flashing coloured lights danced on the waves in its wake. They turned right and kept on walking along the pathway.

Conversation had turned to superficial things now: TV shows they watched, YouTube videos they'd seen, memes on social media. Their chatter was comfortable and easy flowing. Whoever was talking used their hands to gesticulate their words. There was an energy between them. Perhaps it was the wine, but Lucy suddenly felt she wanted more than just talking. As they came out of the tunnel leading under Southwark Bridge, she moved closer to him, so that their hands might accidently touch. When she felt the opportunity, she brushed his hand and he didn't respond. She brushed it again and this time interlinked her little finger into his. He jerked his hand away like a bolt of electricity had hit him.

"Oh, I'm so sorry," he blurted. Lucy felt her ears burn.

"No, no, it's me that should apologise, I'm sorry. I thought…."

Before she could finish, he looked at her. Those brown eyes….

"I'm sorry. I just wasn't ready for that. It's just a natural instinct. You know, this hasn't happened to me in years. I'm so far out of my comfort zone." He glanced away, a furrow on his forehead. An awkwardness descended on the both of them.

"Me too," Lucy countered softly. This was so strange for her too. This hadn't happened in a long time either, yet it felt so right. She nervously swept a stray lock of hair behind her ear, waiting for him to say something. Do something. Her legs quivered like they were balancing on the river's waves. It seemed there were a thousand thoughts going through his mind behind those eyes. Waiting for a verdict.

They looked at each other in no-man's land, both unsure what to do or what to say. She realised she was foolish: they had had a nice evening, but she had only met him today, he was only in London for a few days, and he was mourning the sudden and tragic death of his wife and kids. What was she thinking? She apologised again.

"Please, don't apologise. I really like you, Lucy. I'm just not used to it after being out of the game for a while. Um, let's try again, shall we?"

He took her hand and intertwined his fingers into hers. It immediately felt natural and they carried on walking. It felt nice but it was far from comfortable. He dipped his free hand into his pocket and they walked along the river in silence, electricity coursing between their skin.

They turned a corner and in front of them was an old ship, lit from beneath, casting gorgeous shadows onto the buildings behind.

"So, what's this then Miss Tour Guide?" The ice began to break again.

"Oh, this?" she said. She had never before seen this black ship adorned with gold and red markings. She struggled to find clues around the vessel and make something up.

"This is an old boat, built in the past." He looked at her and smiled.

"Oh really, and where did it sail to?" he said playing along.

"It sailed to lots of different countries, on the sea, where it plied its trade with spices and rum," she guessed.

"Yo ho ho, and I guess there were pirates on board too?"

"Yes! Lots of pirates and scallywags." He walked up to it and read the board in front of it.

"The Golden Hind-e!" he announced.

"Yes!" Lucy shouted, "this is the Golden Hind-ee. I was right, it is an old boat and was built in the past. If you don't believe me, I'll give you your money back!"

They collapsed into a fit of giggles, their hands propping each other up as they bent over laughing. They continued down the pathway, turning down narrow cobbled streets where men in suits spilled out of bars and walking haphazardly down the way. Other couples were arm-in-arm, hand-in-hand; tourists in their colourful tops and shorts, maps sticking out of their back pockets.

They navigated round Borough Market, closed for the evening, stalls all boarded up. Lucy pointed out the house where Bridget Jones' Diary had been filmed, and Joe nodded politely. Crossing over the busy streets outside London Bridge they were back on an almost spotlessly clean path with a stream running through it, heading through a spacious atrium and back out onto the river where Lucy spotted her destination. Coming into view, lit up like a mirage in front of them with its twin towers spiking the night sky, was Tower Bridge. Red buses and white vans criss-crossed over it. Joe got out his camera and took a selfie, this time putting his arm around Lucy's shoulders and pulled her tightly in. She could smell a faint whiff of cologne. To the left of the famous bridge were the sand-coloured walls of the Tower of London, the White Tower within with its four turrets nestled inside the estate. The river glinted with lights reflecting on small waves, Canary Wharf's skyscrapers in the background providing a modern backdrop. The hum of boats plying their night-time trade and the distant traffic created a surreal soundtrack to the giant city.

Lucy turned to Joe, their eyes locked and she planted her lips softly on his.

Chapter Seven

The morning after being in the bar with Josh, Lucy turned over and let out a groan. She clearly wasn't used to drinking champagne. She revisited the previous night, Josh and his mates in a very loud bar, his mates egging him on but eyeing up all the other girls. Girls in short skirts and low tops. Their glamorous make-up and styled hair a million miles from her look, if you could call it that. Plain and simple, girl-next-door was the 'look' she was going for. She glanced at her phone and the display read ten o'clock. She sat up in surprise, thinking she had to go somewhere or be somewhere. Then she remembered she didn't have anything to do or anywhere to go. She unlocked her phone and opened Facebook. A few more likes on her London post and a message in Messenger. She opened it up, it was from Josh at 3:29am.

Hey Lucy, great to see you last night. Looked like you had a bit too much of the champers! [Emoji smiley face] *Hope you got home ok. I messaged my mate at the PR agency. Drop him a note on the email below and tell him you know me. See you soon! Take care alright?*

Underneath that message was an email address. Give him credit, she thought, he stuck to his word. She rubbed her eyes and swung her legs off the bed, went to the kitchen and downed a pint of water. She wiped her mouth with the back of her hand and went to stand in the shower, the water seemingly washed away the previous night's alcohol. Wrapped in a towel she sat down at her desk and opened her emails. A few unread emails had come through, rejections from a myriad of applications she had sent off. She copied and pasted the email address Josh had given her in his message and wrote a covering letter that showed off her English skills and willingness to work hard. She opened up her CV and re-read it for the millionth time, double-checking grammar and spelling. Then she attached it to the email and sent it off.

Nothing ventured, nothing gained.

She got up and poured herself some cereal and milk and sat down at the small round kitchen table, looking out of the window to a brick wall. She slipped on some jeans and a cardy and ventured outside. The wind whipped up as she opened the door which almost slammed back in her face. She risked it again and managed to power herself out. She struggled to close the door as the wind tried to force itself in. Litter and dust blew around her feet, her hair flew in front of her eyes. It was an impossible walk, particularly combined with a heavy head and low energy. She turned and went back in, the door swinging easily open as the wind seized its chance to enter. She had to muster all of her energy to put her back into the door to close it again. Once the lock clicked, the air was still and silent. Lucy trudged upstairs to her flat and back to her room. She opened the laptop. An email had appeared from Josh's friend at the PR agency. *That was quick.*

Hi Lucy, nice to e-meet you. Yes, Josh mentioned you. Thanks for sending your CV. I've sent it on to Emma. She'll be in touch if interested. BR

A 'we'll-call-you' email if ever she saw one. She sighed and opened up Google to keep looking for vacancies. She looked at recruitment agencies, but it was difficult to know what she really wanted. They pigeon-holed you into a box, with 'essentials', 'desirables' and 'experience'. There weren't many 'have no experience whatsoever but am really good at writing' on job applications, even entry-level ones. She looked at bar work, of which there was plenty, but nothing paying anything near she needed to pay a rent on a new place, unless she wanted to work 24/7. At this rate though that would be a good option. As she was just about to give up, an email pinged through.

Hi Lucy, this is Emma. I was forwarded your CV. We are looking for someone at the moment with your skills. Do you want to come in for a chat? BW

Wow, that was quick. Thanks Josh. Her first foot through the door. She immediately replied.

Hi Emma, thanks for your quick response. That would be great, thanks. I'm available today if that works. If not, let me know when you are free, and I'll work around you. KR

Maybe she had responded too quickly. Keep them keen and all that. But she thought, what the hell, she had nothing else to do, and was pretty desperate. She looked through her wardrobe for something appropriate to wear. Nothing said PR more than a white low-cut top with a black blazer, a short skirt and tights. She put them on in case Emma responded, wishing to meet her that day. She checked her emails. Nothing. She went to the kitchen and made herself a cup of coffee and imagined what it would be like working for a PR company. The parties, the air-kisses, the dinners in expensive restaurants. None of those really appealed to her. Maybe she was not gregarious enough for that kind of job. She went back to her laptop and hoped that there wasn't an email, that they had forgotten about her. Instead, there it was, an email from Emma.

Hi Lucy, today is looking tight. I'm free tomorrow at 11am. Address is in my signature. See you then! KR

11am tomorrow it was then. Fate had decided her path. She wrote back in the affirmative, highlighted the address and popped it into Google. A map came up with a red marker plum in the middle of a smorgasbord of streets, multi-coloured pins and words. She panicked that she wouldn't be able to find it, amongst all the bustle of a packed city. It was close to Covent Garden, and the map showed it was in walking distance of Waterloo Station, where her train pulled into. Just a hop over Hungerford Bridge and past the Embankment. That seemed ideal, she thought to herself. Maybe it wasn't as bad as she thought. She changed out of her interview clothes and into something a bit more casual and googled the company she was going to. She did a bit of research on its clients and its history and set the laptop down. She lay down on her bed and waited for tomorrow.

Emma was bubbly and sweet, full of optimism and positivity about how amazing the company was and how fabulous their client list was. Lucy didn't need selling on the company, she just needed a job. She had passed the written test: a fake press release for a fake company about their fake new product launch. Emma barely glanced at it when she had finished. She would start next week, and just needed to sort out her references and paperwork.

Was it really this easy to get a job in London?

She messaged Josh with a superlative-ridden thank you, how grateful she was, and how they needed to catch up soon. He replied immediately with a blue thumbs-up icon.

Out of curiosity she clicked on Josh's profile to see if he had posted any pictures of the night they met up. She scrolled down what seemed like endless photos of him in bars with friends that he had posted just over the past couple of days. She got to the date and sure enough there were half a dozen photos of him and his friends posed in selfies, the camera high up getting a full view of the bar. The photos were clearly taken after she had left as they were on the dancefloor, with bottles of beer in each of their hands. Some pretty blonde women were smiling opening mouthed in the photos too. They had obviously quickly moved on from her. He had tagged in his friends with the comment – *top night in London's hottest new venue, thanks for the invite,* and he had tagged in a person who she didn't know. It was hard to believe she was there at the same night. He hadn't tagged her into his photos. For the rest of the world, there was no footnote of her being there, like she didn't exist.

Her first day in the office of her new London job wasn't as exciting as she thought it would be. She was paraded, the guys either eyeing her up or narrowing their eyes as she shook all their hands. She didn't remember any of their names or what they did. She thought there was a John in IT and a Frankie in Finance, and a Billy as an account exec. Lucy was a 'copywriter' and was to sit next to Jessica, who would be 'showing her the ropes', as Emma said with a knowing wink.

Jessica, or Jess as she was instructed to call her, was an account manager with ambitions to be sitting in Emma's office within two years. She kept playing with her straight bleached blonde hair, which made Lucy in turn unconsciously mirror her actions. She had to force herself to stop when she realised what she was doing. Jess didn't say much about the job itself, more about all the perks you got and the restaurants they would go to with clients. She loved meeting the clients face-to-face as that was where her strengths were. Lucy didn't doubt that for a second. She could hardly get a word in edgeways.

The first day passed without much incident. She was set up with an email and password from John, or perhaps Frankie, and was shown all the shared folders. She clicked around the little yellow folders with interesting names of companies she had heard of, getting to know the history and the pitches. An email icon popped up in the bottom right-hand corner of her screen from Emma, who was asking if she could write a short paragraph for a piece of copy she was preparing. She gave her bullet points and Lucy fashioned it into a readable paragraph with positive adjectives and spin. She sent it back and immediately got a reply with 'Thanks Luce!'. Ugh, she hated that nickname. Knowing she'd done a good job, earned some money in London and actually spoken to some people, she was satisfied. She thought she would be able to fit into the company, work well and survive. She went home that day happier than she'd ever been since arriving in London. She emailed her mum that night with an update, knowing she would be as relieved and as happy as her daughter.

Chapter Eight

Lucy must have taken Joe by surprise as he didn't move when their lips touched. They held the kiss for what seemed an eternity, not moving a muscle. She gently pulled away, but he came back in and the sides of their noses rubbed against each other as their lips touched. She put her hand on top of his grey hoodie, her fingers resting on the stitched JW fabric. He kept his arms by his side letting the moment fill him. With their mouths closed they stayed connected; electricity bounced between their skin. She pulled back and momentarily saw him with his eyes closed, before he slowly opened them revealing his deep brown irises.

"You taste like candyfloss," he purred. She threw her arms around his neck and hugged him tightly and he buried his face into her hair. He put his arms around her waist and rested them on her hips. She squeezed her eyes tightly shut and then opened them, seeing the lights of Tower Bridge hazily reveal themselves like in a Richard Curtis film. She hoped a few fireworks would go off in recognition.

This felt real.

Someone liked her for who she was now, without history or prejudice. He turned his head and kissed her on her neck. A shiver went down her spine. He pulled away, noticing.

"Lucy, I, er, haven't done that in a while. Forgive my rustiness."

"Please, it's ok. It was lovely. A perfect evening." She beamed a playful smile. He grinned back and turned towards the bridge.

"Wow, you chose the perfect location. Wait, let me get a photo."

He pulled out his phone and took another selfie, with the bridge glistening in the background. Their cheeks touched as they grinned for the camera.

"My turn," she said, as she took a snap with her phone.

As the camera clicked, she put her hand on his cheek and turned his head so that his lips met hers. She felt giddy and she felt happy.

"Come on," she said, interrupting the moment, teasing him. "Tour's not over yet." She took his hand and pulled him along the waterfront.

"Oh, what else is there to see?" he joked as he mockingly pulled her back into an embrace, his American accent softening which Lucy didn't notice. They kissed again, this time for much longer, forgetting the world around them.

They walked with their fingers intertwined, passing the big gleaming buildings along the riverbank, and alongside the shell-like County Hall as Tower Bridge loomed larger. They walked up the stairs and stepped on the bridge itself. Traffic had thinned out now, just black cabs and red buses trundling along the carriageway. They walked along the bridge, stopping at the halfway point to look down at the water through the gap where the bridge lifts up. They stood astride it, Joe behind her holding her waist. She lifted her arms to recreate the Titanic moment, the bit where Jack took Rose to the edge of the ship and she thought she was flying. She felt just like Rose. They laughed and carried on to the Tower of London, the place almost deserted by the usual throng of crowds. They went past the old boundary wall that marked the beginning and end of the City of London and headed up to Tower Hill tube station. As they sauntered in, the blue-capped staff member urgently informed them that the last train would leave in three minutes. They bolted down the escalators, laughing out loud as they did and jumped on the train that was waiting on the platform. They collapsed into adjoining seats and took a breath. There was an unanswered question between their lips. *What now?*

"Lucy, I've had an unreal time tonight, thank you," he said with an exaggerated accent.

"You are SO welcome," she replied in an awful American pronunciation to which he smiled.

"Look. I know we only met today. It's been a great evening and I don't want it to end." Lucy gulped and looked hopefully into his eyes.

"Me neither," she replied.

"As I said, this is still pretty new to me. I really want to see you again but don't want to take advantage." Her heart sunk a little.

"Do you mind if we call it a night and meet again tomorrow?" There was the answer, the awkward moment passed. A part of her felt disappointed, a part relieved.

"Yes Joe, yes. You are so sweet." She took his head in both her hands and gave him a long kiss. The doors closed and the train rumbled off. She turned so they were both looking the same way out of the window, her head rested on his shoulder, their fingers still laced together.

"Thank you, Lucy," he murmured. She felt him looking up at the map of stations lined up in a row, to see what stop he had to get off.

"Bayswater, that's where I'm headed," he said. Lucy counted the stations.

"I'm Embankment, then I go down to Waterloo," she replied. She squeezed his hand and he squeezed hers back.

"Same time tomorrow, outside Starbucks?" he asked. Lucy was tempted to take the day off.

"Yes. What would you like to do?"

"Not sure, you're the tour guide, what do you suggest?"

"I'll take you to a cute little restaurant I've been to. One of my clients took us there once."

"OK, sounds like a date," he said. Lucy sat back suddenly at the word 'date' and they looked at each other. The word hung in the air. She felt warm inside: she was going on a date, in London, with a handsome man from a country she loved, who seemed to know her, say the right things and do the right things. He was perfect.

"Yes. It's a date," she said confidently and lent in for another kiss. Her lips not wanting to leave his, he squeezed his hand around hers. He didn't try to touch any other part of her body, not her thigh nor her hair or anywhere else a wandering hand might go. The train passed through stations, the doors opened and closed, and the train moving off as she laid her head on his shoulder. Her eyes started to close as the rhythm of the rocking train lulled her into a sleepy daze. The announcer declared that they would shortly be arriving at Embankment.

"Next stop for me Joe." She looked despondently at him, giving him one more time to invite her back to his. She was willing.

"OK Lucy," and he kissed her again.

"I'll see you tomorrow. Same place, same time."

She nodded and gave him one last kiss as she stood up. The doors opened.

"Wait, gimme your number," he called out. Lucy panicked as she went to take her phone out. The warning beeps of the closing doors started to sound.

"Don't worry. I'll be there," she said as the doors shut in her face.

Joe gave a thumbs up as the train started to rumble off, which turned into a shy wave as he disappeared from sight. For the first time in her life, she felt real.

Lucy hardly slept that night as the evening with Joe replayed in her mind. What she had said and how it might have come across. She saw his face, his eyes and she dreamt of what tomorrow might bring and what a future might bring. As soon as these thoughts entered her head, she tried to erase them: this was a holiday romance for him. Nothing would come of it. It just felt different, familiar. On the other hand, if it was just a holiday romance, surely she'd have been in his hotel room now, wrapped in clean white sheets, nestling in the crook of his shoulder. Something definitely felt different with Joe. Maybe, just maybe, it would be longer than a holiday romance. She reminded herself he'd just lost his wife and kids in a tragic accident. But that was over a year ago. How long does it take to grieve? He himself said that he wasn't ready, but then they slipped into being a couple.

These contradictory thoughts whirled inside her head into the early hours of the morning, each with different scenarios and outcomes. She imagined what he would say and what she would say back. Where they would be and what they would be eating. She thought of the touch of his lips on her lips, their fingers knitted together and never letting go. The permutations of different conversations spun through her mind. She checked her phone clock. 2am. She tried to switch her focus, to work, to her mum, to her unhappy, confusing teenage years at school but she kept coming back to Joe. Joe's eyes, Joe's hair, the beginnings of a small dimple on his cheek. His East Coast drawl. The touch of his fingers. The touch of his lips.

She didn't know when she drifted off back to sleep but when her phone alarm trilled which suddenly woke her, the room already filled with light. She jumped out of bed and into the shower. Standing in front of her wardrobe, she pondered what to wear. Something that wouldn't look out of place in the office but flirty enough to meet Joe later that day. She settled on a flowery white dress that banded around the waist that showed off her small cleavage and wrapped a black shawl around her shoulders. She looked out of the window and the sun was shining. She slipped on her pumps and checked herself in the mirror. Her hair was almost dry and there was a bounce to it from the conditioner. She twisted her body around to get a profile look, the hem of the dress twirled around like a ballerina, and she was satisfied she looked girly enough. Nothing she could do about her pale legs though. She checked her face for pimples and brushed a small smattering of blusher over her cheeks. That would have to do she thought to herself. She popped her phone into her bag and put it over her shoulder. She checked one final time in the mirror and left the flat, a warmth in the air and a spring in her step.

She stopped by the Starbucks as usual and Al greeted her with his usual smile.

"Ah Miss Lucy! Well, you look nice today! Important meeting or a hot date?!" He accentuated the word 'date' in a staccato way, with a broad grin across his face.

"Something like that Al," she bashfully replied.

"Oooh, well good luck! The usual Miss Lucy, with an extra shot?"

"Yes please Al, thank you."

"And anything else to accompany your beverage this morning?"

"No thanks Al, I'm fine."

She glanced around the café as she waited for her order. Someone else was sitting in the seat that Joe was in yesterday. Despite the same types of people as the previous day, minding their own business and carrying on with life, the café felt different, like sunlight was shining on the place. She got her mug and took a seat at an empty table towards the back. She smiled into her coffee as the lukewarm liquid went down her throat, warming her insides. Her mind went back 24 hours to when she bravely chose a seat opposite Joe and what had happened since.

Carpe Diem.

She was proud of herself. Her mindset had changed. She was happier, positive, feeling like anything could happen. She finished her drink and headed out of the door to the office. She strode through the almost-bare reception and nodded to Johnny, who was staring intensely at his computer screen, biting his fingernail.

"Alright Johnny." she said. It wasn't a question.

"Yep, alright Lucy." he replied. Again, not a question.

She saw the top of Jess's head and felt excited that she finally had something worthy to say to her. She bounced into her chair and swung round to face her.

"Blimey, look at you. Bliiiiiiimey, look at YOU!" said Jess. She did a double take at her bare legs and her white flowery dress.

"What happened Luce?! No, no let me guess. I can't think of any clients you are going to see today. It's not *that* warm outside. Hmmmm…." She tapped her fingers mockingly on her chin. Lucy smiled an embarrassed smile. She felt her cheeks reddening.

"It can only mean one thing… A HOT DATE!" Lucy smiled bashfully and gave her a nod. Jess squealed. A couple of people popped their heads up over their computer screens to see what was causing the ruckus.

"Luce!" She jumped up and threw her arms around her neck, whilst Lucy was still sitting and hugged her tight. She had to prise her off.

"Calm down Jess!"

"Tell me, tell me, tell me." She was still squealing. Lucy reached over and turned her computer on, conscious that people were still looking, and giving herself a bit of dramatic pause.

"Who is it Luce?" Jess was beyond excited, thirsty for gossip, gagging for details of a possible love life of her work neighbour.

"His name is Joe and he's from America."

"Ooooh!" she clapped her hands with her fingers pointing up, her palms not separating.

"I met him yesterday morning in Starbucks and we agreed to meet up after work. We had a lovely evening walking along the river."

"Wait, wait, wait." She held up her palm to stop her.

"You met him yesterday morning. And you didn't mention it to me? Luce! I'm your work buddy!"

"I didn't know, it was just some guy that I met and decided to meet him after work."

"Babe, you gotta tell me these things. Let me give you some advice, where to go, what to do." She arched her eyebrows with a telling nod.

"Tell me then, what did you do?" she inched her chair towards hers. "So, you walked along the river. Aaaaaand….."

"Aaaaaaand…. We had a nice dinner," she countered.

"Aaaaaannd…." She was egging her on.

"Aaaaaannnnd…. We had a little snog."

"Haha I knew it! Good on you Luce! What was it like?"

"It was lovely Jess; he was a true gent. Perfect even."

"Uh-oh, what does that mean? You didn't go any further right?"

"Yeah, we said our goodbyes and agreed to meet tomorrow. Which is today."

"Oh Luce, you sly little minx. Keeping it all quiet from me. Well good for you, you need a man in your life." Lucy didn't want to tell her his details, that he was a widower and only in London for a holiday. She didn't want Jess to burst her bubble. When the time was right, she would tell her. She couldn't handle the advice and the judgement right now. She just wanted to go with the flow and see what happened. *Carpe Diem*. She turned back to her computer and fired up the email app.

"Oh, Luce I'm so happy for you!" Jess could hardly contain herself. She reached over and squeezed her knee.

"So, where you going tonight? Somewhere dark and romaaaaantic?" Lucy got the feeling she didn't want the conversation to end.

"Yeah, somewhere nice to eat. Do you know anywhere?"

"Do I *know* anywhere? Luce, you're talking to the queen of restaurants!" She spun back round to her screen and tapped furiously on her keyboard. Lucy thought that might do the trick and keep her quiet for a while. Fifteen minutes later she got an email notification from Jess with the subject line 'restaurants'. Jess wheeled herself over to Lucy's computer.

"Right," she said. "I've sent you a list of places I've been to, ordered by priciest at the top and cheapest down the bottom." She opened the email with Jess looking on. Blue lines highlighted the hyperlinks. Jess took over the mouse and clicked on each link, opening up each website and the photos of the venue. She went through one-by-one giving her an analysis of each one, scored on romance, quality of food, ambience, how hot the waiters were, wine, slowness of service, temperature and where to sit. The information was overwhelming. Lucy listened but nothing sunk in. Twenty minutes later Jess asked:

"Well?"

"Well, what?"

"Which one tickles your fancy, so to speak?" she winked at her.

"Oh, um." She chose the first one on the list.

"Oooh, great choice. Let me know how it goes!" She picked up her notepad and pen and got up from her chair. As she passed Lucy, she put both hands on her shoulders and gave them a squeeze.

"Oh Luce, I'm so happy for you!" and she disappeared into Emma's office and shut the door, no doubt telling her the good news. Emma would be delighted at Jess' social transformation.

Chapter Nine

Lucy couldn't think too much that day. Her mind was somewhere else. Jess came and went, each time squeezing her shoulders and giving a squeak every time she walked past her. Emma was in and out of her office, giving her an appreciative smile every time their eyes met.

At eleven-thirty, Jess came bounding over to Jess' desk, a huge smile on her face.

"Get your things, you're coming with me!" she said as she picked up her coat from the back of her chair, slid her notepad and pen into her handbag and slung it over her shoulder.

"What? Why? What are we doing?"

"You're coming with me for a client lunch. Em can't make it and said you should come with me. They are lovely and they'll love you."

"OK. But I need to be back for five. Remember?"

"Yeah, yeah. It's just a lunch. We'll be back in time for your hot date!"

Anxiety rose up into Lucy's chest. She knew that more often than not these 'lunches' went on to the early hours of the morning. She reluctantly switched off her computer and got up.

"Yay!" Jess said, clapping her hands. "This is going to be so much fun!"

The Uber cab pulled up along the cobbled, curved driveway of the red-bricked St Pancras hotel, it's huge Gothic-style dominating the landscape. Lucy had seen this sight many times – her train depositing her in the newly-refurbished – and gargantuan – train station attached to it. She had never been in the hotel part though, yet it was clear Jess had as she breezed through the glass doors as if was a resident of the luxury hotel.

They turned into the restaurant before Lucy had time to admire the impressive skylit lobby.

As she entered the restaurant, the space took her breath away. The ethereal atmosphere and curved arches made it church-like, whilst the exposed brickwork and high ceilings made her feel tiny in such a huge space. It reminded her of the Turbine Hall of the Tate Modern and her mind went back to Joe. A white-topped bar ran along the entire left flank of the room, with a multitude of square tables and booths dotting the remaining space. A mixture of blue and brown plush leather seats sat askew. The large room made the tinkling of cutlery and murmured voices dull into a humdrum of background noise.

Lucy was still looking around when Jess pulled her attention.

"Impressive, isn't it? We always bring new clients here. Come on, they are here already."

She waved over to a couple sitting in a booth, their backs against a high white leather seat. They both stood as Jess bustled over, Lucy a few steps behind, their mobile phones laying on the table next to the forks.

"Hi Jack, hi Megan, you haven't been waiting long, have you?"

She leant over to air-kiss them. Jack was wearing a smart blue blazer, a clean white top and dark blue jeans, his hair clearly thinning on top. Megan was almost the spitting image of Jess, yet considerably older, with bright blonde hair, wearing a tight, black skirt and white blouse.

"No, not all. Lovely to see you Jess," she said, air-kissing her back.

Jess turned to Lucy.

"This is Lucy," she said, by way of introduction. "She is a super member of the team that will be working on your account."

This wasn't true of course. Jess had briefed her in the cab over: what the account was, personalities involved, the brief and, importantly, what she should and shouldn't say.

"Hi," Lucy responded, extending her arm out.

"Oh, hi Lucy," Megan said, accepting the handshake. Her head tilted slightly and her eyes narrowed just a fraction of a millimetre.

"Nice to meet you Jack," Lucy said purposefully, reaching over the table to shake Jack's hand. He hesitated for a split second before taking her hand.

"Right!" Jess said loudly, causing the people on the neighbouring table to glance at them. "Let's order, shall we?"

She sat down on the cushioned seat and picked up the menu sitting between her knife and fork.

"The mussels here are to die for," she said to herself.

Megan and Jack turned out to be good company, the wine flowed and Jess was in her element. Lucy couldn't help but admire her patter, the way she complimented the clients and made them believe that they were best friends. It was a ruse of course: to wine and dine the clients, make them feel good and valued. Lucy joined in with the banter and the stories, enough to be just involved but not overpowering the conversation. Jess was an expert at that, allowing them to talk to make them feel important (she had briefed her in the cab – *always let the clients do most of the talking, this meeting is all about them*).

Eventually, they talked a bit about the brief and the work that was needed to do. That was the part where Lucy stayed quiet and let Jess do all the talking. She couldn't believe the amount of BS that was coming out of her mouth. Yet the clients were raptured, and the free-flowing alcohol certainly helped. The conversation turned away from the work soon enough and they were back to laughter and tales. Warmth was coursing through Lucy's body and she actually felt like she was having a good time.

A text message notification rang from her phone. She apologised as she turned her mobile over, which sat on the white tablecloth, speckled with food from their meal. It was from Josh.

Are you currently sitting in a posh restaurant in St Pancras?

Lucy spun around in her seat, looking around the large restaurant. A man in a blazer was waving at her from a table in the corner. It was Josh, sitting on his own. Lucy immediately stood up and waved enthusiastically back. She turned to her companions.

"Would you excuse me for just a minute?" she said excitedly.

"Of course," Jack and Megan said, almost simultaneously. Jess gave her a cautious nod.

Lucy walked quickly over to Josh, darting between tables and diners. He was already next to his table with his arms outstretched. Lucy hugged him.

"I thought it was you!" he said, "I could've recognised those red curls anywhere!"

"Oh, good to see you Josh," Lucy beamed back. "I seriously owe you one for setting me up with this job."

"Ah, it's nothing. Glad I could help. Is that who you are with now?" He glanced over at the table Lucy had come from.

"Yeah, it's a client meeting," she said, putting air-quotes over the words 'meeting'.

"Haha! Yeah, I've had a few of those. Alcohol flowing, is it?"

Lucy blushed.

"Can you tell?!"

"Er, slightly!" Lucy felt her cheek with the back of her hand. She was certainly very warm.

"What are you doing here?" she asked.

"Meeting up with a mate. He's doing well," he said as he glanced around the restaurant. "Nice place, isn't it?"

Lucy followed his gaze. It sure was and it was thanks to him that she was here.

"Well, when he comes why don't you join us? You know, when our clients are gone. My colleague Jess is over there, she's a right laugh."

He peered over Lucy's shoulder, trying to decipher which one Jess was.

"And it's the least I could do. To say thanks for getting me the job."

"Yeah. Yeah, ok then. Give me the signal when we should come over. He should be here any minute so I'll get us some drinks and come over."

"Perfect!"

She turned to go and noticed Jack and Megan getting up from their seats. It looked like they were readying themselves to go. She hurried over.

"Sorry about that, someone I know from university. A bit of a coincidence."

"We've got to get back to the office. It was so lovely to meet you, Lucy."

Lucy extended her arm but Megan scoffed.

"Oh please!" and gave her a big hug, almost knocking her off her balance. Jack put one hand in his jeans pocket and shifted on his feet. When Megan released Lucy from her embrace, he shot out an arm.

"Great to meet you too," he said, shaking her hand whilst Jess hugged Megan and went to air-kiss Jack. He leant in awkwardly, not knowing which way to go to and in the process almost brushed her on the lips. Jess laughed nervously and flicked her hair back.

"You take care now, and I'll get those ideas over to you tomorrow."

As they left the restaurant, Jess sat down and cocked her head at Lucy.

"Well, what did you think?"

"They were lovely. I had a great time."

"See! I told you! Let your hair down a bit. Let the champers flow and let yourself go."

"Yeah, you're right."

"Damn sure I'm right! Who was that guy anyway?" She said, picking up her flute and taking a sip.

"Ah, an old uni friend. He's a policeman. Actually, he set me up with this job."

"No way!" She turned to look at him, to see if she knew who he was. He waved at her.

"Oh Lucy, let's get him over. This calls for a celebration! He looks so alone over there too."

Jess beckoned him over and he shot out of his seat, knocking the table. He swaggered over, his wine glass dangling between his fingers.

"Afternoon ladies," he said, smirking at Jess who stretched out an arm.

"Jess," she countered and motioned him to sit in the space vacated by Jack.

He slid across the white leather seat and flicked crumbs away. He opened his blazer and pulled out a pair of black rimmed glasses. They suited him.

"Nice to meet you. My mate literally just bailed on me, so you've saved me actually." He looked over to Lucy. "She rescued me from embarrassment."

"Shut up! I owe you one anyway."

"Lucy said that you got her the job. She's been amazing so far," Jess said.

"Glad to hear it! Yeah, I know Jonathan. He's an account director or something."

"Jonathan?" Jess replied, astounded. "He's the owner."

"Oh, is he?" Josh said casually. "A friend of a friend, you know."

"Hmmm, friends in high places," Jess said, raising an eyebrow.

"Yeah, s'ppose. It's who you know, not what you know in this city," he replied, winking at Lucy. "Ain't that right Lucy?"

Lucy bashfully smiled.

"As Jess said, this calls for a celebration. What do you think Lucy?"

"Yeah, why not!" she said, her eyes momentarily going out of focus. She looked at Josh who seemed to be looking into the far distance. It was hard to tell with those glasses. Maybe he was looking right at her. Jess beckoned a passing waiter and ordered a bottle of red as Lucy looked at the display on her phone. Enough time for another drink and then get to Joe.

"This one's on Jonathan," Jess said, straightening her back and raising her glass.

"To friends in high places."

And they all chinked their glasses together and took a large glug.

With warmth flowing through their bodies, conversation flowed. Other diners glared at them whenever a loud, raucous laugh left their table. Josh seemed to be loving the company of two women, particularly a very attractive blonde who was getting tipsier after every minute. Lucy noticed that she twirled the end of her hair more and more frequently as time elapsed. True, she had never seen her outside of a work setting before. It was like her guard was down, with no ulterior motive of getting clients to feel good about themselves. Josh was on-form, cracking jokes and anecdotes of some of the police work he had done in his job. Whenever Jess asked about what Lucy was like at university, he somehow managed to divert the conversation back to Jess, asking about her and what she liked doing (it seemed like he was playing Jess' game back to her, letting her talk about herself to make her feel special). Occasionally his attention seemed to be distracted, asking for questions to be repeated. Perhaps it was the drink getting to him.

"So, Lucy," Josh said casually, running his fingers along the rim of his glass. "Have you met anyone special yet?"

Jess sat bolt upright and put her hands flat on the table. "Luce! What time is it?"

Lucy flickered her eyes into focus.

"Oh shit!" She flicked her phone over and read the dial. 4:45pm.

How did that happen?

"I got to go," she said, scooping up her things and stumbling over her chair. Jess opened up an Uber app.

"What's going on?" Josh asked.

"Lucy's got a date," Jess smirked.

"Oh really!" Josh replied. "Good on you!"

"Yeah, but I'm so not going to get there in time," she replied, busying herself.

"I'm getting an Uber for you, I'll come with. I need to get going."

"Ah, so soon!" Josh countered, clearly disappointed that he thought he might get Jess by herself.

"Yeah, sorry Josh. Let's meet up again. That was fun!" And she leant over and pecked him on the cheek. She beckoned the waiter over and asked for the bill.

"Can I, er, have your number then?" he asked, trying to sound casual as the women busied themselves to leave, Jess searching her bag for her credit card.

"I'll get it off Luce," she paused. "If that's all right."

"Yeah sure," he said, a lightness to his voice. Lucy winked at Josh and gave him a hug. She mouthed a 'thank you' and he nodded silently back. He hugged her again and whispered a *take care* into her ear.

"You're doing so well," he said and squeezed her arm. Lucy smiled shyly. Jess grabbed her arm and pulled her away.

"Come on! We don't want you to be late!"

The two women bustled out of the restaurant, knocking into a few chairs as they went. Jess' high heels clanked on the wooden floor as they hurried out. The cool air hit them as they left the building and stood on the cobbles outside. Jess had her eyes glued to phone.

"Damn it. Twenty minutes." She looked around. The Euston Road was at a standstill.

"Come on, quicker to get the tube."

"We'll never make it Jess. It's almost five already."

Lucy imagined Joe making his way to the meeting point, butterflies in his stomach.

"Do you have his number?"

"No, I didn't get it. My social calendar isn't exactly bursting so I didn't think I would need it."

"Oh Luce, I'm so sorry." Her eyes darted left and right trying to think of a solution.

"Where did you say you were meeting him?"

"Outside Starbucks on the Strand."

"Luce, call the office and get Johnny to run there."

"I'm not doing that!"

"Luce, bloody do it. I've never seen you so excited before. Call him. In fact, if you don't do it I will." She swiped up her phone and called the office.

"Damn it, pick up Johnny! What time is it? He's probably gone home the skiver." One of the benefits that Emma was keen to push home was that no one should be staying past five o'clock, in the office at least – entertaining clients was a different rule.

"SHIT." She turned her screen off.

"I'm so sorry Luce. I'll make it up to you."

"Don't worry Jess, it's fine. It's not your fault." She pictured Joe standing outside Starbucks, looking left and right for her through the crowds.

"Yes, it is. I ordered more bottles of –"

"Starbucks!" Lucy exclaimed.

"What?" Jess looked at her, "what about it?"

"I'll call Starbucks and ask them to go out and meet him. And explain."

She was already bumbling in her bag looking for her phone. She whipped it out and fired up Google. She typed in Starbucks on the Strand and two red pins appeared on the map. She located the correct one and saw the 'call' button. She hurriedly pressed it and held the phone to her ear. Jess looked at her, her fingers crossed in front of her flushed face. Someone picked up, and cheerily greeted her "Hello Starbucks how may I help you today?"

"Oh hi, I'm wondering if you can help me…." Her voice trailed off at the voice at the end of the phone sounded familiar.

"Al, is that you?"

"Yes madam this is Al."

"AL! This is Lucy, Lucy that drinks a flat white and shot every morning!"

She felt a relief over her body.

"Ah Miss Lucy! What are you wanting, placing an order in advance?"

"No, no. Al, listen. I was supposed to meet a guy outside Starbucks tonight but I'm late. I can't make it and I need to tell him. Can you go outside and see if he is there?"

"Oh Miss Lucy, yes the hot date! I remember! I am sorry that you are waylaid. I'm not really supposed to leave my position. I can see outside now but I can't see anyone really. What does he look like?" The question left her a bit surprised.

"Oh, well he is about six-foot-tall, dark hair, American. He was there yesterday morning in a grey hoodie and a baseball-type shirt. You may remember him; his name is Joe." She felt like she was clutching at straws, thinking Al might remember his name when taking the order.

"Hmm, no I don't remember and I don't see anyone matching that description. Hold on Miss Lucy, for you as a valued customer, I will go and look."

He placed the receiver down as she said 'thank you Al' through the phone. Jess was still crossing her fingers looking hopeful. She mouthed that he was going to look. Al came back on the phone in what seemed like an eternity later.

"Hello Miss Lucy. No, there isn't anyone there matching that description. I asked a couple of fellows who were standing outside but no one called Joe."

Her heart sank and Jess noticed her reaction. She put her arms around her neck.

"OK, thanks so much Al," she said, her phone squeezed against her ear.

"I'm so sorry Miss Lucy. I'll see you tomorrow."

"Yeah, thanks Al." She hung up and Jess muttered her apologies.

"I'm so sorry Luce."

"Please don't worry. He's just a jock anyway."

Jess knew Lucy was hiding her disappointment.

"Next time, get his number!"

"Next time don't invite me out for lunch! Especially when it lasts till teatime!"

Jess playfully punched her arm.

"Maybe this is the universe talking. Maybe it's meant to be."

"In that case I need to have a serious chat with the universe."

They giggled but Jess could tell Lucy was upset.

"Glass of wine?" she asked, hopefully.

"Yeah, why not. But not with Josh, if that's ok. Maybe just the two of us?"

"Agreed. But I do want his number."

They walked slowly along the pavement, past Kings Cross and into a posh-looking pub. They went in and Lucy ordered a couple of glasses of house white and placed them in front of Jess who had found a round table for two in the corner, flicking through her phone.

"Thanks Luce," she took a glass and swallowed a glug whilst still looking at her phone. Lucy was not even sure she tasted it. They sat in silence for a while; Jess absorbed in her phone and Lucy feeling guilty for Joe. She let out a big sigh. What must he be thinking, and doing? Being stood up by the girl that wanted to go back to his place. Maybe he felt rejected and was regretting not inviting her back. Perhaps he was with another girl right now. She tried to shift her thoughts and started a conversation.

"That was a good lunch though. Is that what it's always like?"

"Yeah, pretty much," she grinned. "I like going out with the clients. Don't really like doing the work," she picked up her glass, looked through it and took a sip.

"Keeps me busy I suppose. I like going out to all the bars, and the guys flirting with me. I never take it too far though, I've got boundaries."

"Doesn't it mess with your social life?" Lucy asked.

"Work *is* my social life Luce. I don't really have any friends outside of work, except for Kaz, but she's always jetting off round the world on shoots. And you."

Lucy immediately started to pity her; how lonely she must feel underneath the bluster. Lonely like her.

"If a client leaves, or I get the old heave-ho, I'll be lost. That's why I always say yes to a drink. Keeps me active. Sometimes when we lose a contract, I meet up with the client socially, thinking they are my friends but they start to lose interest. My flirting means nothing if it doesn't lead to anything or doesn't get them extras on their contract."

90

"Have you ever, you know, even after they aren't clients anymore…. Gone further?"

"Nah, thought about it though. Just not my style. Plus, never really had anyone I fancied. They're usually too old for me."

She took another swig of her wine. Lucy checked the time and realised she had to travel right across London to get home.

"What about exes? Surely you must have had loads, Jess."

"Yeah, a few. Nothing special. Mainly when I was at uni. I guess I'm a professional now or waiting for 'The One'." Her eyes glazed over, her mind looking into the past.

"What about dating sites, I imagine you'd do well on them."

"Ew no! I'm not that desperate Luce," she looked up horrified, and started to backtrack.

"No, I mean dating apps are ok, but just not for me you know."

"It's ok Jess, I'm not on a dating app." She smiled at her and took a sip of her wine.

"Oh, thank God. I'm sorry Jess for ruining your evening."

She placed her hand on her knee.

"Stop apologising! I'm glad I'm here. It's too late now anyway! Let's get another one in – your turn."

They sat and chatted for a while. They took it in turns to order each other a round and soon it was pitch black outside. Lucy had sat next to Jess for over three months but tonight was when she found out most about her. Her brother had died when she was a baby and her mother hadn't been able to cope. It had been a strain on her relationship with her dad, who had left soon after. It had been just her and her mum as she grew up, and they still lived together in a two-bed flat just down the road. She had been bullied at school and had flirted with the guys as a way of protection from the nasty bitches, as she called them. She had to do what it took to survive the bullies – just like Lucy. She was glad to get away to uni and let her flirting develop into one-night stands and short relationships. It was her 'wild years' as she called them and vowed to learn to not be such a slut. She had felt guilty being away from her mum. When she moved back in after uni her mum had fallen in love with a hairdresser on the high street, who had moved in not long after. The upside was she got free haircuts. The downside was knowing the guy cutting her hair was sleeping with her mum. She sighed and took a gulp of wine. Her mum was getting more action than her.

That's when she 'fell' into PR. It meant she was out most nights with clients, which allowed her mum and boyfriend to have some time alone together. Her mum was happy, that's all that mattered, and her boyfriend was a laugh. It seemed that she had waited for Jess to become an adult before she could think about herself. She was pleased the way it had worked out. And no, she hadn't seen her dad since he had left. She had found a few photos, but he was as alien to her as the next guy. Just like Lucy and her relationship with her father. Maybe they weren't so dissimilar after all. Lucy yawned, conscious of her journey home and work tomorrow.

"Look Jess, is it ok if I go? I've got a bit of a trek to get home."

"Oh jeez, Luce, I'm so sorry. I feel so bloody guilty. Listen why don't you stay at my mum's tonight? I've got a settee in my room and we can go into the office together. I'll even lend you some clothes, so you don't look like a dirty stop-out."

Lucy tried to resist, saying she needed to get home, which was nonsense of course and Jess saw right through it.

"It's decided then." She got up, went to the bar and ordered another round.

Two hours later they were back at her mum's place, two friends passed out in her room.

Chapter Ten

The next morning the sunlight shone through the open curtains into Lucy's eyes. She blinked hard, trying to remember where she was. Her head pounded. She looked over the side of the double bed. Jess was curled up on a settee, facing away from her, hugging a pillow, still wearing her clothes from the night before. She sat up, her crumpled white dress around her waist. This wasn't the strange room she had envisaged waking up in. She thought back to Joe standing outside Starbucks and wondered how long he had waited for her. Then she remembered calling Al who couldn't find him. Maybe he didn't recognise him, maybe Joe didn't wait that long. She pictured Joe's face, disappointed and angry at her for standing him up. She got up and looked in Jess' full length mirror. Her hair was a red mess of a bird's nest sitting atop her head. She tried to smooth it down and rubbed the sleep out of her eyes. She crept to the door in search of the toilet. The door creaked as she slowly opened it and standing almost in the doorframe was a hulk of a man, his dressing gown slightly open with a large round belly protruding over the loosely done up straps. A white vest struggled to cover his hairy paunch. He was as shocked to see her as she was to see him. He looked at her square in the face then eyed her up and down - his eyebrow cocked over his left eye. He moved his head back to peep through the door.

"Erm, I'm Lucy," she stammered. "I work with Jess. We had a few drinks last night and she said I could crash here." She felt the colour of her cheeks redden at the speed of her voice. "On her sofa."

"Of course you are love. And of course you did. Jim. Jess' mums', erm, fella," he replied, a smile creeping onto his face. He leant back to take a peek into Jess' room.

"As you were," he said to himself, turned on his heels and almost danced to another room, the door slightly ajar, the corner of a bed just visible. Lucy went into the bathroom and locked the door as she heard voices, a deep male voice and a female voice. Then she heard footsteps and Jess's door creaked open. Then the footsteps retreated. Lucy splashed water on her face, washed her hands and dried herself on a clean smelling towel hanging on a silver rod. She unlocked the bathroom door, tiptoed out and back into Jess's room. She sat on the edge of the sofa, next to her curled legs.

"Jess," she whispered, "Jess." She nudged her legs. Jess responded by turning on to her back and opened her eyes wide.

"What? What?" She looked around the room, dazed. Her eyes found hers.

"Oh Luce, what time is it?" She curled back around and hugged the pillow. Lucy got up and looked for her phone. The screen lit up. 7:30am.

"Half seven Jess."

"Ooooo crap." She sat up and rubbed her eyes. Her usually immaculate blonde hair was ruffled and curling up at the ends.

"How much did we drink last night?" she said rhetorically. She swung her legs round off the sofa, got up and walked out the door to the bathroom. Lucy was left sitting on the bed. She found her phone, swiped up, opened Facebook and had a quick scroll to fill the time. She heard the toilet flush and Jess came back into the room, a folded towel in her arms.

"Here have this, I'll grab some clothes for you." She took the towel and had a shower. It was always odd having a shower in someone else's place, grappling with the knobs to get the temperature right and the weird air of a new environment. She towelled herself dry, wrapped it tightly around her and darted into the bedroom. Jess had laid out a few clothing options on the bed, and she picked out the most conservative of the selection whilst Jess went to have a shower. She sat on the edge of the bed waiting for her to finish – she didn't want to meet Jess' mum and fella on her own – looking around the room.

After what seemed an eternity, Jess eventually came back in, a towel round her body and one in a bun wrapped around her head. Her body was long and sleek. She sat down at her dressing table in front of the mirror and started to brush her hair, long strokes from the roots to the tips, her slim, feminine shoulders naked above the towel. She was talking about last night, and apologising, wishing that she wasn't such a cow and that she hadn't ruined her date. Lucy's feet were tapping on the floor, she wanted to get going. She thought about going to Starbucks to see if Joe was waiting there, the same time as they had first met. Jess picked up one of the clothes choices that she had laid out on the bed for her and slipped into a knee-length skirt and a flowery blouse. She opened the door, walked out and Lucy followed like a naughty schoolgirl. They went down the stairs where they could hear the rattle of teaspoons and clunk of crockery, cupboards opening and closing. Lucy walked in behind Jess, keeping her head low, her cheeks felt red. Jim was standing by the kitchen counter, a mug of tea resting on top of his belly, now hidden behind a black t-shirt.

"Morning," he said cheerfully and with a hint of mischievousness behind it. Jess' mum spun round and looked at them both. Her eyes lingered on Lucy more than Jess.

"Have a good night girls?" She asked, although it sounded like a rhetorical question.

"Yes mum. This is Luce, we work together."

"Oh, hi Luce," she said in an enthusiastic tone. She looked back and forth between them. Jim's eyebrow was still cocked. Jess noticed it.

"Oh, piss off Jim. It's not what you think." She rolled her eyes and turned away. Jim continued to grin, knowing he had got the attention he was after. He moved over toward Jess, and lowered his voice, bending down to her ear – pretending to whisper but knowing full well Lucy would hear.

"It's ok if you are Jess. I'm a modern man, your mum loves you for who you are. It's the 21st century you know. People are more open to, you know. It." He shot Lucy a look. She responded by going bright red.

"As I said Jim. Piss off." He raised his spare hand in mock-defeat.

"Ok, whatever you say honey. We're here if you need us." Lucy got the feeling Jim joked about everything.

"Don't listen to him sweetheart," Jess's mum said looking at Lucy. "Just a bit of fun, ain't it Jim." She poked him in the stomach and her finger disappeared.

They laughed and Jim looked at Jess's mum like Joe had looked at her the night before last. Jess's mum grinned back. Her eyes were alight. She turned to get back to what she was doing as Jess hurried about and a mug of tea was put in Lucy's hand. She declined the offer of toast and cereal, happily watching this family's routine at the round table, hands around her mug of tea, moving around each other like a rehearsed dance: they left the room and came back, picked things up and put things down; a smattering of noise and a few sentences of updates. Like families were supposed to be – non-judgmental and getting on with things.

When Jim passed by Jess's mum, he affectionately brushed his hand over her body – sometimes her bum, sometimes her back, sometimes her arm. The way she responded to Jim's touch was completely natural, mockingly moving his hand away when he reached for her bottom, fussing over him. Lucy looked at Jess's mum and thought of Jess as a baby, her mum on her own, having to deal with a death, a life and a future of loneliness. And then to find happiness. She watched her and felt glad she had met Jim, like she deserved another chance at love. She had gone through hell and come out the other side. She thought of Joe and what he must have gone through over the past year. And then she felt bad again for standing him up. Jess breezed back into the kitchen and grabbed her bag from the floor.

"Let's go Luce. Bye mum. Bye Jim. Don't be a cock today!" she turned her head back, her long blonde hair swirling in the turn.

"Burk, buk, buk, burrrrrk," Jim replied, jutting his head back and forth.

"See ya, nice meeting you Luce. See you again," Jess' mum called out as they shut the door. Lucy never did catch her mum's name.

The front of the station was full of people: hawkers, people waiting and commuters walking past. They quickly navigated through them all, meandered through the crowded, cobbled streets and walked right through Covent Garden with its high arched roof and independent stalls and shops. A couple of human statues were out already, hoping to catch the early tourist. Jess powered through a few steps ahead of Lucy and ended up outside their offices in no time. Starbucks was beyond the office. Lucy thought about going on, just in case. The time read 9:15am.

Too late.

Jess breezed into the reception, Lucy a few steps behind catching the glass door before it shut. Johnny looked up at them and nodded a bored 'hello'.

"Hey Johnny, running late today!" Jess trilled as an excuse that she couldn't stop to chat. They both went through the doors into the open-plan office. People were walking about with mugs in their hands, steam coming from the rims.

"Morning!" Jess shrilled over the entire office. She took off her coat, dumped her bag by her desk and booted up her PC. Lucy reached over and switched on her PC, and realising a need for her morning coffee, went to the kitchen and put the kettle on. She'd never done that before; she usually got her flat white and shot and that saw her through for most of the morning. She waited by the kettle, the water inside bubbling and making it shudder. She pulled down a couple of mugs and peered inside inspecting its cleanliness, dumped in a couple of spoons of instant and grabbed the milk out of the fridge. She turned and saw Em half-sitting on her desk, chatting to Jess. She took the cups over and stood awkwardly, holding them out. Em turned to face her.

"Well, someone made a good impression!" she beamed. "Jack and Megan loved you! What on earth did you do to them?"

Lucy blushed.

"Nothing. Jess did all the talking. She was great."

"Ah, modest. Well, maybe you two are the new dream team." She clicked her tongue, smiled at her and walked away. Jess raised her eyebrows in triumph.

"Success!" Jess said but noticed Lucy didn't share her enthusiasm. She took the cups and rubbed her arms.

"I'm sorry Luce. About your date."

"Don't worry about it," Lucy replied. She had had a thought that she would wait outside Starbucks later at 5pm, just to see if Joe turned up. Maybe, just maybe, she could rescue it. But first she had a day of boredom to get through.

Chapter Eleven

Later that morning Lucy was called into Em's office for a conference call with one of her clients. She struggled throughout, the alien voices jostled out of the little speaker on the table, talking over each other. The accents on the phone were all women, so without a face to go with the voice, they all merged into one. She kept looking up at Em to help her out. Throughout the call, Em and Lucy exchanged Post-It notes to try and interpret what was transpiring. After an hour the meeting was called to an end, and Em pressed the red button on the speaker. She breathed out a long sigh.

"So, what do I need to do?" Lucy enquired, hoping that Em had followed, and understood, the conversation.

"Not entirely sure Luce," she replied. "I'll drop them a note, copying you in, with a summary of the conversation, and see what they come back with." She stood up and went back to her desk. Lucy got up and walked out the office. Just as she was coming out of the door, she almost bumped into Johnny.

"Oh, there you are. I dropped you an email and I was ringing your line. You've got a visitor." He turned on his heels and walked back to reception. She was slightly taken aback. No-one came to visit her and she didn't have any clients that would just drop in. She called after him asking who it was but he just shrugged his shoulders as he disappeared along the corridor, not looking back.

She followed him and got to the door just as it shut from Johnny's exit. She looked through the round glass embedded in the wooden door and couldn't believe her eyes. It was Joe, standing in the reception area, looking around at the vast atrium. How had he found her? She took a deep breath, her heart thumping against her chest, opened the door and walked out.

He looked up immediately and gave a relieved sigh. He walked over to her and they met halfway.

"Joe!" she said, surprised. She didn't know what to do with her hands for a greeting, and neither did he. They let them rest by their sides, awkwardly.

"Joe, I'm so, so sorry. We had a client lunch and I couldn't get away. I'm so sorry. I didn't know how to contact you. I had drunk quite a bit and didn't notice the time." The words tumbled out of her mouth. Johnny, sat behind the large wooden desk feigning interest in his computer screen, looked up at her. Lucy felt his presence.

"Erm, shall we?" She beckoned him over to the small table by the window. That day's Metro laid skewed on top. She motioned him to sit down.

"Joe, I'm so sorry. I didn't know what to do. I didn't have your number, or your name, or even where you were staying." The excuses seemed to roll off her tongue into a heap on the table between them.

"I even called Starbucks to get Al to let you know..." He raised his hands up, palms towards her and shook them.

"Lucy, Lucy. It's ok. I thought something like that might have happened. I didn't think you were the type to stand me up. On purpose." She relaxed. Her shoulders dipped in relief. His deep brown eyes bore into hers. She felt Johnny looking over and shot him a look. Joe followed her gaze.

"Look, there's a little café over the road. Why don't we go there?" he said, motioning across the street. She looked out the window and saw a tiny white-fronted café immediately across the road, a couple of metal tables and chairs outside it. She'd never noticed it before.

"Yeah, good idea," she replied. They both got up in unison and hurried out the large reception area, crossed the road and ducked into the café. A smell of salad, coffee and toasted bread hit Lucy's nose. She realised she was hungry having not had any breakfast at Jess's house and it was nearly lunchtime. He ordered a flat white for the both of them and they sat down at a plastic table inside. He hugged his mug with both hands.

"I'm so sorry Joe. I just didn't know where the time went. I'm really sorry." The apologies spilled out of her mouth again.

"Please, don't worry. You're here now. We're here now." He had his palms up towards her. He put them back on his mug.

"How did you find me? I mean, how did you know where I worked?" she asked, sounding more accusing than she intended.

"Well, to be honest, I didn't. It was pure luck. I waited outside Starbucks this morning in case you turned up like you did the first time we met. But you obviously didn't. Then I remembered you said when we first met that you worked around the corner, and I saw you turn left outside of Starbucks, so thought I'd go into some offices nearby, ones that looked like a PR-kinda office. I thought it might be pretty simple but boy are there lots of offices around here, and they all look like PR offices! The first one I went to, I asked for Lucy and realised I didn't know your last name! I felt a bit of an asshole to be honest." He looked at her and smiled. She smiled back. Fair play to him for using his initiative, and his keenness.

"So, I just said Lucy with the amazing red curly hair, about this short." He put his hand up to just above his neck. She giggled and consciously touched her hair.

"I got rejections and so I kept moving on, until your man in there said, 'just a minute' and I thought I'd hit bingo. Of course, it took a while to find you, and I still wasn't sure if it was going to be you. Imagine some other Lucy with red curly hair coming out and we look at each blankly!" He smiled a crooked smile. Lucy had a touch of jealousy in case he liked this other imaginary Lucy with the red curly hair. She cupped her hands around his, which were still wrapped around his mug. He looked up at her and smiled a big, bashful smile. He moved one of his hands out so that it could envelope hers, wrapping it around the mug.

"Well thank goodness it was me. Thank you," and they smiled and stared at each other, the intensity returning.

"What did you do last night, you know, when you realised I'd stood you up?"

"Well, I was pretty peeved but couldn't do much about it. I walked up to Co-vent Garden and ended up in Chinatown. Had some noodles by myself and then went back to the hotel. Then I cried myself to sleep." She looked at him inquisitively. He broke out into a large grin.

"You'd want that would ya?!" He chuckled, a heartfelt friendly chuckle that warmed her insides. Their fingers still intertwined around her coffee mug, exploring each other's fingertips.

"So, tonight?" he said tentatively. "Same time, same place?"

"Absolutely. Nothing will stop me this time." She smiled a broad smile. They got up and gave each other a tight hug.

"You're damn right. I now know where you work!" he smiled.

"You hungry? It is, well, almost lunchtime," Lucy asked, not wanting to let the moment end.

"You betcha!" They walked out of the café hand-in-hand and turned towards Covent Garden. The streets were filling up with tourists and office workers looking for something to eat. They spotted a black metallic van selling paninis and sandwiches. He paid for their lunch, went to the piazza and stood watching an energetic man with large dungarees entertaining the crowd, his shouting voice faltering as he struggled to be heard over the busy streets and the flapping pigeons.

"What do you fancy doing tonight?" Lucy asked, breaking the silence that was borne from munching on their sandwiches and watching the show.

"I don't really mind," he replied. "Actually, scrap that. I want to see the real London. Not this tourist trash. I want to go out and see where Londoners live and what they do."

"I'm not sure it's that exciting to be honest Joe," she smiled, tucking a stray lock of hair behind her ear.

"Maybe not for you but for Johnny Foreigner here it might be." Lucy didn't really know much about where Londoners went. Apart from where she lived the only place she'd been was to where Jess lived the previous night.

"OK, well let's go down to where I live, we can walk about and see what takes our fancy."

"That sounds ideal Lucy. Soak up the atmosphere of where y'all live."

"OK. That's a date then," she said.

"It better be!" He replied and put his arm around her shoulders and pulled her into him.

"Second time lucky." Lucy resisted pulling away and stayed in the crook of his shoulder, watching the performer end his show with a call to put money in his hat. The crowds dispersed quicker than you could say 'Co-vent Garden'.

"Er, you just met … *Joe*?!" Jess was wide-eyed as Lucy sat back down at her desk from lunch, telling her that he found her and they just went on a mini date.

"Yep," she replied, brimming with smugness and warmth.

"Whaaaaaaat! Are you kidding me! How did he find you? Why didn't you bring him in?!"

"He said he went into PR-looking offices around Covent Garden, looking for a Lucy with red curly hair." She purposely left out the word 'amazing' from his description.

"OMG! What a guy Luce! A bit stalkerish but cute! Why can't I find a fella that looks for me huh?!"

"He's a very sweet guy Jess. We've rearranged our date for tonight."

"Ah I'm so sorry for last night Luce, but so happy for you! Yay! Well done you!" She clapped her hands together, fingertips pointing up again.

"Where you going to go?"

"He wants to see the real London, somewhere off the beaten track. I thought I'd take him back to my area."

"Oh yeah!" she grinned. "Classic. Just a hop, skip and a jump into Luce's bed. Sly old devil you!" She play punched her and licked her lips. "You'll going to tell me *all* the details tomorrow, aren't you?"

"I'm not sure about that," she blushed.

"Oh, come on!" She raised her voice a bit. "You can tell me anything, we shared a room together last night!" A few chairs scrapped back, a few male faces appeared over their computer screens. Jess saw them and rolled her eyes.

"Oh behave boys, nothing to see here," and she turned back to her computer, giving Lucy a wink as she went. Lucy felt her face flush red.

Five o'clock finally came around. Lucy switched off her computer and Jess span round to face her, crossing her fingers in front of her face.

"Good luck Luce, I'll be thinking of you." She stood up and gave her a hug, squeezing tightly. "Go get him!"

Lucy turned to go, walked down the corridor and headed out towards the doors.

"LUCE! LUCE!" She turned, knowing full well it was Em.

"Glad I caught you. Can you pop in for a minute? Need to pick your brains on something."

"Uh, actually I'm just on the way out to meet, um, a friend. Can it wait till tomorrow?"

"It will take just a couple of seconds, promise."

"Oh ok. As long as it's quick."

Lucy followed her to her office as she eyeballed Jess who rolled her eyes. She stepped in and Em had a PowerPoint document open on her computer screen. She pointed to it.

"I've got to fire this off to a potential client tonight. Can you help with the words, you're *so* good at it?"

She glanced at the screen. The slide was full of bullet points and words filling the whole screen. It would take a while to sort out all the mess into short, coherent points.

"What exactly do you want me to do?" Lucy asked.

"I don't know, it looks way too busy, don't you think?"

"Yes. It does Emma. I mean Em." Lucy pulled up a chair from the table, heavily dropping it to the floor and sat down in front of the screen. She sped-read what she had written, trying to think of shortcuts.

"Well, what exactly do you want this slide to say? What do you want them to feel at the end of it?" she enquired. Lucy had sat through too many presentations already which had little or no point. Em pondered for a second, her finger on her chin. It seemed like a lifetime.

"I want it to say something like 'you can trust me, I produce extraordinary stories, with a twist'."

"Well, why don't you just use that? Just change 'me' and 'I' for 'us' and 'we'. And all this filler just put in your back-pocket notes and talk around it."

"Oh my God Luce, you're a frigging genius. Right, what did I say?" She swept the mouse over all the words, cut and pasted it into the notes section underneath the slide. Her hands hovered over the keys and looked expectantly at Lucy.

"Oh, um, you said 'you can trust me, I produce extraordinary stories, with a twist'." Her fingers danced over the keyboard as Lucy spoke, leaned back and admired her work.

"Bloody perfect."

"Just change the 'me' and 'I' for 'us' and 'we' and you're done." She edged towards the door. Em's face was locked onto the screen, the glow reflected on her face. Lucy opened the door and slid out.

"Thanks Luce," she cried out. Lucy hurried down the corridor, giving Jess a little wave as she went and gave her the thumbs up signal.

Lucy turned onto the Strand quickly, almost bumping into an irate suited man. There was a light drizzle in the air as she half jogged and half walked, dodging the throng of people moving across the street. She craned her neck to see if Joe was there, standing outside Starbucks. She couldn't see clearly among the sea of heads and a smattering of umbrellas. She got closer and she could see his dark hair. He was leaning against the glass of Starbucks, his hands in his pockets, looking left and right along the road. She called out to him. He swivelled his head towards her and smiled, a relief over this face.

"Jeez Lucy, I thought you stood me up again!" She stopped in front of him, unsure how to greet him. Should she hug, kiss or take his hand? She did neither and stood in front of him, smoothing down her hair catching her breath.

"I'm sorry. The boss called me into her office. She had a mini-emergency." She air-quoted the word emergency.

"Thanks for turning up this time," he said sarcastically and he moved awkwardly to give her a hug. She hugged him back and held him there.

"Shall we go?" she eventually said, grabbed his hand and pulled him across the road. They walked across the east side of Hungerford Bridge, the side that looked out to St. Paul's Cathedral. The light drizzle had turned heavier and people brushed past them, their collars up and their umbrellas threatening to poke them in the head. They stood at the halfway point of the bridge and Joe pulled his camera out. He took a picture of the drizzly skyline, the tall buildings behind St. Paul's Cathedral as dark as a silhouette.

"Nice view," he said looking at her. He grinned and kissed her on the cheek.

They carried on down the steps, under the train arches and headed into Waterloo Station. The blue and silver arch of the old Eurostar terminal stretched and bent outwards, the underground escalators next to it deposited hundreds of commuters onto the concourse, joining the throng and crowds of people moving around. Lucy glanced up at the digital destination boards and saw that a train left in five minutes, from the platform at the far end of the station. She grabbed Joe's hand and led him quickly, snaking through the people waiting for their trains, him following her like a dutiful carriage behind an engine.

"Have you got an Oyster card or do you need to buy a ticket?" she said, realising he might not have one and they'd need to turn back to the ticket machines.

"Oh, er, yes I do. In here somewhere." He patted his pockets and fished out a worn-looking blue card.

"Great. Here we are." They scanned their cards on the reader and the gates opened. Still holding his hand Lucy jumped on the train and pulled him in. There were no seats left and a couple of people were standing in the vestibule. She pulled him over to the glass barrier separating the standing area and the seats and he leaned and pushed her back into the glass, kissing her full on the lips. She could sense other commuters watching, silently tutting but she didn't care. This is what happy felt like and she was happy.

The train doors closed and it set off. Joe pulled his face away and looked out of the window. The London Eye and Big Ben ducked in and out of view behind office blocks as the train trundled on. The famous sights morphed into the grittier side of London, the bits that weren't in the tourist brochures: council estates, warehouses, cemeteries, factories, backends of terraced houses and streets leading into the distance. Joe looked out of the window while Lucy was still pressed up against his body. She studied the side of his face. A small bit of stubble protruded out of his chin, his skin was smooth except for a few ancient potholes of acne, his nose was curved, and his lips were full. The ends of his sideburns were untidy. She lifted her finger and smoothed them down. He looked at her and smiled. He leaned in and gave her a kiss. The train stopped a few stations on and she pulled him out. A horde of people followed them and they all walked in unison towards the exit. The sound of people descending stairs echoed around the covered walkway. Fingers locked together, they stood outside the station and they looked both ways, taking in the panorama.

"Well, this is suburban London, what do you think?" A few pigeons took off on the other side of the road and roosted under the bridge that their train now rumbled over.

"Different," he said and smiled at her.

"There's a pub over there, and a restaurant there, and another pub just down the road. Any ideas?"

"Whichever one you recommend Lucy," sweeping his arm out in an arc in front of them.

"Uh, let's try that one," she pointed in the direction of a nice-looking pub with green awnings and crossed the road to get to it. A few suited men were standing by the bar, ties loosened, pint glasses half drunk. There were plenty of tables free so they headed towards a small round one in the corner surrounded by a sofa. She sat on the faux-leather seat and he sat next to her, not on the wooden chair opposite. She rested her head on his shoulder. He picked up a menu and held it up so they could both read it. They studied it for a few moments.

"Chosen?" he asked.

"Yeah, I'll have the fish and chips."

"No way, that's what I'm gonna have!" he laughed and put down the menu.

"So, this is what you Londoners do in the evening huh? Not much different to the States, except we have nicer bars and sports on the TV." She squeezed his thigh and he instinctively covered her hand with his to keep it there. She looked up at him and he met her gaze. He leaned down and kissed her, putting his other hand on her cheek and chin, as if to hold her face there.

"This feels so nice," he said, pulling away. She purred. And it did. She straightened up and they sat next to each looking in front of them.

"What do we need to do to get a drink in here?" he said looking around the bar.

"Oh, it's not table service you know. We have to go up to the bar."

"Oh really?! I didn't know that. Here I am wasting my time kissing you thinking some dude is going to come and take our order." He kissed her on her forehead and squeezed himself out from behind the table. He looked back.

"Fish and chips right, and a white wine?"

"Yes please, that would be great. Thank you." He went to go to the bar, then turned back.

"Um, large or small?"

"A small one please."

"Are you sure?"

"Yes. No! Make it a large one."

"Alrighty then."

He turned to go to the bar and theatrically wiggled his bum as he did. He looked back over his shoulder to see if Lucy was watching. She covered her mouth giggling like a schoolgirl.

They stayed at the pub until closing time. She was a bit giddy from the three large glasses of wine he had bought her. He had been on the cokes. They'd talked pretty much the whole time, any silences comfortably filled with kisses and exploring their clothed bodies. He had traced the outline of her face with the tips of his finger a few times, from the fringe of her hair, along her ear, down her jawline to her chin. It eventually rested on her lips. He swapped his finger for his lips and pressed firmly. The pub landlord called for the final time that he was closing up so they headed to the exit. The cool air hit her. They held hands and looked out to the train station.

"Um, do you want to come back to mine, you know, for a nightcap?" Lucy asked hopefully.

"Sure Lucy, I'd love that," he said as he looked at her, confidently and firm.

She took his hand, crossed the road and headed towards her flat. The shops petered out and turned into new build flats and terraced houses. They all looked the same but Lucy had memorised the route now, the identical becoming familiar. She stumbled as she attempted to put the key into the lock, dropping it onto the floor.

"Sorry. Must be the drink," she giggled and she felt her heart beat faster as it slid into the slot and the door opened, a hot flush rising to her face. He glanced around the flat, peeking his head into the rooms as they went past the open doors – bathroom, kitchen, bedroom.

"It's awesome Lucy. Small but perfectly formed."

She looked at him and gave a smile. She put her arms around his neck and kissed him hard. He put his hands around her waist and found the top of her skirt, Jess's skirt, and slid his fingers between the fabric and her skin. He teasingly pulled it up and then down, his fingers caressing the top of her knickers. She sunk into the moment and let his wandering hands explore her body. He pushed his hips into hers, pressing his lips hard onto hers, causing her back to arch. She pushed his shoulders back and he released his grip. She playfully bit her bottom lip and again he pushed his mouth hard against hers, the passion coursing through her veins. Lucy jutted her hips into him, shocking him but secretly liking it. He slowly opened his eyes and looked deep into hers. That look again. She wrapped her arms around his neck and let him kiss her neck. As if cooling the moment, she dipped her head and slumped her shoulders.

"I really like you…" she began. Joe pulled back, looking heartbroken. "… do you mind if we… don't."

"Yeah, sure, sure," he said, his eyes lighting up. "Of course, honey. Let's take it slow. I'm just happy to be here. With you."

Lucy smiled shyly.

"Thank you."

She took his hand and led him into the bedroom. They collapsed onto the bed, legs intertwined and lips locked, eventually falling asleep clothed in each other's arms.

Lucy woke with her head in the crook of Joe's neck, his chin rested on her forehead. They were cuddled up together, hardly any air between them, his arms completely encased her. He was stroking her upper arm, her face nuzzled against his chest. The first shards of light were poking through her curtains. She took a deep breath and his arms expanded. She gently closed her eyes; the feeling of warmth and security ran through her body. She wished the sun would set again so they could stay trapped in this cocoon. Her phone alarm beeped, stirring his sleep. He purred at the sound, shifted his legs and rubbed them against hers. She leaned out of bed and turned off the alarm, feeling the cold away from the inner sanctum. She got up and walked to the bathroom, locking the door behind her and glancing in the mirror; her hair was a complete mess and needed washing. She turned on the taps of the shower and when the water was warm enough stepped in and let the water wash over her head, filling her ears. She ran her arms over her body, feeling for the scars that used to be there, now healed, and hugged herself, the hot water running over the warm sensation she had inside.

They both had a mug of tea and a slice of toast each sat in her small kitchen. She was dressed for work and he sat casually at the table. He was looking at her.

"What are you going to do today?" she asked.

"I might check out the local area here. Hang out and see what I can find." He paused. "Lucy, we need to talk about this, where it's headed kind-of-thing."

"Oh," she replied.

So soon.

"Well, I was only planning to stay in London for a few days. Then I was going to move on, you know. I was thinking, maybe, I just extend my trip here for a bit longer. I've got nothing to go back to. Maybe I could crash here, if that's ok with you, save on the hotel bills," he asked hopefully, not knowingly. Lucy was startled at the suggestion. Was it too soon? If he was only going to be there for a few more days....

"Er, yeah, that would be nice." There was a strange air between them.

"Only if you are happy with that. We seem to have a good thing going here, maybe it will give us some time together, and we can figure it out from there."

He made a compelling case. She was not sure what was holding her back. Maybe it was her future being mapped out. Maybe it *was* all a bit too soon yet she had never felt this way about anyone before.

"Yeah sure, it's fine. Um, yeah, no problem. Why don't you get your stuff and meet me here later? How does that sound?"

"It sounds yankee doodle dandy, sweetheart," he joked and she smiled back.

"Look, I've got to go. I don't have a spare key so why don't you leave when you want. Give me your mobile number so we avoid another disaster like last time."

"Oh, well. Yeah. Erm, my number is from the States. Data roaming will be expensive for you," he stuttered. "Just meet me outside at say half past five?"

"Let's make it 6pm, just in case," she winked and took a glug of her cooling tea.

"It's a date," he replied, stood up and kissed her on the lips.

"Pick something up for dinner darling," she mocked as she picked up her bag and left the flat, closing the door gently behind her.

Chapter Twelve

"Weeeeeellllllllllll….?" Jess intoned as Lucy came through the door to the office, a slight spring in her step.

"None of your business," she retorted as she swung her bag down and sat in the chair, her lips in a wide, bashful smile. She leaned over and switched on the monitor.

"Oh, come on! You look like the cat that got the cream! I take it you had a goooooood night then?" She winked at her and Lucy couldn't help but grin.

"Yeah, it was an amazing night!" she beamed, her eyes sparkling.

"Brilliant! Come on Luce, tell me what you did!"

"We just went for a few drinks in a pub near where I live, then he came back for a nightcap."

"Oooooh!" It came out like a squeal as she clapped her hands with her fingers pointing up. "I knew it, I knew it! What was he like?"

"Now that really is none of your business Jess," she laughed, turned and typed in her password. Jess got up, picked her phone up off her desk and walked past her, bending down to whisper in her ear.

"I 'ave ways of makin' you talk," she said.

"Eh?" Lucy responded, crinkling her nose up as she looked round.

She picked up a notepad and pen from her desk, skipped off and disappeared into Em's office.

The morning crept by for Lucy. She couldn't hold a thought in her head apart from Joe.

The whole evening was just perfect. Joe was just perfect.

She glanced at the clock on the bottom right of her screen to check the time more than once a minute, willing 5pm to come. It was painfully slow. She got up and made herself a coffee, went to the loo and mooched over to other desks. Jess was locked in a heated debate in Em's office, Post-It notes, A4 paper, iPad and laptops strewn over the small table. She went to lunch at twelve on the dot and took a full hour to break the monotony of clock-watching, wandered up and down the Strand, into Covent Garden, skirted the Thames along Victoria Embankment and through the U-shaped courtyard of Somerset House. Office staff, delivery people and tourists intermingled with one another, traipsing the streets in a million different directions. A helicopter buzzed overhead and buses rumbled past. She got back to the office and as she passed by Johnny looked up.

"Luce, that American guy was just here looking for you again. I told him you were out for lunch."

"Really? Here?" her brain buzzed.

"Er, yeah," he replied, his eyes glancing left, confused at the doubt of his story. "About 40 minutes ago. He said he'd come back later."

"Oh. Thanks Johnny." She continued back to her desk, cursing that she'd just missed a lunch date with the person she'd been thinking about all morning.

Jess was sitting at her desk, eating a wrap with a crisp packet open. A few crumbs were scattered in front of her keyboard. She was staring at the screen, keys tapping at the keyboard whilst chewing. Lucy sat down and typed in her password.

"Apparently Joe just turned up," she said to Jess nonchalantly, "while I was out."

Jess turned to her, eyes wide.

"No! Really? Here! Oh man I wish I'd known. I wanna see what he looks like! What was he doing?"

"I don't know. Guess meeting me for lunch?" She shrugged her shoulders and turned back to her monitor. "He's coming back later."

"OMG, you've got a keeper Luce, a proper keeper!"

A few people left the office mid-way through the afternoon in a fit of bustle and panic. A client had asked to see Em and the team for an emergency meeting. There was a crescendo of rustling paper, the printer spitting out documents and people swearing at the 'bloody thing'. *'WHY DOESN'T IT WORK WHEN YOU WANT IT TO!'* Drawers banged and the sound of running feet to and fro filled the space. Then quiet when most of them left. A few lonely sounds filled the void: Jess tap-tapped on her keyboard, the hum of the air con and computer cooling fans, a few people at the back of the office; finance, IT, HR: the non-client facing people. And Lucy. She turned her chair a full circle, her feet dancing as she went around. Her office phone rang, breaking the silence. Jess glanced at it. It was Johnny at reception. Lucy met Jess' eyes who had a puzzled look. She knew visitors didn't come to see her. Then her eyes opened wide in excitement.

"It's him, it's him isn't it!" she squealed. She jumped out of her chair and ran to the double doors. Lucy jumped after, leaving the phone to ring.

"No, don't Jess! Don't!" she playfully chased.

Lucy saw the tall figure of Joe leaning against the reception desk, his back to the office, casually looking at Johnny who had the phone to his ear, waiting for her to pick up. Jess reached the door and peered not-so-subtly through the round porthole.

"That's him isn't it? It's him!" Joe must have heard a commotion and turned around to look through the door. As he did, Jess spun round with her back to the glass. She slid down on the floor. Her face had gone white, like she had seen a ghost.

"Jess? Are you alright?" She bent down, crouching in front of her.

"Luce, that's him. That's Joe, right?" She said with a quiver in her voice. Lucy straightened her legs and peered through the porthole. Joe was looking at her and waved. She waved back and raised her index finger to indicate to give her a minute. He nodded and looked back to Johnny.

"Yes Jess, it is," she said, crouching back down.

"No Luce. No, it's not."

Her face was contorted in confusion.

"Yes Jess, yes it is," she repeated. "What's going on?"

"No. No. No." She replied, her eyes going crazy, moving left and right trying to understand something impossible. She looked up at her. Her eyes were red, scared.

"Luce, look at me. That is not Joe."

"What the bloody hell are you on about Jess?"

She got to her feet, grabbed her by the hand and pulled her into the ladies' toilet, Lucy almost falling as she was dragged.

"Jess, what are you doing?!"

They entered into the ladies, and Jess checked all the cubicles to see if they were empty.

"Jess, what are you on about?" Lucy repeated, more urgently this time.

She took a deep breath, her hands on her hips, looking down. After composing herself she looked up, and deep into her eyes. A full-on drama-queen.

"Lucy…" She said her full name, for the first time, just like her mum would. "That is not who you think it is. His name is not Joe. He isn't American. He's, he's, well, English!" She looked at her intently, willing her to believe her.

"Jess, what the hell are you talking about?!" It was Lucy's turn to get angry and frustrated. "His name is Joe and he is from New York!"

"No Lucy," she said her full name again. It sounded odd coming from her. Her voice dropped an octave.

"He's an utter bastard, that's who he is." She looked away; eyes glazed over as if remembering a bad dream.

"Jessica!" Lucy shouted, using her full name. It produced a reaction and she looked back at her.

"I have no idea what you are talking about so do you care to enlighten me? What the flipping hell are you talking about?!"

Jess walked away towards the end of the bathroom, past the sinks, and came back, her hands on her hips, taking deep breaths looking along the floor.

A forced dramatic tension?

Tears started to form in Jess' eyes.

"Nathan. That's it, Nathan. That's his name. It must have been a couple of years ago, when I was working at my previous job in the City, in Canary Wharf. I was out with a client and we had a few drinks. I was in a good mood and didn't want to go home when they left. So, I called Kaz to meet her and we hit a few bars, the type that all the bankers go to. We thought we could snag a rich one and get champers for the night. So, we got talking to a bunch of guys, flirting away. They were buying us loads of drinks: champagne, vodka red bulls. Kaz and I were getting so much attention from these lads, and we were lapping it up. We went along with them to another bar they were going to and got a private table. We were sitting around, laughing and dancing, bottles of Cristal kept coming, that kind of thing. Pills were being passed around and some of them were doing coke. I think Kaz might have snuck off for some but I didn't. I don't do that kind of thing." Jess was talking quickly, trying to get the story out.

"Anyway, a couple of guys were starting to get a bit touchy feely with me under the table. I kept brushing them off but their hands kept coming back. They were constantly mentioning going back to theirs, just the three of them, and I kept knocking them back. It seemed they were just trying hard but there was no malice. No pressure. Then one of them went off as he wasn't getting anything from me and the other guy started to be more forceful. He was drunk, off his tits and leaning all over me. I kept pushing him away, but it just spurred him on. I was trapped behind the table between the wall and him. He was putting his hands on me more and more and I kept pushing them away. Again, it just spurred him on."

Jess' eyes were starting to fill with tears. She brushed them away with the back of her hand. She took a deep breath.

"Wait, wait, wait," Lucy said before she could start again. "What's this got to do with Joe? Don't tell me it's him, that's impossible."

She looked at her, frightened, but didn't agree or deny.

"But that's impossible!" she cried, a bit too defensively. "That's not Joe! You don't know him! You've just glanced at someone through a door, for a split second! Maybe it's your mind playing tricks."

Tears formed in her eyes. Jess grabbed her by the shoulders with both arms and looked sternly in her eyes. The physical action shocked her.

"Listen to me. LISTEN TO ME!" Tears flowed down her cheeks. Her mascara ran making her look older. She took a deep breath.

"Anyway. He got more and more touchy feely and I shouted out for him to stop. A few of his mates looked over and laughed. One of them catcalls over, and said, 'he's harmless love, just having a laugh with you!' He leaned into my ear and whispered, 'Yeah babe, I'm harmless', and nibbled on my ear." Jess shuddered at the memory.

"He muttered, got up and joined his mates. I made a move to find Kaz. Him and his mate stared at me as I stomped off, called me names. I walked around the bar looking for Kaz. It was full of blazers and suits. I started to hate them. The music was getting louder and I couldn't find Kaz. I don't know if it's the booze, the music or the heat in the bar but I got really dizzy and the room started swirling."

Tears were now running full flow down Jess' cheeks. Her hands were shaking. Lucy listened, dumbstruck at the story, not knowing where this was leading to and what it had got to do with Joe.

"The next thing I know I woke up on my bed, in my flat, on my own. I had no recollection of how I got there or what time it was. There were clothes scattered everywhere around on the floor. Cupboards were open, drawers empty, paper strewn about, pillows and cushions on the floor. It was a mess. My head was a blur, like I'd drunk way too much alcohol, but it was a different feeling. I looked around for my bag and phone and couldn't see them. That's when I noticed. I was still wearing the black dress and crop top I had on the previous night, but I didn't have any knickers on. So, I panicked."

She wiped her nose with the back of her hand.

"I got up off the bed and there were small flecks of blood on the sheets. I checked myself but there wasn't any blood on me, and it wasn't that time of the month. It didn't *feel* like anything had, you know, happened. But I was crapping myself. I looked around the floor my knickers, I just couldn't find them. I went into the kitchen and it was the opposite of the bedroom. It was clean. Not a hair out of place.

"I downed a pint of water to try and clear my head. In the bathroom, there was a smell of vomit and saw some sick on the side of the toilet bowl. The hand towel next to it was screwed up and damp in the middle. Luce, I never leave my towels like that. The only thing I could remember from the night before was Mr Touchy Feely and the sneers and falling down."

She took a deep breath, steadying herself by putting her palms on the basin.

"I needed to call Kaz but couldn't find my phone. I didn't know how to contact her. I mean who knows their mate's phone number these days? I thought about Skyping her mobile so went to get my laptop but I couldn't find that either."

Tears continued to stream down her face, her eyes were red raw, reliving this horrible moment. Lucy let her continue, trying to decipher what this meant to her, and Joe. Surely Joe was not in this story.

He's American for Christ's sake.

She was suddenly conscious he was being stood up again but couldn't tear herself from Jess' attention.

"I was stuck in my flat. I thought of all the possibilities of what might have happened. Luce, when you are in that state your mind goes nuts. Suddenly it didn't feel right, you know, down there. Stupid I know cos it felt alright a few minutes before but your mind goes places. So, I thought of all the worst things and panicked. I felt the need to clean myself so I went in the shower and scrubbed myself all over. I washed every inch over and over again. I even used three different shampoos! And then I put all the towels and bed clothes in the washing machine. I know now how bloody stupid that was but I was in a panic Luce.

"I got dressed and ran to Kaz's. I didn't even know how to order a cab without my phone. She opened the door ready for work, sprightly. She said how much of a good time *I* must have had last night. She was smiling so wide. I just started yelling: why did you leave me, where did you go, what happened? She told me to calm down. She said I was snogging that bloke on the sofa and that I looked well into him so she left me on her own, that she was busy with one of the others. When she wanted to leave, she tried to call over but I didn't reply and the guy she was with told her not to worry and he would make sure I was ok. So she left. She said she called and left messages and texts but assumed that I didn't reply because I was 'busy'. Then she asked why I didn't just call her rather than come around and then the penny dropped. I could see it in her eyes. I told her what I just told you, and she yelled at me for putting everything in the wash. We called the bar to see if my purse had been left there and nothing had, so we cancelled my cards and my phone. Then we called back the bar to see if they knew those guys, and if they had any CCTV. They just said the bar was packed last night, and no they didn't have CCTV. I thought about going to the police but what could I say. I went out, got drunk, came home missing my phone, cards and knickers. They'd laugh at me. Standard blonde girl night out."

She pointed to her hair with her index finger, and then made a gun with her hand and pretended to pull the trigger.

"Jess, that is absolutely terrible. I'm genuinely sorry and disgusted that that happened. But seriously. What's that got to do with Joe?"

"The guy next to me at the table, getting all handsy. The guy I *think* came back to my flat and took my knickers, phone, bag. That's him, that's him outside in our reception, speaking to Johnny."

Lucy looked at her incredulously.

"What, what are you talking about? That is an American guy called Joe. We spent the night together last night. He has been nothing but charming, polite, humble. A perfect gentleman. The opposite of what you are saying. Two years ago, he was married and living in Colorado!"

She opened her palms out showing how defensive she was being. Jess looked at her, confused.

"I don't know what he has told you Luce, but that guy out there is him! Definitely!"

"You are being ridiculous Jess!" her voice started to rise. She was glad she was in the toilets and not out in the open-plan office.

"You've just glanced at him through a window in a door. He wasn't even looking at you! Your mind is playing tricks on you. How come you remember his name but nothing else?!"

"I know Luce. It sounds crazy. I remembered his name because it's not a name I hear that often. Some bits have come back. I remember saying to him it's the first time I'd met someone with that name. And I also remember his mate calling him Nath when he wasn't getting anywhere and went off."

"Yes, Jess it does sound crazy. You are crazy." Lucy was getting more and more worked up, shouting now.

"It's the first time I have ever met someone who is into me, and I'm into him, and whilst he is waiting for me you drag me in here and tell me this, this, *story*."

Jess looked up abruptly at the word 'story' as if she had made it all up.

"Look, Jess. I am sorry this happened to you. I really am. I've never been in that situation before so I have no idea what you went through or how you felt, or how you are feeling. But this has got nothing to do with Joe. So, I'm going to go out there now and say hello to him."

"LUCE NO!" She took a step forward, getting into Lucy's space. The words shocked her.

"No, Luce you can't. Please trust me on this one. Don't go out there."

"I'm sorry Jess, I am. Don't try and ruin this for me. I had to stand him up, I stayed at yours and missed him when he said he was waiting for me outside Starbucks this morning, when every other day that's where I'd be. And now you are telling me not to even see him. For the first time in my life, this feels right. *He* feels right. Maybe it's you Jess, maybe you are jealous of me finding someone when you don't have anyone yourself. You think you're so popular but you don't have anyone. You kept buying drinks to stay with you because you've got no friends."

Jess slapped her. She slapped her hard across the left side of her face. As soon as she did it, she looked at her with horror. Lucy could tell she immediately regretted it.

"Oh shit, I'm sorry Luce. Fuck! I'm sorry." Lucy looked at her with cold eyes but didn't say a word. Only her lip quivered. She turned, stormed out of the ladies and ran to the doors. She swung them open and Joe looked at her.

"At last!" he said but stopped abruptly, seeing in her eyes that she was about to burst into tears. She grabbed his arm and dragged him out into the dirty streets of London.

Chapter Thirteen

"Ouch," Joe said as he gently caressed the left side of Lucy's face where Jess' hand had struck it. It stung a bit and she could feel that it had gone red. The last time she had been slapped across the face was when her dad hit her in one of his drunken rages during her late teens. Lucy remembered it well because she had just bought a new red dress. That was a long time ago and usually it was a full-fisted punch. The memories of the tears filling her eyes, willing the dams not to burst whilst being strong, brought it all back. They were in the little café opposite the office, Joe making cooing noises, trying to calm her down. Her bottom lip was trembling. Jess had sent texts and rung her number several times. She declined them all and eventually switched off the phone, buzzing as it closed down. Lucy told him she had had a work argument that got out of hand. It was nothing and it meant nothing. A stressful day. He swallowed.

"It's your thing," he said, "I'm here for you."

He took her hand and kissed the top of her knuckles. He smiled his sweet innocent smile.

Jess had got this all mixed up, mistaken identity.

She pushed it to the back of her mind and concentrated back on Joe. She leant in for a kiss and he obliged.

"I'm sorry Joe. I guess you weren't expecting this. What are you doing here anyway?"

"Don't worry babe. It's fine. I'm glad I'm here for you. To tell you the truth, I got a bit bored in suburban London. There are only so many estate agent windows you can look in."

A horn beeped somewhere in the distance.

"And the shock factor at the price of those houses wears thin when you see so many of them. So many numbers, they don't seem real." He grinned at her and kissed her tenderly on the cheek, the part where it was red.

"Are you ok?" he asked, earnestly.

"Yeah, I'm ok. I don't fancy going back into the office. My boss is probably going to be out for the rest of the day. Let's go do something." Joe looked delighted.

"Awesome. Lucy is playing truant huh? Right, I think dinner is in order."

"It's not even three o'clock," she said, playfully.

"Well why don't we have afternoon tea, that's what you Brits do, doncha?" He said 'afternoon tea' in a shrill English accent. "My treat."

"It's always your treat," she said, putting her coat on and picking up her bag.

They walked past the theatres on the Strand, heading east. Airplanes lined up above their head, aiming for Heathrow. Lucy spotted a short road on the other side of the street leading to a grand silver sign with a gold knight standing sentry over the top of it. She motioned towards Joe.

"That's the only street in the whole of London where you drive on the right."

He stopped and looked down the short road, taxis turning in.

"So it is! Good spot tour guide," he exclaimed. "Savoy," he read the grand silver sign. "What is that, some kinda hotel?"

"Yes, it's one of the poshest in London."

"Well in that case ma'am, shall we have afternoon tea?" He looped his arm and she threaded hers through his and they crossed the busy road, walking down the short street and into the decadent lobby, a black and white checkerboard stretching out in front of them. A capped concierge eyed them.

"We've come to have your afternoon tea," Joe drawled.

The concierge snapped to attention on hearing the American accent, used to tourists coming in and spending their money on cheap scones.

"Certainly sir," he said, his accent not quite English. "Through the corridor and to the left."

They followed his instructions and turned into a beautiful ornate room, filled with plump armchairs, sofas and table-clothed tables, adorned with tiered stands, plates, teacups and saucers. A silvery-blue gazebo-like birdcage sat in the centre of the room beneath a huge stained-glass dome, which flooded the room with light. A baby grand piano sat within the gazebo, like a large black bird trapped forever. Gold-framed portraits of distinguished-looking lords and ladies from the past decked the walls between marble pillars. Elderly people in expensive-looking clothes sipped tea, men in double-breasted blazers and ties, women wearing brooches and hats. Joe and Lucy felt they were the youngest people there, and the least well-dressed. A maître-d in black tails approached them and escorted them to a table for two. As they sat down, he took the two ready-folded napkins on the table, gave them a flick and placed them gently over their laps. Next, he took the menu that was standing up in the centre of the table and handed one to Lucy first, and then to Joe. He took a small step backwards, gave a little bow and walked away. They looked at each other and giggled.

"How utterly charming," Joe said, with a cut-English accent. They looked at the menu of treats and a waiter, also in tails, came over and read out the available teas from heart. They both chose Earl Grey and he nodded his head and muttered 'Excellent choice'. Like the concierge, his accent was not quite English too. They both chose from the menu and he took them away, bowed again and left, not writing anything down. They looked around, taking in the environment: teaspoons gently clattering sides of cups, cubed sugar in little pots and the tinkling of the pianist adding to the grandeur of the large room they were in.

Joe leaned over and whispered in her ear, "This is nice isn't it". She looked at him, smiled and lent over to squeeze his hand. At that moment, Lucy noticed a tall, broad-chested man in a pinstripe double-breasted jacket and his woman, in a tan coloured, shin-length light coat, walking towards them. She thought it was strange for them to be making such a beeline towards their table, an urgency in their step. The lady had a feather in her hair, walking slightly behind the smiling who had grey hair combed backwards. He was looking at Joe: he was headed straight for them.

"Excuse me for interrupting," he said, in a posh private-school, home-counties-accent. Joe and Lucy both looked up.

"Don't I know you?" he held out his hand for Joe to shake.

"Er, no I don't think so, sir," Joe replied in an American drawl. The man stepped back, a shock on his face.

"Oh, do excuse me. I'm so sorry. I must have mistaken you for someone else. You look just like someone I used to know. A British chap so I'm dreadfully sorry."

His wife looked on aghast.

"Oh, I'm so sorry," she apologised, taking her husband's hand. "His mind isn't what it used to be!" and tried to pull him away.

"Oh, no problem sir," Joe replied, "I must have one of those faces."

"The spitting image! I'm so sorry for interrupting."

"Come on now Charles," the wife said, "let's go and not disturb this lovely couple any more than we have."

"Yes, dear. Apologies again." He gave a short bow of his head, his face etched in confusion. They disappeared deep in conversation and Joe and Lucy burst into giggles.

"Well, well!" she said, "are you actually famous? Are you who you say you are?" A flash of Jess' tear-filled eyes shot into her mind. Joe smiled bashfully, not looking at her, then returned her gaze. A shiver went down her spine. The waiter came and placed a silver teapot between them on a silver tray and disappeared again. Lucy looked around, seeing if she could spot Jess. Was she watching them, asking this man and women to come over and place another doubtful seed in her mind? A clattering of dropped teacups in the distance took her attention. Joe didn't seem to register the disturbance as he used the strainer to pour the tea into the cups. They took a sip, Lucy extending her little finger out theatrically as she tilted the cup to her mouth to break the tension. Joe watched and adjusted his hand accordingly. They both giggled as the hot water hit their lips, but Lucy's mind was suddenly wary.

They devoured their little scones, jam and clotted cream, crustless sandwiches and elegant little cakes and pastries. Joe paid the extortionate bill and gave a generous tip. Jess played on Lucy's mind again, and she thought about Joe's work and how he could afford all these treats for her. Maybe he had a very different attitude to her about money: play now, pay later. Or maybe it was because her salary barely paid her bills that she was more cost-conscious. She thanked him and said next time they needed to split the bill as long as it wasn't at the Savoy.

Outside the hotel's small entrance street, they turned left and walked past the gold-plated fronts of the shops on the south side of the Strand. Joe led her into Charing Cross station where he had put his suitcase in left luggage. He gave in his ticket and the attendant brought out a jet-black carry-on case, the red letters of Tumi stamped on the front pocket. They headed across Hungerford Bridge and into Waterloo Station. The concourse was starting to get busy with commuters heading home for the evening. Lucy's mind was elsewhere, playing tricks on the doubts that Jess had put in there, getting lost in a million different thoughts and scenarios. And every avenue led to a shake of her head.

Surely not.

He pulled his suitcase into her room and laid it down whilst Lucy went to the kitchen to flick the kettle on. She grabbed a couple of mugs down from the cupboard as she heard him unzipping his bag followed by a rustling of clothes. She poured the water on to the teabag and added a dash of milk to both cups.

"Tea's up!" she called.

"Thanks Luce," he called out from the bedroom.

Luce.

That was the first time he had said that. She pictured Jess again but shook it from her mind and took the mugs to the bedroom. His case was open, a few bits of underwear, toiletries and a razor were spilling out, a can of deodorant and a travel shaving kit were in a transparent bag.

"A man of few possessions," she remarked.

"I don't need much," he responded. He put his arms around her waist and kissed her.

"Watch out!" She exclaimed, her arms outstretched holding two hot mugs of tea.

"Sorry!" he said, grabbed one and wrapped his hands around it, gathering warmth.

"I'd rather put my hands around you," he said, looking up with a wink.

"What a line!" she replied and they placed their mugs on the floor and rolled into each other's arms, eventually falling asleep fully clothed.

The next morning, Joe got up and headed to the bathroom. Lucy lay back with her arms above her head, tilting her eyes to the window, the early sunlight streaming through the curtains. Her stomach growled so she thought about putting some toast on. She swung her legs around to the side of the bed and saw his suitcase open, the lid jutting out towards the bed. She looked around, contemplating. Jess entered her mind.

How much do I really know about him?

She got up and flicked the open lid closed with her foot. The front pocket was zipped open and a piece of white paper was poking out, torn at the edges. A touch of curiosity entered her mind, the seed of mistrust planted by Jess. A clue to who Joe was before. Again, Jess's face popped into her mind. She listened out for Joe; she could hear the shower running. She crouched down and carefully slipped out the piece of paper. It was a letter that had been hastily torn up and shoved into the pocket, the edges of the paper jagged and bent in the corners where it had been put in. Lucy separated them out. The date appeared on one of the scraps – three days ago. It was a letter from a bank, a familiar blue logo appearing above the date. It was a warning, a reminder to pay a bill. She searched through the fragments for the name and address. She found a shred which said, 'Dear Mr Clyne'. She put the scrap to the back of the pile, and another and another. Finally, there was a name and an address at the top of the paper. Her heart stopped dead still. The colour drained from her face. A sweat prickled her skin. A funny feeling entered her stomach.

Mr N. Clyne.

And a London address.

Ealing.

West London.

N.

N for Nathan. She heard the taps turning off, the water stopped and a towel scrapped from the rail. She put the fragment with the address on into the pocket of her black trousers, shoved the remaining pieces back in the suitcase and jumped into bed, her brain whirring. Jess' face appeared in front of her mind, her red eyes and streaked mascara, her scared eyes and the white face. Joe came in with a towel around his waist, his torso smooth and naked. His hair was wet.

"Morning babe," he said, leaned over and kissed her on the lips. Lucy quickly pulled away and got out of bed.

"Fancy some toast?" she asked, pulling on a dressing gown.

"You betcha," he said and walked over to his suitcase.

You betcha she repeated in her mind.

Classic American.

Lucy absent-mindlessly put the bread in the toaster, pulled down the jam from the cupboard and got the butter out of the fridge. She flicked on the kettle and it started to rattle. She opened another cupboard to get a couple of plates but there weren't any in there. Over at the sink, a pile of dirty plates had begun to form. She sighed and put the hot tap on, wiped a couple of plates and dried them with a tea towel. Her mind was doing flips. Why did he have a letter from a London address from three days ago? Was it his letter? If not, why was it in his bag. What other names began with N? Nick. Noah. Noel. Norbert.

Don't be so ridiculous!

Was Jess right? If she was, why did he have an American accent? Had the suited man in the Savoy really recognised him and been bamboozled by the accent? It had been her choice to go and sit at his table in Starbucks. She pushed all these thoughts from her mind, the absurdity of it all. It was simply playing tricks on her. The toaster popped up and the kettle switched off at the same time. She pulled out the toast, burning her fingers and she let go of it as it flew onto the floor. At that moment Joe came in scooped it up, threw it on the plate, blowing and shaking his fingers. He moved over to the kettle and poured the water into the two mugs and dropped a teabag in each.

"Are you ok babe?" he asked.

"Yeah. Yeah, fine. Just, erm, got to get ready for work," she said as she went into the bathroom and locked the door. She sat on the toilet seat with her head in her hands, her brain confused. She ran through the different scenarios, unsure what to do. Should she confront him? She had never been good at confrontation, and if he lied how would she know? It's not as if he would confess like in a procedural American cop show. 'Jeez Luce, you got me. Darn it. I almost had you going. Sorry.' Then what? Should she speak to Jess? It would just add suspicions to her doubts, fuelling her conspiracy. And there was no evidence, just a torn-up letter. It could all be completely innocent; an acquaintance that he went to pick up the mail for? A piece of litter he found on the floor and shoved it in his bag to put in the rubbish later? All not very plausible but possible.

She got in the shower and let the water run over her head. She thought about Joe, she thought about Jess and her story, she thought about the man in the Savoy, she thought about N Clyne and lastly, she thought about herself. What did she want out of this? She just wanted to be loved, less lonely and share her time with someone. That wasn't too much to ask, was it? She thought if she was happy why should she care. Joe wasn't a figment of her imagination – she felt him, touched him, smelled him, kissed him. He was standing in her kitchen right now. But what if it was all based on a bed of lies? What if he really was Nathan Clyne from London? Deception, trust and misinformation was commonplace in this world now, just look at her Facebook feed and Instagram posts. People she barely knew posting boastful updates and pictures, designed to make them look good and her look bad. Who knew what they were *really* feeling? She knew that was not good for anyone but yet she still did it – several times a day sometimes.

Look how wonderful my life is, don't you wish you were like me?

Lucy knew mental illness was at an all-time high. Her therapist had said it so many times.

"People these days are so confused. We just don't know for sure what is true, who is lying and who isn't," she would say. "It's hard to understand who *we* are any more."

With the thought running around her mind, she looked down at her naked body, her legs, her feet. When she was growing up, she was bewildered with what was going on with her body and her place in the world. Magazines and newspapers body shamed people and contorted her thinking of who she should and shouldn't be. She felt for the teenagers now with the onslaught of social media messages bombarding them with even more personal attacks and confusion. Her head started to spin again. She turned off the taps. The sound of the water was replaced by urgent banging at the bathroom door. Goosebumps appeared on her skin.

"Lucy! Lucy! Are you alright in there?" It was Joe hammering on the door.

"Yes," she called out, "I'm fine." She wrapped a towel around her body, unlocked and opened the door. He had his hand on the door frame.

"Jeez Luce, I've been knocking for ages. I was about to break the door down." She shivered slightly when he said 'Luce'. She wasn't sure if the shiver came from being against the cold air, or from thoughts of who Joe really was. Or might be. She shook her head.

"Sorry, I had my head under the water." She closed the door again and looked in the mirror. Water was dripping down from her red hair to her shoulders and onto the towel. Her curls were starting to spring back into place. She turned her face to check for any red marks, traced her finger down from the cheek along her jawline to her lips, remembering Joe doing the same a couple of nights ago. She sighed a deep sigh.

She had made a decision.

She needed to find out. She would go to the address in Ealing today, and investigate it for herself.

Chapter Fourteen

Lucy finished her toast and asked Joe what he was going to do, trying to let the words out casually.

"I'm going to retrace our steps along the river, maybe head into the Tate Modern and sit in that massive hall and get on with some writing. It's a very cool space, very inspiring for my literary works."

"That's a great idea Joe!" she said perhaps a bit too enthusiastically, knowing he would be out of the way, headed somewhere other than Ealing.

"I need to head off." She sprang up and grabbed her bag.

"Wait, I'll come with you."

"No, it's fine. Take your time and I'll see you later."

"Don't be silly. I'll only be a minute."

He rushed into the bathroom and cleaned his teeth. He came back wiping water from his mouth. He went to give her a kiss on the lips but she turned her head and it landed on her cheek. They left the house and as he took her hand they walked to the station in silence. At the river, they pecked each other on the lips and said goodbye. He said he remembered the route from there and she stepped onto the stairs of the bridge. She stopped and watched him walk with his rucksack on his back. He turned and saw her. He stood, waved and blew her a kiss. Spinning on her heels, she briskly made her way across the bridge.

At the other side she went into Embankment station but instead of going straight through, she turned left through ticket barriers. She had switched on her phone earlier and had a million more texts from Jess. She had been tempted to read them but decided against – she wanted to focus on the real information she had discovered. Opening up the contacts she thought about letting the office know she was skiving off work but dismissed that. Finding another name, she quickly typed out a message and pressed 'send'. She got down to the platform just as a Wimbledon train was arriving and jumped on in order to change at Earls Court. The train rumbled on and her heart was thumping – she'd never even bunked off school before and she suddenly felt a wave of guilt. Her heart beat faster, like it would burst out of her chest. A large part of her hoped for nothing. She got off at Earls Court and the open-air station chilled her bones. Pigeons were scurrying and pecking around the platform floor. The destination board pointed to an Ealing Broadway train arriving next. When it came, it was virtually empty, with few people going the opposite direction to Central London. She found a seat and thought of what she would do when she got to the house.

At Ealing Broadway station, she pulled out her phone and the scrap of paper with the address on it, opened up Google Maps and typed in the address. It was a 15-minute walk. She walked down the busy Uxbridge Road, against the flow of commuters heading to London, past shops and cafes, which eventually led to office blocks and then to restaurants and more cafes – Persian, Lebanese, fast-food takeaways. The female voice on her app instructed her down another busy road, red buses trundling alongside her. She passed a large allotment, overgrown bushes covering a tired metal fence. She walked past side roads with terraced houses jammed packed together, road after road, street after street. It was not too dissimilar from where she lived. All very suburban and middle-class. A silver-bodied jet roared overhead, causing her to look up. American Airlines.

What a coincidence.

The female voice instructed her to turn into the next street and every house looked identical. The same small front garden in each place, some with a bike in it, some with a few flowers and some trying to standout with purple stones and an ornamental flowerpot in the middle. The voice announced that she had reached her destination. She looked at the door numbers and found the one she was looking for. She stood outside it for a few moments, not knowing quite what to do next. Should she knock on the door? At that moment, an elderly woman bundled out of the next house along. She had her back to the street and she was talking down to something. She reversed out of her door and Lucy saw she had a lead and a tiny mongrel pulling at the end of it.

Come on now, let's go for a little walk.

She turned and saw Lucy.

"Oh hello!" She said cheerfully. Lucy was a little surprised by her greeting. She was not quite sure how to explain how or why she was stood outside her neighbour's house.

'Hi. How are you?" She said.

"Oh, not too bad thanks. Surviving." Her eyes went to the top of her sockets.

"Are you looking for Nathaniel?" she asked. Nathaniel. N. Nathan. It hit her like a rocket, a punch to the stomach.

"Erm, yes. Yes I am. Have you seen him?"

"No love, not for a couple of days. I saw him the day before yesterday, I think. Or was it yesterday? I can't really remember; they all blend into one these days love."

"Erm, can I ask you a question. It's going to sound really odd. Do you mind?"

"Well, it depends on the question don't it love!" she chuckled. "Go on, fire away."

She pulled her phone out of her pocket and loaded up the photos app. She picked a photo of the two of them posing along the Thames, Tower Bridge in the background framing their two heads, her hand on his cheek ready to pull him in for a kiss. She showed the photo to her.

"I just want to double-check to make sure I've got the right address. Is that Nathaniel?" she said tentatively.

"Yes love, that's Nath. What a lovely picture. When was that taken?"

"Erm, a couple of days ago," she replied.

"Then he must have been with you then, innit!" she chuckled again and pulled on the lead.

"Come on Joe you little rascal, off we go to the shops." She opened her gate and walked out of her front garden.

"Joe?" she said, surprised. "Your dog's name is Joe?"

"Yes love. Named after my husband. American he was, died in 'Nam during the war in the 70s helping refugees escape. Smashing fella he was. This little monkey is a cheeky bugger just like him!"

"Sorry, I have just one more question. How well did you know Joe, I mean Nathaniel? I mean, er, did you know him well?"

"Well? Mmm let me see. Yeah, pretty well. He used to come around for tea and cake at a weekend sometimes, usually when he had a headache from the night before, hehe! Mind you he don't come around that often anymore. Probably too busy. My Joe used to love my cakes. He used to say, in a terrible English accent 'Make me one of your delicious Victoria Sponges'; he would have liked Nath too." Her eyes glazed off looking into the distance.

"And he trusts me enough to have his key in case he loses it. Good job as well as it happens pretty often!"

"Oh, you *do* know him pretty well then," she flashed a grin and became more friendly as an idea popped into her head.

"Yeah, I suppose so. I've lived here all my life. Nath moved in, um, let me see, four, five years ago now."

"Ah, that's so nice. I only moved to London a few months ago, still finding my feet. It was so great to meet Nath. We get on like a house on fire. He asked me to swing by to pick up some DVDs for him but he doesn't seem to be in." She flashed a smile again.

"Well, why don't you take the key, let yourself in and pop it through my letterbox when you're done," she said, pleased with her own idea, giving her a wink.

"If you're sure that's ok." she replied innocently.

"You look like a lovely girl, and Joe isn't barking at you, and you've got a lovely photo of you and Nath cuddling up. Hold on a sec love, I'll go get it." She moved to go inside, then she stopped, paused and turned around. Lucy held her breath.

"Actually. Would you mind holding Joe for a sec whilst I do it? It's a nightmare getting him out the house at the moment." Lucy let out a sigh of relief.

"It would be my pleasure. What's your name again, sorry?"

"Margaret dear, Margaret. Hold tight love," she said, giving her the lead.

She took hold of it as Margaret went back into the house. Joe laid down on the ground and rested his head on his paws. She quickly came back.

"Here you go love," and they swapped keys for the lead.

"Just remember to pop it back through the door when you're done. Tata love."

She waddled out of the gate and turned down the road towards the shops, Joe pacing behind her. Lucy looked at the house and then the black door. Taking a deep breath, she opened the gate and walked up to the door, sliding the key into the lock, half-expecting it not to fit.

It couldn't be this easy, could it?

The lock clicked as the key turned and the door creaked open. She stepped in looking down the wooden-floored hall and let the front door click shut. A set of wooden stairs climbed up to a second storey. Everywhere was spotless and minimal with no pictures on the bright white walls. She passed a room on her left, the living room. There were two fashionable sofas facing each other with a distressed wood table in between on a wooden-slated floor. A solitary remote control sat atop the table. A high-end giant television was bolted to the wall in between the sofas on a whitewashed wall. Wooden blinds covered the windows, causing a slatted shadow to appear on the floor. She turned and walked towards the back of the house.

An open-plan kitchen opened up into a large living space, bi-folding doors spanned the entire width looking out to an immaculate lawn. The kitchen looked like a showroom, not a crumb or a speck of dust. An Aga oven sat on one side, a Smeg fridge on the other. A set of knives rested innocently in a block on the counter. She opened the fridge, its door a giant Union Jack. It was empty apart from a half-empty plastic bottle of milk and a tub of butter. A trendy glass table was positioned between the kitchen and the bi-folding doors, with four transparent matching chairs tucked in around it. She turned around and walked back down the hallway to the stairs. Her pumps padded softly on the wood as she walked up slowly looking around her as she went.

At the top of the stairs was thick, heavy carpet. Her shoes sunk into the fibres. She opened the first door on the right, a bathroom. Spotless with a few bottles of men's products – shaving gel, shampoo, hair gel and shower gel – and a razor, all neatly arranged with the brand names facing out. A whiff of Joe's cologne hit her nose. The shower was a walk-in, the dividing glass gleaming as if brand new. She moved on to the master bedroom, the double bed the centrepiece in the room, a stylish brown leather headboard rested against the back wall, oodles of light coming in from the large windows overlooking the street. It was like a show home, unlived and unloved. She walked in and opened the cupboards. Rows of suits, collared shirts and smart trousers lined up. She brushed her hand over them, they were silky and smooth. She thought of Jess.

A banker.

Within the cupboard there were two rows of drawers. She opened one: underwear. The same style and brand that Joe wore were folded up neatly next to each other. The one underneath was packed densely with socks, colour-coded and in pairs. She shut the drawer and it closed with a bang. The noise reverberated through the house and the hairs on her skin pricked up. She looked over her shoulder but the room was empty. Not a single picture or photo was on the wall for her to look at.

Exiting the bedroom, Lucy walked along the hallway to the only other upstairs room, its door closed. She pressed on the handle and it opened silently. Inside was a large bookcase on the opposite wall to the door, filled from top to bottom with box files. All of them were neatly stored, uniformed and all lined up, with no spaces between them and cursive writing neatly scrawled on each one, in exactly the same place on each label. There were four shelves going up and she counted 15 box files across. That's 60 in total. It was like art. They felt fake, like those rows of books in Ikea – the ones which are all stuck together. Each label had a women's name written on it, in alphabetical order. Starting at the top left was Abi, then Anna, then Beth and Briony. Lucy reached up and followed the names with her finger. At her head height, on the next row down, was Gemma. She pulled it down off the shelf and opened it up. Inside were scraps of paper: ticket stubs for trains, attractions, buses; restaurant menus; letters and envelopes. A perfume bottle sat at the bottom of the box. She lifted up the loose papers and behind were photos. Hundreds of photos of the same woman. A young pretty woman with long straight brown hair and an obviously large bosom. She flicked through the photos, some were taken from far away, some were close-up and some were with a man. Selfies.

With Joe.

Happy, smiling, kissing, cheek-to-cheek, like the one she just showed Margaret. Except Joe looked different, his hair was shaved and he had long sideburns. He was wearing a checked lumberjack shirt. At the back of the file was a lock of hair, brown and straight like the girl in the photo, taped to a white piece of card. Lucy closed the file and carefully put it back and traced her finger along the bottom row. Sara. She pulled the file out and opened it. Inside were ticket stubs and letters, menus again. She pushed them aside and found hundreds of photos, this time of a woman that looked like she was in her forties with natural blonde hair, set in a side parting. She had a mischievous glint in her eye that showed a younger spirit. Some of the photos were taken from very far away, some close-up. Cheek-to-cheek, kissing, photobooth photos.

With Joe.

A different Joe.

He was wearing very skinny jeans and a tight black shirt, the famous red lips of the Rolling Stones logo emblazoned on it. Lucy looked behind all the paper and there was a lock of hair taped to a white piece of card. Blonde and straight, exactly like the woman's hair in the photos. She carefully pushed the file back into its place.

Lucy traced her finger along the middle shelf. She was looking for Jessica, or Jess. She found it.

Jess.

She pulled it out and opened it up. The same items. Ticket stubs, menus, a white piece of card with jet black, thick hair. She looked at the photos but it's not the Jess she knew looking back. The woman was Afro-Caribbean in complexion, her hair in braids stretching in rows behind her head, revealing a beautiful natural face. She didn't look older than twenty. Hundreds of photos again, the same thing. Joe was in them, again the same face but a different look. He had long shoulder length hair and a small goatee. His clothes were big and baggy. She placed it back carefully, making sure they all lined up with each other as when she found them. She traced her finger to the right, looking for L. She found it.

Lucy.

She took the box folder out. It was lighter than the others. She bent down and sat on her knees, the folder out in front her, like she was praying to the bookshelf of folders, the door sat open behind her.

Hesitantly she opened the folder.

The pizza menu of the restaurant they went to, covering the whole space with crease lines down the middle and through the centre, the edges crumpled like it has been stuffed into a pocket. She took one of the crumpled edges and peeled it back. Behind were hundreds of photos, all of her. Her heart missed a beat, a lump hit her stomach. Her brain went into meltdown. There were photos of her going into Starbucks; coming out of Starbucks; a far-away shot of her coming out of her house; going into the office – her office – taken from across the street, which looked like it was in the café she had never noticed; a blurry photo of her bedroom window of which she could just make out her silhouette; one from the street into a sandwich shop buying her lunch; shopping; one of her on a train, her face peering out from behind a Metro newspaper; one from behind walking across Hungerford Bridge. The timespan must be a few months. She felt like she was going to be sick. Thank God he didn't know where her mum lived.

Or did he?

She flipped the photos forward. Screwed up bank statements, torn letters, an empty bottle of conditioner. Things she had thrown in the bin. And there it was: a piece of white cardboard with a piece of red curly hair taped to it.

She thought of Jess. She was right. Lucy didn't know who Joe was. Or Nathan. Or Nathaniel. She felt bile come up into her throat, and she swallowed it down. Her legs felt weak and she couldn't move them off the floor. Her head started to spin. She saw Jess' face, then Joe's, then Margaret's, then the suited man in the Savoy and then all the different versions of Joe like an animated flicker book. She put her forehead down on the shag pile carpet, the folder in the space between her belly and the floor. It was like she was locked in prayer, asking for forgiveness to the wall of folders. Folders with women like her. She gathered her thoughts.

Think Lucy!

She tried to make sense of it all. The words, the accent, the touch of his hands, the caress of his lips. The *perfection* of it all.

The photos of Joe flashed through her mind. A distant memory jolted through her brain like a lightning strike. A familiarity. Those eyes. She had seen them before. A long time ago, a lifetime ago. Or was her brain playing tricks again, trying to fit everything together in a convenient jigsaw puzzle? Her mind was racing, silent noise filling her head. She felt like throwing up.

Suddenly, the door behind her clicked shut. She sat up straight, alert, frozen. Nothing happened. Then she moved her body an inch and heard a large, dull thwack. It seemed to have come from inside her head. She fell forward hitting the carpet, bouncing on the soft fibres. Her head pounded. She tasted metal in her mouth. It was warm. Her head was resting down on the floor, like she wanted to go to sleep. Footsteps paced around her. Her eyes closed to force the pounding out of her head.

Shush, she warned it, *I'm trying to sleep.*

She slowly opened them to see a bright blue trainer in front of her, with a black Nike swoosh across it. She heard words. She felt the sick coming back up and this time she let it out, spitting as she did. The blue trainer stepped abruptly back, swear words filled the room. Her eyes slowly closed again, she felt herself slipping away. She tried to force them open. She heard the words. *Luce! Luce! Luce!* The trainer was dancing around the room, moving around and around in circles. She heard crying. *Luce!* It was Joe, he was calling her name. She tried to speak but it came out a whisper. She could feel blood dripping through her hair and the warmth trickled down her cheek. She whispered more.

"Luce what have you done? Lucy!" the male was voice panicky, crying almost. It was unmistakably Joe's but not a hint of American in it at all. She whispered more. The trainer came back into view. She whispered louder.

"What is it Luce, are you trying to say something?" She heard Joe's voice, loud and clear, English, mocking. She saw his knee come down to the floor. She felt his hand cradle her head, his soft, moisturised hand. His face came down to her and he looked her in the eye. It was unmistakably Joe.

"Luce, why did you come here?" he was pleading, desperate. She whispered.

She saw his trainer appear in front of her eye. The blood filled her mouth, she could feel herself slipping further and further away.

"What, what is it?" he called out, pleadingly "Luce? Lucy!"

"Lucy" she spluttered, determination in her voice, "is not the name you used to know me by."

Part Two

'Joe'

Chapter One

"Joe! Joe! JOE!!" The stern voice echoed throughout my bedroom, coming from the rear of my house. I opened my eyes in a daze.

"JOE! Come back here boy!" I came to and recognised Margaret's voice. I heard fierce yapping, punctuated by his name being shouted at.

That bloody dog.

She couldn't control him. I moved into this new place two weeks ago, buying my first house outright from the bonus I got from the bank. My first year and a million-pound bonus. I was a natural. Neither I nor my seller were in a chain so the sale went through quickly: knocked 20% off the asking price too, exchanged and completed in a couple of months. You don't really vet the neighbours when you buy a new pad. I met Margaret briefly when I viewed the place. She was just bringing the dog back from a walk and seemed nice enough. A doddering old widow. She invited me round for tea and cake which I must get around to doing again. The dog seemed sedate enough that day so I didn't even think about the issues it might bring.

It must have been getting on to eleven am on a warm summer's morning. The weekend. I turned over in my bed and looked out towards the big window at the front of the house. The blinds caused shards of light to filter through the window, casting horizontal shapes on the blank walls. I was never a fan of pictures and photos, preferring the minimalist look. Clean and tidy, just the way I liked it. When Margaret's back door shut, the wall shuddered. That's another thing you didn't think about when buying a terraced house in London – how close everyone and everything was. Squashed together, hearing and sensing every movement and action, yet at the same time being locked away in our own world, borders and barriers keeping people out and away.

I tried to get back to sleep but it was no use. My brain was awake and buzzing. I swung my legs round and put my feet into my woollen Gucci Princeton slippers, tucked tidily just under my bed, heels together pointing out to the window. I slid around my new house. The spare room was bare and empty, even the lightbulb hadn't got a shade around it. The bathroom looked old and uninviting – an avocado green bath and basin stood amongst dirty, worn tiles. It needed updating and was another reason why I knocked the price down. The stairs had a threadbare red carpet, it looked like it was last cleaned in the seventies. I ripped up a corner on my first day in the place to see what was underneath. To my surprise the original flooring, pretty much intact from when it was laid down. Just needed a bit of sanding, polish and TLC and it would add £10k onto the value of the house. I'd get someone in to sort that out.

Downstairs the kitchen was in much of the same state: dilapidated appliances and mouldy floor tiles. The Guccis deserved better than this. They didn't even have a dishwasher. It all needed to come out and be replaced, a few modern white goods and some decent brand names. I stripped down the brown and cream patterned wallpaper in the front room the first week I moved in. It was so satisfying peeling the nicotine-stained paper from the walls, coming off like a piece of Velcro. I brought a 60-inch widescreen smart TV the day before I completed and it arrived the day I finished tearing off the wallpaper. I set it up, the only item in the whole echoey room.

I pulled on a white Boss t-shirt and faded Diesel jeans and headed out the door. Margaret was taking Joe for a walk so I said a neighbourly good morning, and she apologised for Joe's barking.

"Not to worry," I said. "I had to get up anyway."

"At this time?!"

"It's the weekend Margaret. Need my beauty sleep. You should try it sometime," I said with a wink.

"Oh, you cheeky bugger you! Where you off to anyways?

"Up the West End to do some shopping. Need a few items for the place."

"Yeah, imagine the place needs sprucing up. Have a good time love."

She sauntered off down the road, pulling Joe along.

I took off in the opposite direction, getting on the tube direct train to Oxford Street, where I looked around Selfridges and paid for a Smeg Union Jack fridge, a couple of French Connection sofas and a Hästens bed. Paid for them all on my Platinum Amex card. I winked to the young, blonde saleswoman and asked her out for a drink. She bashfully said no but gave me a flash of her pearly whites. John Lewis was next on the list so I hurried along Oxford Street, past the queue of stationary red buses and dodged the other shoppers, hands full of crappy paper Primark bags. The vast central atrium of the department store, with the escalators criss-crossing over the empty central space, sucked in the noise.

Peaceful.

I headed up to the second floor and sat for an hour with a suited and booted man planning out the layout of my kitchen and bathroom. As always with my careful planning, I had brought the exact measurements with me and he plotted them into his computer. A 3D image of the space appeared on his screen and he dragged and dropped white goods in like a jigsaw puzzle, including the Smeg I had just purchased in Selfies. I chose a colour and with a click all of the surfaces changed. When finished designing, he clicked a button and a bill printed out itemising all the purchases. We chose a date for installation and I paid again with my flexible friend.

Bish bash bosh.

Home decorating done and a team of lads would come and sort it all out whilst I was at work, earning yet more money.

There was a men's grooming salon on the ground floor so I had a spontaneous haircut and shave, accepting a glass of bubbly whilst I waited for them to lather. By mid-afternoon I was back on the tube heading back west. Walking up the street after getting off the tube, I spotted a carpet and flooring company, a small thin backend of a place. A bell rang above the door as I waltzed in. An old man, his hands worn from years of hard graft, came out of the back with a brown cardy and glasses on the edge of his nose. He looked over the rim and looked me up and down. I asked him for a price to rip up the old carpet, sort out the wooden stairs, the floorboards in the front room and hallway, giving him the exact measurements and haggled him down 25%. You always get a better deal at the local shops, especially for something like carpets. He agreed and promised to send a guy in on Monday to check it out. I said I was at work and if he wanted the job the guy would come around tomorrow, Sunday. He huffed and puffed but reluctantly agreed to come himself at 10am. I gathered that this was the biggest job he had had all month. I popped into the fish and chip shop next door, ordered a saveloy and a large chips and ate it on the floor of the front room, the TV providing all the necessary entertainment and light I needed.

Monday morning I was in the office at 7am, wearing my favourite Paul Smith wool suit and matching cufflinks and tie. First one there as always. I had booted up my two monitors and watched as the flashing numbers scrolled across one of them and green graphs pulsated on the other. On the far wall was a bank of screens listing stocks, bonds and futures, some highlighted in red, some in green and a few in black. Asia was already awake. The office started to get busier as my loser colleagues arrived.

"Alright Matty!" I shouted when I saw my partner in crime.

"Nathstar!" he responded, dragging his knuckles along the floor.

"Good weekend fella?" I asked as he swung his leather Ted Baker bag down, his hair wet from showering in the gym downstairs.

"Not too shabby. Went out on the town Saturday night, got in about 4."

"Legend," I replied.

He was already booting up his two monitors as he watched the bank of screens ahead, taking in all the information from the weekend and the Asian markets.

"How's that bird of yours," he said without looking away.

"Which one?" I replied and gave a suppressed laugh.

"Haha! Legend. I can't keep up mate."

Since getting this job, the women have been easy. Whenever we went down after work to the trendy bars in Canary Wharf, they were gagging for it. A few rich bankers, throwing their money around, they went crazy. Offer them a glass of Cristal, a bit of coke and they were putty in your hand. At the start it was easy, too easy. Buy a couple of drinks, talk to them for a bit and then take them home. Always their home. It was easy to get rid of them as there weren't any ties. I couldn't believe it when I landed this gig after graduating from Oxford. Not only was I earning a shedload of dough, I was also sleeping with fit, beautiful women. Work hard, play hard. The pressure was on but at the end of the day you were playing with other people's money. They knew the risks. It's like spinning the roulette wheel and you won whether it landed on red, black or even green. And when it did land on your colour, you got a nice hefty bonus, a slap on the back and another blonde in the sack. Work hard, play hard. Even if you did screw it up, the Government was there to bail you out.

First year in, I went mental – wide-eyed with a bulge in my Calvin Kleins. I was knackered. Late nights and early mornings. The weekends weren't enough time to recover, especially after a traditional late Friday night. I had actually started to get bored after the first year. Going to these bars and picking up women was too simple; it wasn't even a contest. So, I used my bonus to buy the house a bit further out and give myself a challenge, stretch myself a bit from the easy pickings. I would clock a good-looking woman on the tube and think about how I could get her, without flashing money, drugs and alcohol around. The challenge was to hook a variety of different women – young, old, black, Asian, slim, curvy – whatever felt like a contest. I decided to research them as best as I could, change myself to see if I could be their 'ideal' man. A chameleon adapting to their environment. I thought it would be a craic and a hobby to do in my spare time. And get some action in the process. Get them to fall for me and then dump them and move on. It would be a longer game but ultimately more satisfying than getting some drunk girl high within an hour.

I chose my first challenge a week later: a brunette with a woollen hat pulled down over her hair to just above her eyes, her face buried in a crappy romance novel, oblivious to the other passengers on the tube. I watched her and studied her. She had a worn, knitted jumper on, the sleeves longer than her arms, ripped jeans and platform shoes. She looked about my age but she would never have gone for me. A couple of stops after my station, she got up, slung a knitted satchel over her shoulder and got off the train. I followed her at a distance pretending to be another commuter. She walked along the main street and zigzagged through half a dozen streets, all lined with semi-detached houses and drives with 4x4s parked on them. I made a mental note that I needed to write the directions so I wouldn't forget them.

As I followed her, my heart was racing and thumping through my chest. I felt alive. It was like I was a lion watching his prey. She turned up the drive into one of the semi-detached houses. A two-year-old Alfa Romeo was parked outside. To the left of the front door was a large bay window with a dining table visible, a couple of candlesticks poking up. A woman, about 60 years old, came into view carrying a large pot with steam coming out of the top. Must be mum. A man, a little bit older, entered uncorking a bottle of white wine. Must be dad. Then she came in and sat down. Her brown hair straggly from removing her woollen hat. She took a spoon and ladled out the hot food from the pot. I watched them from across the street until the streetlamps were brighter than the darkening sky, imagining their conversations, what the girl liked and didn't like, what my character could be. I turned and headed back to the tube, trying to retrace my steps I came. I felt exhilarated. I felt challenged, and most of all, I felt I could do this.

Chapter Two

I was offered another promotion. Nothing unusual in that, considering the progress, and dough, I was making for the bigwigs above me. The promotion was a biggie: Not only did it give me a chance to travel it also meant my colleagues would be well jealous, so I snapped it up. Their faces were a picture! Some had been there years longer than me!

The major downside was that I had to put my little side projects and challenges away every now and then because I was travelling to a new time zone every other week – Singapore, New York, Frankfurt, Beijing. Jetlag was the minor downside, which meant the thrill of travel dissipated quicker than I thought. At first, I loved the lounges, turning left to the business class seats, the airmiles, the swanky hotels. Over time, I started to hate airports, the security checks and the numpties who should know now to remove your flipping belt and shoes before you get to the x-rays. Worse when you hadn't slept properly. And for god's sake put your toiletries in the transparent bag; they're not going to make an exception just for you, you know.

At first the five-star hotels were exciting, then staid and then downright boring. Soulless and superficial, like the women I was bedding in a different country every night. Waking up at god-knows-o'clock in a god-awful identikit room. It started to play on your senses.

This was one such trip. I'm tired and I'm jet lagged. It had been pretty much non-stop since I landed at JFK. I barely slept on the plane over, finalising the presentation and proposal for the big meeting I had with the potential investors on Wall Street. I didn't even have time to put my flatbed down and enjoy a movie. The chauffeur had whisked me away in his sleek sedan and when I got into the mirrored elevator at the Wall Street office, I straightened my Louis Vuitton tie and smoothed down my hair. The meeting was intense and we only broke for 20 minutes for lunch. They picked apart every detail of my proposal and questioned everything. I was used to massaging egos from rich investors and trust-fund beneficiaries, so it was a piece of pie getting the deal over the line – it's the time and the incessant questions that frustrate me. Having done it so many times now it was getting tiresome, and the travelling to and from the States was messing with my body. I hadn't been to the gym for over a month. The late-night drinking and the early morning rises to get into the office to beat the others were starting to take its toll.

Deal completed, we all shook hands, my Hugo Boss cufflinks danced over the paperwork. I gathered up my things and they offered to take me for a drink. It was impossible to say no in those situations, and the business-travel mindset kicked in: don't sit in your hotel room, go out and enjoy the place. Especially if it was all on expenses. They took me to some hokey-cokey place in Greenwich Village, the walls stripped bare showing off exposed brickwork and trendy naked lights hung from the ceiling. It was full of suits and women with tight black dresses. A line of coke went around the table and I obliged. It was quality stuff. Several moments later a gaggle of women joined us, sniffing the white stuff and helping themselves to champagne. I got chatting to a blonde who drooled over my British accent, and she sat next to me the whole night, kissing my neck and caressing my thigh, wanting more.

Next morning, I left her in my hotel room as I dragged my Tumi out of the room to catch the red-eye home. I jumped in a yellow taxi and it stunk of sweat. I told the driver to go to JFK, terminal 7 and opened the window. My head was still swirling and the last thing I needed was vomit-inducing smells. I looked out at the early-morning scrum of traffic, people and couriers. The air felt dirty and everything was in shadow. I looked up to see an endless row of office windows stretching up. I never quite saw the sky from this side of the taxi. We pulled up outside the terminal and the driver jumped out and retrieved my Tumi. I paid him in cash, dropping a 30-dollar tip.
Get some deodorant, my friend.

He looked up surprised and was overly friendly all of a sudden, wishing me to 'have a nice day and a good flight'. I entered the terminal and headed to the business class check-in, got my boarding pass and made a beeline for the lounge. God, I could do with a hair of the dog.

After sinking a couple of fingers of whiskey in the lounge, the flight was called and I made my way to the gate. There was already a queue of passengers lining up, carry-on cases parked behind them, passports out and boarding passes sticking out. I looked down the line looking for talent. Boarding hadn't started yet so I took a seat on one of the rows of plastic chairs with a thin material covering the seat. I couldn't wait to get onto my flatbed. I looked around the passengers that were sitting down and spotted a redhead a couple of rows across with her head down and her carry-on open. She was busying herself with the contents. All I saw was a mop of red curly hair looking at me, dangling down covering her face. She had blue jeans on and her legs were closed together, her pale arms moved frantically around her case. She eventually zipped it shut and looked up taking a big sigh. I looked at her, transfixed.

Wow, she was a stunner.

Not in the conventional model-sense, but in a completely natural, girl-next-door way. There was a *je ne sais quoi* about her which I couldn't quite put my finger on – a warmth, perhaps even a familiarity from the past. Her red curly hair rested upon her shoulders framing a beautiful porcelain face. She had dark eyes which stood out against her pale face, a hint of a cleft chin and two cute dimples on either side of her mouth. The way she looked around was totally innocent and unassuming, bashful even. Her beauty hit me in the chest, it felt as if the wind had been taken from me. I considered waltzing over to her with a chat-up line but the thought of it felt like a pit landing in my stomach. All of a sudden, I felt like an idiot – I'd chatted up tons of girls in the past yet felt too nervous to go up and talk to her, like *normally*. Maybe the hangover, or the whiskey I had just downed was having an effect on my confidence.

I instinctively reached for my Galaxy in my pocket as I had done with countless other women I had spotted. Holding the phone upright in my hand, I expanded the screen and the lens zoomed in. She filled the frame and I clicked the button, taking a few photos. She looked left and right, allowing me to snap all angles, oblivious that I was doing this. My heart beat faster and faster. She delicately tucked a loose curl behind her ear, revealing a small, hooped earring and a stunning square jawline. I watched her through my screen. She looked behind her at the queue of passengers waiting in line to board and got up. Her perfect bum, tight around her jeans, filled the screen and I continued to click. Picking up her carry-on she walked over and joined the queue. I grabbed my Tumi and stood right behind her, millimetres from her red curls and slowly inhaled the air, letting her scent tickle my senses. It smelt like candyfloss – sweet, sticky and childlike.

Yummy, yum, yum.

The hairs on my arm stood on end.

My eyes followed the strands down her neck and onto her shoulders. The blades protruded against her pale, freckled skin and disappeared behind a white cotton sweater. I enjoyed the feeling of being in her space. A uniformed woman came down the line, checking our passports and boarding passes. She took the redhead's British passport and boarding pass and I tried to read it as it passed. I saw the seat number but didn't memorise it. I was looking for a name. I saw an 'L' but the surname was hidden behind the attendant's thumb. She tucked the long white card into the passport, handed it back to her and wished her a pleasant flight. She then took my boarding pass and looked up in surprise.

"Sir, you can board in the business priority line. Just head down the line to my colleague."

She pointed her fingers to the front of the line and to the left where a couple of men in suits showed their passes to another uniformed employee wearing a blue hat and walked straight down the tunnel, dragging their carry-ons behind them. I thanked her and left the line, walking past the queue of economy passengers. I had a strong desire to look back along the queue, so I quickly glanced. A few of the passengers looked at me with envy. The redhead was staring blankly forward, not even noticing me. She looked stunning standing amongst the bored passengers, her red hair stood out like a lighthouse in the dark.

Turning left on the plane, I tucked my Tumi into the overhead locker and slumped down on my flatbed. As I did a steward appeared with a tray of assorted drinks perched on it and handed me a flute. As I took a swig my mouth salivated at the thought of candyfloss – a memory bounced into my mind of stuffing it into my mouth when I was a kid at school at some kind of gypo fairground. I leaned back and pulled my phone out of my pocket and called up the gallery. Swiping through the images of the redhead, I was transfixed. Everything about her shone beauty. She looked completely innocent and unperturbed, without a care in the world. A girl next door, in the classic sense. At a guess I would say she was about the same age as me too, perhaps slightly younger. I looked forward to getting off the plane and checking her out again.

In the meantime, I kicked off my Church's, ordered more champagne and switched on the entertainment. As soon as dinner was cleared away, I was putting this bad-boy bed down and getting some well-deserved sleep.

When I got off the plane at Heathrow, I slipped into airport mode. I grabbed my Tumi and raced off the plane, overtaking the first class and other business passengers to get to passport control before them. I wanted to get out of the airport as quickly as possible, getting ahead to avoid queues and wasting time. I got through using the automated passport machines and skipped baggage reclaim pulling my carry-on fast through the green channel of customs. By the time I got out into arrivals, a record six minutes after leaving the aircraft, I remembered the red headed girl. What an idiot I was. I considered hanging around the arrivals to wait for her but didn't have the patience. Beside I had already spotted my driver with my name on his whiteboard. I clicked my tongue and put her out of her mind.

There were plenty of other fish in the sea, and challenges in my research pipeline.

Chapter Three

I was sitting opposite a dullard in a dull, featureless restaurant – the one I had chosen and it was as boring as she was. Somewhere along the line I had made a mistake. I had done the research, taken the photos, followed her around and created a pen portrait of her likes and dislikes. I had made an educated guess as to who her perfect man should be based on what she had been up to, the books she had read, the parts of the newspaper she flicked right past and those she slowed down to absorb. The charity shops I visited to create a look that I thought she would dig were the worst part of the research – I had to have a shower after visiting them along the high street: god knows what diseases I would have picked up.

She seemed like a difficult challenge; one I hadn't gone with before, so the research part was longer than usual. I first spotted her in a red charity vest, trying to get people to stop as they bustled about their lives, clipboard in hand, iPad ready to show terrible images of starving children. A chugger who I usually avoided like the plague, crossing the street to duck their tired opening line. This one though had a certain charm and a certain smile. I watched her patch from a nearby café. I saw how she danced from one foot to the other, trying to grab the attention of a passer-by, always men. Every time, she managed to snag a good-looking guy. At the end of her shift, she went back to the headquarters and emerged wearing a multi-coloured beanie hat then headed off to Dalston on the bus. God, I hated travelling on buses. She wore headphones most of the time so I didn't know if she was listening to podcasts, music or hippy whale-singing. She lived in a run-down ex-council flat with three men, who looked like they inhaled more weed than air.

I decided my act would be a fed-up banker who was sick of the corporate, money-grabbing world and wanted to 'give something back'. When I spoke to her on the street, I told her how wonderful the charity she worked for was, and how aligned it was with my new values. She lapped it up thinking this could be the bonus she was looking for. I chatted to her for ages, making all the right noises and saying things that I knew that she would respond to: that I volunteered at the foodbank at weekends, and had a direct debit to Oxfam (her eyes lit up when I said this). I bemoaned how the women I mixed with didn't understand why I would want to give my hard-earned money to little black kids in a foreign country and that the women I met weren't on my level. I said I need to be more grounded with the obscene amount of money I made, which is why I didn't wear the expensive suits, choosing instead to get them from second-hand shops. She cooed and nodded her head. At the mention of money her demeanour changed. We agreed to go for a drink after work.

When we met, I asked if we could try a new Vegan place that I was dying to go to but none of my colleagues would touch with a bargepole. She nodded enthusiastically and we sat in a dimly lit, bare restaurant. She was talking incessantly about the Establishment and how they controlled every element of our lives. There were words and phrases I needed to say, nod in the right places, to feign interest and hopefully get her into bed. Unfortunately, it made things worse. She continued to expunge the education system, saying it was designed to create obedient servants to work in factories, and how out-of-date that now was.

"Where was the creativity? Where was the focus on saving the planet?"

Yadda, yadda, yadda.

"We are all taught the same things and conditioned to act in a certain way, the way the elite wants us in order to control us. Why did we need to regurgitate dates when we could now google them? Instead, why don't we teach our kids the softer skills, like compassion and kindness."

Blah blah blah. You didn't earn a million through kindness, love.

I nodded knowingly, telling her she was *so* right. It egged her on.

She continued to blather, spitting food at me in her fury.

"Why, in exams and tests, we were forced to sit in silence, on our own in rows, sweating and stressing at an answer we didn't know! In that very room, we knew full well that someone else, probably sitting next to them, knew the answer. In what world would that happen in real life?"

I knew exactly the kind of world that happened in because I worked in it, but I bit my tongue. Instead, I nodded enthusiastically as if she had found the answer to the world's problems.

"Don't get me started on private school."

Hmm, not sure I can stop you, love.

"What's the point of single-sex schools? And in what environment in today's world were men made to work separately from women?"

Again, I bit my tongue thinking of the male office I had just came from, although some women were starting to infiltrate the ranks. My brain was dying inside, I didn't even think bedding her was worth the pain. I pushed the beetroot burger around on my plate and complained that my stomach had started to hurt. I put on a pained expression and went to the toilet. I sat on the seat for a good twenty minutes flicking through my Facebook and Twitter feeds. I saw England were 2-0 up and scrolled through the written commentary on the Sky Sports app. When I returned, she had a concerned look on her face.

"Look, I've had a grand old time. I've got a bit of a tummy issue. I think I better head off. Really sorry but listen. You've really made me think about some of the things you've said."

I thanked her again and apologised, deliberately forgetting to make future plans or a text or a meetup. I paid the bill and walked out of the restaurant. What a waste of time and energy that had been. I went down the golfing range that night, smacking the little pimpled ball as hard I could.

She reminded me of another failure of a challenge I had had. I had spent a week researching this brunette who was a proper airhead, but she had had a certain something about her, a sense of a kinkiness just beneath the surface. She was easy to photograph as she was out and about all the time, flirting with a particular type of guy – tattooed, badboy, skinhead. She was a challenge completely out of my comfort zone so she was a red rag to my bull. Every so often she would come out of some guy's house a bit battered and bruised, but with eyes looking up at the man as if he was the best thing in the world. During my research I followed her into Soho and she sneaked into a sex shop. She came out with a brown paper bag. Of course, I was intrigued. She went home and a couple of hours later she walked out, empty-handed. She closed the door behind her but I noticed the door didn't catch properly. I hadn't seen anyone else go in or out of that place for days so I went in.

I couldn't believe how clean it was: clinical, spotless, metallic. I looked around and opened drawers and cupboards. Nothing unusual. I went into her bedroom. Again, spotless, not a crease in her bed. It all seemed out of place. I walked around, testing doors and cabinets, looking under her bed, searching for that brown bag. Nothing. I noticed a hatch on the ceiling in the hall. I pulled a lever and a ladder clattered down, almost knocking into my head. I climbed up, felt around for a light, found it and switched it on. A red light blinked on. A dungeon. A room Christian bloody Grey would envy. Toys, whips, chains, handcuffs neatly hanging on the wall. It could have been the film set. My mind started racing, my lips turning into a smile. Talk about out of my comfort zone. This would be a fun one.

I morphed into the kind of guy she liked. Even got a couple of semi-permanent tattoo transfers done on my arms and legs, which lasted a couple of weeks before new skin grew replacing them. I got my head shaved with a number one at Jack the Clippers in Mayfair, the lads in the office had a right giggle at my expense. The joke would be on them when they heard why I'd done it. So, I got a date with this chick, Megan her name was, and we headed to some grimy vegetarian place in Shoreditch. She was chewing on a tofu dish and she started talking Capitalism and Nihilism, going all Karl Marx on me. I hadn't been expecting this. I thought the conversation would be reality shows leading to filth. I guess people aren't what you expected. So, she was blathering on about 'banker wankers' and I was starting to get uncomfortable, I felt an anger rise inside her. She ordered another beer and carried on a tirade. I wanted to give her a slap, not in the way I was intending tonight. Then she started prattling on about mental health, and how our brains couldn't cope with the amount of information that we were being exposed to.

"It's taken us millions of years to evolve to this point, and for millennia all our small brains had to cope with were something like sixty stimuli a day – weather, food, shelter, sex."

I wanted to tell her my brain wasn't coping with this nonsense right now.

"In the last ten thousand years or so the number of things our brain has to cope with has exploded, to the point in the last ten years we have around 60 million messages going into our head *a day*."

She took a swig of beer direct from the bottle.

"From 60 to 60 million in a tiny amount of time in our evolution, and that's just external stimulus, never mind stress, anxiety and remembering everything we needed to remember, like paying the bills."

I remembered wondering how this conversation could ever lead to heading back to her secret dungeon. I kept nodding and agreeing, hoping it turned her on, thinking about her other fellas who didn't seem to be the type to be discussing Charles flipping Darwin. Maybe that's why she got knocked about, trying to get her to shut up. She was still talking, asking me why, after all this evolution, childbirth was so painful. She paused, waiting for an answer. I shrugged my shoulders.

"Because our brains are developing and getting bigger at a faster pace than the evolution of a woman's vagina."

Hmm, now we might be getting somewhere. Getting in the right area.

She was still talking, saying it was no wonder mental health was at its highest, our brains were getting frazzled, and social media didn't help – all that comparing and keeping up with the Jones'. Kids these days were never off it.

Not just kids, I thought, *I've seen you on it constantly*.

She paused and stabbed a piece of tofu, holding it up as if she was going to ram it down my throat. During dessert, she started going on about how the Earth was spiralling towards the Sun (*'have you ever noticed that everything spirals towards a gravitational centre: galaxies, hurricanes, water going down a plug. Doesn't it make sense that the Earth was doing that too?'*), and that was the real reason for global warming. I had had enough. I made my excuses, got home and threw all the photos of her in the bin. I would have to find a dungeon via someone else. The next day I went to the gym and pounded a punching bag for a solid hour. It made me feel good again. Yet every let-down was a learning, that's how I looked at it. Not that every tart was a fiasco: my hit rate of success to failure was verging on 50-50. Every challenge made me a little bit better, honed my skills where I went wrong and every disaster led me to a different place.

Feeling sorry for myself after hitting a few golf balls after I left the chugger dullard failure, I thought about who might be out and about. I called up my Facebook feed again as I walked to the tube and I saw a few of my colleagues out on the town, pissed and taking selfies in a bar. I called one of them and when he answered music blasted down the phone.

"Alright Phil" I shouted. "Where are you?"

"Alright mate. At the opening of a new bar down the South Bank. We've just arrived and it hasn't got going yet. Although we've been on the piss since five!" A cheer erupted down the phone from the others he was with. I checked my charity-shop watch that was part of the act. It wasn't even seven yet.

"I'll be there soon mate. Get me a beer," I said.

"Mate, it's free champagne!" and hung up. I hailed a black cab and instructed him to take me home. No way I was going to turn up at a bar in the clothes I was wearing. I needed to get changed into my Paul Smiths and put my Breitling back on. I told the cabbie to wait outside my place and slipped him a fifty note for the inconvenience. I threw on a casual suit, clicked in the cufflinks and slipped on my Church's. On the way out I dumped the clothes I was wearing in the black bin outside. I jumped back in the cab and he sped off to the bar, arriving just after eight.

A waiter stood by the entrance and offered me a champagne flute which I grabbed and took a sip. I immediately saw Phil and his cohorts with some of my colleagues from the office, all standing in a tight circle. I made a beeline for them. They all cheered when they saw me, and there were hugs all round. They were properly wasted, probably had snorted a line of coke each too. I looked around the place, it was starting to get a buzz. The usual array of hot women and tight dresses: the sparkly ones usually meant not wanting to get wasted and passing out on the toilet floor. Many of those were BOBFOCs – *Body Off Baywatch, Face Off Crimewatch* – not worth the hassle or the time as you were bound to get a dig the next day in the office. Phil's group were recounting a night out they all did once together, laughing at all the in-jokes and memories. I felt left out so I looked across the bar. I did a double take when I noticed a curly-haired redhead standing by the ladies on her own.

Surely not.

She looked the spit of the woman at JFK. I excused myself from the group to take a closer look. I walked over but kept my distance. It was definitely her. The dark eyes, pale skin and the unmistakable red curly hair. I pulled out my Galaxy and scrolled through the photos.

When was it?

I tried to recall the date. I flicked through thousands of images, reconnaissance photos of women I had been researching. It must have been a couple of years ago. I scrolled through more and found the date. There she was. I zoomed in on the photo and looked up. It absolutely had to be her.

I thought about going up to her but I suddenly felt nervous. I'd done no research on her and I found I couldn't just go up to her and speak, just like at the airport. I didn't have the confidence to be myself. She was not the type to go up to with a bottle of Cristal and a flash of my Breitling. She seemed unpretentious.

Girl next door as I recalled labelling her at JFK.

I ran through various chat up lines and they all seemed crass. She was anxiously looking at the front door. Maybe she was waiting for a boyfriend in which case I would look like a right numpty, and Phil would never let me live that down. I took a deep breath and just considered going for it. Let the old charm work through, be myself. I steadied myself and took another deep breath.

Here I go.

I took a step forward and she danced on her feet. She had spotted someone and fervently waved. I looked towards the entrance and a dickhead in a cheap suit waved back, a group of wankers followed him in, grabbing a champagne flute each on the way in.

Please don't tell me she is dating this loser.

She looked for a route to him and zigzagged across the floor. I went over to cross paths. As she breezed past her hair brushed my face. My mouth salivated.

Candyfloss.

When she reached him, he hugged her. She looked awkward and wasn't sure where to put her arms. Definitely not dating.

Phew.

Jealousy subsided in me. He was all over her, shouting down her ear. She drank three or four glasses, downed dregs and picked up another fresh glass whenever the waiter glided past. His mates had left them to it. I could tell she was not liking the company and she was getting tipsier, swaying on her feet and her eyes were going. I covertly took photos from my position, zooming in and cropping out the loser. The dark lights didn't help and the images came out blurry. I moved to get a bit closer, keeping my distance but fixing my eyes on her. Eventually, she stumbled to the toilets, accidentally going to the men's before realising her mistake, the silly mare, and forcefully pushed the Ladies door open, her legs wobbling from the drink. When she emerged, following a couple of women who had obviously just taken a line, I wondered if she had too, then dismissed it immediately. She didn't seem the type. It looked like she was making her excuses to the prick and leaving. I was right: she left him and headed to the door.

I followed her out: she was stumbling and walked in a zigzag line. I kept my distance. She meandered over to a black cab with his yellow light on, waving for his attention.

Shit.

She got in, spoke to the cabbie and he drove off. I ran forward looking for another taxi. I saw one in the distance and urgently flagged him. He spotted me, turned off his yellow light and pulled up. I told him to follow her cab, slipping a fifty-pound note under the glass, Queen Lizzie looked up at me, wondering what I was doing. We saw them waiting at a red with their yellow indicator flashing. We pulled up behind them. I asked the cabbie to keep a distance and we followed them along main roads with few vehicles on them. It was easy to keep them in our sights. About 40 minutes later, their cab pulled up outside a row of identical houses in the South West suburbs. I spotted her get out, paid the cabbie through the window whilst fumbling for her keys. She made her way in and I asked the cabbie for the name of the road. I typed it into the notes on my Galaxy. I told him that I was glad my friend got home alright, she was a bit worse for wear, and to head back to the bar. I slipped another fifty under the glass and he took it like a cash machine. We headed back along the same route and he dropped me off at the same place I was picked up. Along the way I thought about the dullard chugger. It was all meant to be, now I had seen that redhead. My next challenge.

I headed back in the bar and spotted Phil. I went up to him and whispered that I was off. He gave me a man-hug. He hadn't even noticed I had gone.

Chapter Four

After all the appliances had been fitted and tested by the workmen, I admired my handiwork. The place was looking good. All remnants of the old place had gone and been replaced by modern, 21ˢᵗ Century, *quality* stuff. I Dysoned the last bits of mess and dust left behind and polished a few smudges off the brand-new Aga. Not that I would be using it much. I must have spent about £30k-£40k on doing the place up, but the value would have shot up by at least £100k. I smiled to myself and went upstairs. I opened my wardrobe in the bedroom and marvelled at the rows of suits and shirts hanging up: Louis Vuitton, Prada, Paul Smith, Hugo Boss, Armani and my pride and joy, the tailor-made pinstripe from Saville Row. I brushed my hand against the fabrics and thought what a life I had created for myself. I was about to land another deal in a couple of weeks, flight already booked to Hong Kong, and was already picturing the drone I had my eye on.

I headed into the living room and collapsed onto one of the brand-new twin sofas. I put my feet up and laid across the whole length, grabbed the remote and spoke into it. It fired up and Netflix buzzed to life. I watched a couple of episodes of Suits and then headed upstairs for a whizz. Whilst up there I went into the spare room and stood in its centre. It was the only room not done up yet, except for the thick carpet which my bare feet sunk into and the new white wallpaper. It was completely empty save for a few stacks of research in the corner. I spun around, considering what I could do with it.

Cinema room? Nah, too small.

Pool table? Nah, the cues would bump against the wall.

Dart board? Boring.

I considered a hot tub and dismissed it from my mind. I left the room, closed the door and left to think about it another day.

I heard the dog yapping from next door and peered through the window, down at the neighbour's back garden. It reminded me to visit Margaret so I got up and knocked on her door. The barking dog went suddenly quiet. I heard shuffling footsteps and she opened it a tiny slither. The dog's nose was sniffling to get out. She shooed him away.

"Oh, alright love. Hang on a sec." She yelled at Joe to get out of the way and opened the door to let me in. "Sorry about that, he's a little rascal."

I followed her in and the layout was the mirror opposite of my place. It's like I had stepped back in time: the carpet was gaudy with green swirls, pictures hung on the wall, black and white as well as faded colour photos of two younger people, a youthful Margaret and a beaming GI. A few photos of children lined the tops of shelves, scattered among china ornaments and souvenirs. She led me into the kitchen, chatted away to herself and to Joe. She popped the kettle on and rattled on about a neighbour I didn't know. As the kettle boiled, she was onto her ailments and decried the state of the NHS. I nodded, absent-mindedly agreeing with what she said. She splayed a few bourbons on a painted plate and put them on a lace tablecloth covering the table. She handed me a cup of tea and sat herself down.

"Now then, 'ow you settling in?"

"Yeah, good thanks. I've got all my stuff in now."

"Yeah, I saw all the chaps coming in. Looked like Piccadilly Circus!" she chuckled to herself. "Are you happy with it? I know that place needed a bit of doing up. Renee and Fred lived there for years. Way before me. I doubt they changed a thing in all that time!"

"It certainly needed a lick of paint, that's for sure," I smiled a winning smile, putting on the good neighbour act. I picked up a bourbon and dunked it in my tea.

"It's a lovely area round 'ere. You don't get a lot of trouble let me tell you. A few idiots but it's pretty rare. We all look out for each other. 'Ere, you should join the neighbourhood watch." She got up and went to a set of drawers. She opened the top one and rummaged through some papers.

She found one with a policeman on the front with yellow branding all over it.

"Sign up online and you get a sticker and all the information. I get an email if there has been any trouble in the area. It's good to know and keeps ya wits about you," she paused and took a bourbon. She filled the silence again.

"So, what do you do for a living then?"

I considered telling her the truth but I wasn't sure how she would respond to me being an investment banker. I couldn't really be bothered to either explain what one was or defend myself. I went safe.

"Marketing. I work for a marketing agency in town. You know, advertising and things."

"Oh right," she said, her eyes glazed over. Right choice. I felt elated at the lie.

"So, what brings you to Ealing then?"

"Well, I was living out East and it wasn't good for the commute to the office."

She murmured an agreement.

"I've got a couple of friends out this way and the area's nice so I started to look round here." She cooed in agreement again. "I found this place and fell in love with it. Thought it was the perfect place to set down my roots." I was spinning the lies as I was talking and was loving it. I was hitting the spots that I knew resonated with Margaret, thinking about her life over the past few decades, living in the same place. Tapping into her maternal instincts. It was like practice for a challenge.

"I really want to get involved in the community and do my bit," I continued. She beamed at me, and tapped my knee, pleased as punch that her new neighbour was a good 'un.

"Well, I'm sure you're going to enjoy it here as I have done. I've seen lots of changes you know but it still feels so friendly and inviting. You must come around for a cuppa and a piece of cake. That reminds me, I need to go shopping." She looked at Joe who was resting in a soft bed.

"You fancy a little walk? Yes you do, yes you do," she clucked at the dog. He raised his ears and his head. Margaret got up, fetched the lead and a treat from the side. She clipped the lead on whilst pushing the treat in his mouth. He gobbled it up. I stood up and thanked her for the tea.

"Oh no trouble Nathaniel" she says, "no trouble at all."

I smiled down at Joe and then at her.

"Call me Nath," I said looking into her eyes. She returned a warm smile. I saw myself out, closing the door gently behind me.

Chapter Five

I got back home from the bar I had just been in with Phil, having been on a little adventure following the redhead. My sleek black Cayenne was parked outside my house – my pride and joy. I had owned it for just under a year and done less than a thousand miles. It was times like this I was glad I had it. I got in and the new car smell hit my nostrils, the black leather caressed my arse, the warmth emanating from the automatic seat heaters. The engine purred to life with hardly a sound when I pressed the start/stop. The streets were deserted at this time of night so I slid out of the parking space without a hitch and turned onto the main road. Still buzzing from the drinks, I typed into the in-built sat nav the name of the road where the cabbie had told me that the redhead lived, and a route flashed up.

Following the green line on the screen, I passed night buses full of revellers, drunk and asleep with their heads leaning against the steamed windows. I overtook them with a smile. Every now and then I beeped my horn at some annoying Uber drivers which were driving slower than my granny. If it woke up a few sleeping babies, then so be it. When one was particularly slow, I put my foot down on the accelerator and got past him. I swerved out and the engine roared as my foot pressed down. I gave the driver the middle finger as I passed on the wrong side of the road. Bright lights ahead of me flashed and I swerved back in, narrowly missing an Eddie Stobart lorry coming the other way. He slammed on his brakes and swerved away from me. His horn faded as I drove away. A few residents would have woken up to that. That was a close one though. I put my right hand on top of the steering wheel, arm fully stretched out. I focused back on the road, rubbing my eye with my left hand. My heart was pumping and I felt mortal. I felt alive. This was fun.

I pulled up a few doors along from where I saw the redhead go in and sat in the darkness. It was almost 3am so I pushed back the leather seats and put my hands behind my head. The trees rustled a bit to let me know they were there, then silence. Dark clouds moved quickly above me; a crescent moon occasionally peeked out giving some light. I drifted off to sleep, the champagne whirring around in my gut, my head fuzzy. I dreamed of the Eddie Stobart lorry, but this time it hit the Cayenne. It span me round and the seatbelt locked, preventing me from moving forward. A woman's piercing scream from the back seat splintered the air at the impact – my sister. I felt blood coming from the right side of my head as the car rested on the pavement. The lorry driver banged on the window, giving me some, telling me how stupid I was, the posh knobhead. I got out, dazed and confused, giving him some back. I was swerving around like a boxer trying to find my target. He was giving it to me large, pushing my shoulders. A crowd had stopped and gathered and were chanting, egging the trucker on.

Chloe Clyne, she ain't fine.

My sister stood amongst them, standing still, staring blankly, tears cascading down her deformed face.

She pooped her pants all the time.

Jesus, I hadn't heard that for ages, years and years.

With a nick nack paddy whack give a dog a bone.

A few taxis pulled up, their doors opened, the drivers half-in half-out of their cars, trying to get a better look at the action.

Chloe Clyne went rolling home.

The crowd's voices were getting stronger. The HGV was jack-knifed on the pavement blocking the road, the damage done. A pram was overturned on the pavement, a woman laid lifelessly next to it, straight, blonde hair sprayed like a fan. Blue flashing lights appeared in the distance, turning red, reflecting off the set-back houses adjacent to the road. The lorry driver pushed me again and I tripped on the kerb and fell over. I looked down and I was in my school uniform, my blazer jacket half off my shoulder, the crest torn off, blood soaked into my shirt. I got up and pushed him back. A couple of cabbies came over and restrained us both. I looked at the Cayenne and the side was smashed in. That wouldn't be good. The police came over, telling me I was going to be expelled from school. They looked me in the eyes and pulled out a breathalyser. I knew how this was going to go. A couple more police cars attended the scene and set up tape around the site. My head was pushed down into the back of the police car, the moving blue lights dancing across my face as I was shoved in. My parents were either side of me, tutting and wondering what to do with me. Mum was crying, dad was lost. A policeman slammed the door shut and I woke up with a jolt.

There was sweat under my arms and the air had a dull light. A suited man with a leather briefcase came down his short garden right next to my car and opened the gate. The sound of his front door slamming shut must have jolted me from my dream. He eyeballed me and walked on. I sat up and stretched out. I looked at the time on my Breitling. 5:45am.

Jeez.

I rubbed my eyes and focused on the redhead's flat. Nothing was stirring, and the curtains were slightly open, just as they had been when I parked up. I imagined her lying on her bed, her nightie riding up her pale thighs. I got out of the car, stretched my legs and reached up to the sky. A wind had picked up blowing my blazer jacket open. The early morning chill breathed through my bones. I got back into the warmth of the Cayenne and the wind helped the door shut tight. I pulled my Galaxy out and booted up Facebook. I searched for Phil, and he had posted photos two hours ago of him and the lads in that bar and a different one they must have moved on to. Looked like Chinawhite. I flicked through my feed, the usual crap filling it up. I shut it down and thought about work, almost time to go to the office.

I wanted to see this redhead again, and I didn't know how long it was going to take. I wondered what time she got up for work. Maybe she had drunk too much last night and was going to pull a sickie. That gave me an idea. I sent a text to the boss, saying I'd been up all-night puking, liquid coming out of both ends. He would like that, wouldn't question it. A few commuters walked past the Cayenne, doors banged shut as smartly dressed men and women left their middle-class houses. Some had toast in their mouth, others were holding silver travel mugs, the black lids keeping strong coffee inside hot. I kept glancing up at the house the redhead had entered the previous evening but there was still no movement. I switched on the radio. That Nick Ferrari bloke was moaning at some Labour MP about the state of the NHS. I immediately switched it off. A text came through from the boss:

Alright Nath, take it easy. See you tomorrow.

The dawn light was stronger now and the bustle of Outer London was coming to life. Women with buggies and school kids in uniform passed by.

That bloody song was going around and around in my head.

With a nick nack paddy whack give a dog a bone.

It took me back to my secondary school days: with the navy-blue blazer and the dull lessons, the girls in their short skirts and the black tights. The song reminded me of playtime, my favourite bit of school where I would go and tease the younger years, nicking their football and taunting them about their virginity and how gay they were, pushing the boundaries trying to get a reaction.

When they had reacted, I distinctly remembered my heart beating faster, adrenaline pumping through my veins. Feeling mortal, feeling alive, feeling special – attention on me. The teachers were having none of it and kept threatening me with expulsion but it drove me on. For some reason a little ginger boy kept coming into my mind and I remembered giving him the knuckle-rub on his head, him crying as me and my mates called him a homo and pushed him about. Now they were everywhere. Homos, not gingers. Although there were a fair few gingers too. Even *gay gingers* no doubt. A giggle escaped my lips. There were probably a few at work too. I glanced out of the car window again up at the flat. Still no movement. Was she going to work or not?

About mid-morning her door sneaked open. The wind had really picked up now and litter was dancing around the street. I switched off the radio again, James O'Brien halfway through another dull monologue about Brexit and how crap it was. I grabbed my Galaxy and fired up the camera. There she was. She was dressed casually, definitely not going to work today. She battled out of the door and the wind whipped up her red curls, covered her face and caused a right mess. It enchanted me and I stared at her hair blowing in the wind, forgetting to click the camera. She had an aura about her. I seemed to remember a *je ne sais quoi* she had about her. Something different from everyone else. A feeling she stirred in me that no other person had before. She struggled out of the garden and her hair was going mental. She tried to tame it but it was no use, the wind was too strong. I took a few snaps on the camera, her hair a blur on the resulting images. She decided quickly against the wind and went back in, the door struggling to shut behind her as it fought against the wind. I pulled up the photos I had just taken. Blurry but still got her body and face in. I scrolled down to the photos I had taken of her at JFK a couple of years ago. Definitely the same person.

What were the chances? It must be a sign.

Well, that was a long wait, but worth the effort, I mused.

I pushed the engine back on and slid out of the car parking space, just as a traffic warden sauntered up the road. I turned onto the main road and smiled as I realised I had found my next challenge. Maybe my last one and then I'm out. I had one space left on my shelves in the spare room. This would be a good one, I could feel it in my bones. I switched on the radio and found Capital, the heavy bass pulsating through the Bose speakers. I turned the volume up, letting the beats fill the car. My heart was racing.

Chapter Six

My Galaxy trilled in the dark. It took my fuzzy head a while to figure out what it was. The light from a lamp post outside shone through the window giving the strange room an ethereal feel. My head was swirling, buzzing. I rubbed my eyes and tried to remember the night and how I had got there.

I must have done a line.

I rubbed my nostrils and leaned over to the source of the noise, the display lighting up. A blonde woman laid next to me, naked, and on her front. Half her face was embedded in the pillow, her long blonde hair spread out on the pillow like a peacock's tail. I reached over her and grabbed my phone. 'Mum' was flashing on the screen. My heart skipped a beat and my head suddenly cleared. I swiped to answer the phone.

"Mum?"

"Oh, thank God Nath. Jeez, where have you been? I've been ringing you for hours." I looked down at the blonde, trying to picture the rest of her face.

"What's the matter Mum, why you ringing me? What time is it?" I mumbled.

"Nathaniel," her voice got stern, she only called me by my full name when something was serious. "You need to come home. Now."

"Why, what's going – "

She rang off and I looked at the blonde. I tried to recall what we did last night. Lifting up the duvet, I took a long look down her naked body. Shame she was lying on her front. I felt a movement on the other side. I looked behind me and there was another girl lying there; on her back, arms above her head, her jet-black skin contrasting against the white sheets. I lifted up the covers and took a good look. My mum's voice snapped me out of it.

Now.

The word reverberated in my head. I slid out the bottom of the bed. Cristal bottles laid empty on the floor, specks of white powder and credit cards left on a glass table. I fingered them, checking if my Amex was among them. I found my clothes: a grey linen Boss suit, the jacket hanging on the back of a chair, my Calvin Klein underwear and socks nearby, my Church's under the chair. As I put them all on, I looked back at the bed with the two sleeping girls, sighed, and let myself out. I scanned about but I didn't recognise where I was. Trendy high-rise flats rose above and surrounded me. I walked down the street hoping to find a main road, and a taxi. Brick-fronted apartments, which could have been warehouses a few decades back, lined the streets. I turned left and right, hoping to find a main road. It was in the middle of the night; the place was deserted. I checked my phone: missed calls from my mum, text messages to call urgently. It was 3:12am.

I heard a rumble of noise in the distance, and I tried to figure a route to get there. Staggering along the pavement I eventually turned onto a main road, a bus stop on the corner. I checked the digital display. A night bus to London Bridge was due in 23 minutes.

Where was I?

I surveyed the map on the bus stop glass and tried to figure out the coloured squiggles and lines. It looked like I was in East London. I looked up and down the road, trying to find a landmark I could recognise. My brain wasn't working properly. I spotted a little yellow light in the distance attached to a black cab coming down the road.

Brilliant.

I waved it down and instructed the driver to go to Ealing. He asked me if I was *'aving a laugh.* I got my wallet out and slapped two fifties under the glass partition. His face dropped as he took them, turned to the road and drove off. I asked how long, and he estimated 40 minutes. I slumped down on the sticky seats and closed my eyes, hoping to get some shut eye before the drive out to mum's.

The driver's voice woke me up. I peered outside the window and sure enough there was my house. The street was empty. I got out and the cabbie tried to give me my change but waved him away. The key struggled to fit in the door and when it did, I almost fell in when it opened. I filled a glass of water and sucked it down in one and put my head under a cold shower; the water shocking my senses. I thought about turning it to warm but went against my instincts. I needed to wake and sober up. My skin started to contract; goosebumps appeared on my skin. I opened the clothes cupboard and picked a pin-stripe Armani suit and plain white shirt. Mum would like that, her boy a success. I slipped on my black Church's and headed out the house to where the Cayenne was sitting. The street was still deserted. I got into the warm leather seats, pulled out and made my way to the M4. Once I passed Heathrow, I floored it and shot out west, my eyes fighting to stay open.

I arrived at Mum's house just as dawn was breaking. Everything looked ethereal in the dim light. The manicured lawns, the crunch of the stone driveway, the ivy creeping up over the house. Everything looked fine and dandy. She came out to meet me, her dressing gown done up. She hugged me tightly. She pulled away and looked me in the eyes. She had been crying, her face was worn and looked ten years older since I last saw her earlier this year.

What happened?

The rough fibres of her dressing gown rubbed coarsely against my skin. She looked at me and told me I looked terrible.

Take a look in the mirror Mum.

I replied that I was tired, considering it was still the middle of the night and what the bloody hell was going on to get me out at this time. She took me into the kitchen and popped the kettle on. She told me to sit down and she sat opposite, a square wooden table between us. The kettle started to shake as it came to the boil.

"It's Chloe, Nathaniel," she started.

"Yeah, I guessed that. What about her?" I asked. My sister was known to get into trouble, causing Mum issues. Last time the police were called as she was having a right nasty argument with a couple of girls who were teasing her.

"She's dead, Nathaniel."

"Wha-"

The words didn't ring true.

There was a silence.

"She's dead."

She waited for it to sink in. Get a reaction. I shook my head.

"What?" The only word I could muster.

"She died. Last night."

"What?" I repeated, still not quite believing what she had said. I could see my Mum but I was sure the words that came out of her mouth were wrong. It must be the drugs, the alcohol, the early morning, or all three. She stood up, walked over to me and hugged me whilst I was still sitting. She started to cry on my shoulder, sniffling and rubbing her eyes. I pushed her away, causing her to stumble onto the kitchen table. She grabbed hold of the edge as the kettle pinged and she wiped away the tears from her cheeks. She put a couple of teaspoons of instant in a mug, one sugar and glug of milk.

"Mum, put the kettle down. What the bloody hell you on about?"

She continued with the drink making, turned with the mugs in each hand and put them down on the table. She looked up, tears about to be released again.

"She was hit. By a car."

She wrapped her hands around the mug, as if a chill just went through her and she searched for warmth. An image appeared in the front of my mind, picturing the scene, my sis lying on the ground, my dream. It knocked me for six.

"When?"

"Last night. She went out. Late. She'd had a row, Nathaniel. With her stupid friends." She scoffed at the word 'friends'. They were more like bullies. I'd known the trouble she had gotten into previously, fighting back with some teenage girls that would pick on her.

"I heard the door slam and she was off. Apparently, she crossed the main road, by the roundabout. The driver said she came out of nowhere."

She reached inside her pocket and pulled out a folded letter. She put it on the table and slid it over.

"Police found this on her. They gave it to me when I went to the scene," she wiped her nose on her dressing gown sleeve. I looked at her and thought back to all the missed calls and texts. She had been trying to get hold of me whilst I was sparked out between two naked women. Dealing with all this shit on her own. I picked it up and unfolded it. The writing was unmistakably hers, the child-like writing, the messy joined-up writing and the awful spelling.

A suicide note.

People with Down Syndrome often suffer from depression but very rarely kill themselves.

I looked at mum. She sniffed.

"I think she was going to the forest to have a go. Got hit on the way." Tears began to roll.

"Oh, jeez mum." I got up and hugged her. She held me tight. I apologised over and over. For not answering my phone, for not being there when the police called, for not holding her hand, for living in London, for travelling around the world, for being a crap son. She sobbed louder and louder at every excuse. She pulled back; tears streamed down her face. She put her hands on my cheeks.

"It's not your fault, Nathan."

I was glad to hear those words come out of her mouth. We sat back down and wrapped our hands around warm mugs. The place suddenly seemed emptier. A photo of the three of us sat on the kitchen ledge, taken a couple of years back. It must have been just before I got the job in the City. I picked it up, took it over to mum and pulled up a chair next to her. The three of us were all beaming back. There was a twinkle in Chloe's and Mum's eyes. We all looked so happy in that moment of time. I looked deeper into Chloe's eyes, what she had been through must have been tough for the hardiest of people. Being forced to go to state school, mixing with all the 'normal' kids, getting picked on daily.

I remembered the day back at school that had changed my life where I had confronted a couple of older kids picking on her. I almost got excluded for that. Then all through school, college and even work, she was bullied and picked on. And all for looking a bit different. True, she wasn't as smart as others, and her mental age was half her real age. It was weird having an older sister who was younger than you in the head. I protected her when I could, but I couldn't be her bodyguard. Facebook, WhatsApp, Instagram, TikTok and Twitter became unbearable for her. We told her to get off them, even snatching her phone once to delete the apps. She went mental and went into a meltdown that we had to call an ambulance for. She was addicted to the scrolling. She was posting incessantly on them, only to receive abuse after abuse back.

We reported it of course but these behemoth, faceless companies did nothing. My sister was getting bullied online, and the comments were nastier from behind the keyboard than to her face. We tried everything and she seemed to get resilient, a thicker skin. But then every so often I'd get a text to say she had been arrested again – some stupid teenagers picking on her and winding her up. Sometimes Mum asked me to go and pick her up and she'd be distraught.

I would always walk out of the police station holding her hand, and she would always ask if we could go and get fish and chips or an ice cream sundae. The police visits became less frequent so we thought she had had a handle on it. I checked her statuses every now and then and the frequency of her posts were getting less. I had hoped she was weaning herself off. I opened the letter and read it again. She wasn't off social media, not even close. She had set up different accounts under different names, still the same profile pic of her face. It brought on the keyboard warriors, safely bullying behind their screens, knowing that they wouldn't be confronted in person.

Cowards.

I fingered the suicide note in my hands. The last bit of Chloe. *It wasn't worth living any more*, it read. *The world would be better if this 'different' person wasn't here. Maybe then people would stop writing nasty things.* It was as if she thought people wrote those things just because of her and only to her. The world didn't work like that. They moved on.

On to the next target.

The next few days had mostly been in silence. Mum shuffled around in her dressing gown and slippers, sorting through letters and paperwork. I helped out around the house, cleaning things up, driving her to appointments, handing her tissues. I would hear her sobs at night. When she spoke, it was of memories of Chloe growing up. Mostly times of heartache, of which I had heard many times before. I just let her talk, supplying her with hot drinks.

"When Chloe was born, the doctors just looked up at me. I could tell in their eyes that something wasn't right. You can tell a lot by people's eyes," as hers glossed over. I stayed silent.

"Without them saying a word I knew our life wouldn't be normal anymore. The hardest thing, Nath, was when friends, family, people – strangers in the street – would look in the pram, expecting a beautiful baby girl. Their reaction spoke a million words. Didn't know what to say. Then pretended that everything was normal. Just pretended, like they couldn't see it. Babbling, cooing then hurrying off."

She took a sip of tea.

"The look in their eyes. Pity, sympathy, disappointment. No-one offered to help. I had to make do with what little support there was."

And then she would sob as her mind filled with memories.

I remembered the tantrums that seemed to go on for hours. Mum found it tough; she had to do most of it on her own because Dad couldn't cope. It was almost as if he had disowned her the moment he laid eyes on her. He wanted another child straight away, to see if the next one came out any better. It was a high risk. They did and when I came out there was an audible sigh of relief. And a boy too. Dad was over the moon. He favoured me and left Chloe with mum. I was a right daddy's boy and I guessed he tried to toughen me up.

Eventually I turned into a man, earlier than I or my Mum had imagined. When I left home to go to Oxford, leaving Mum, Dad and Chloe at home, Dad couldn't cope again – with all the women in the house, Chloe's issues and the constant bullying and the fighting. He left, leaving mum on her own. We hadn't seen or heard from him since.

Two months later, the coroner concluded that Chloe had died as a result of injuries sustained from a road traffic collision. On her death certificate, it simply read 'accident'. The funeral was a small affair. Half of me expected Dad to turn up; the other half was right though. Chloe was disowned by him in life and in death. Just me, Mum and a couple of her support workers who had known her over the years.

Only four people.

I could feel the anger boil up inside me. The online bullies made me furious enough but for my Dad not to bother coming made me incandescent with rage.

So, the day after the funeral I went on a 7-day bender.

I'm not proud of it.

Snorting, drinking and picking on big fellas for a fight. I wanted to get my anger out and didn't mind if I got a kicking or two. My brain felt like it was raging with fire. When I woke up in hospital, concussed with broken ribs it was my mother's face I saw. She was sobbing, telling me to sort myself out, pull myself together, how it was her fault.

"It's not your fault mum, it's mine. I should have been there for you. And for Chloe. I'm so wrapped up in me. I'm a selfish prick."

"Don't talk like that Nathan."

"It's true."

"It's not. We all make mistakes. Mine worse than others. I'm not going to let you destroy yourself. Losing one child was bad, I couldn't handle losing two."

I sat up in my hospital bed and looked at her. She seemed to have aged ten years. I felt sorry for her. Pity. Shame on myself.

I went to stay at her place for a fortnight; went cold turkey on the drugs, told mum to get rid of any alcohol in the house. I sweated it out and flung a few mugs against the wall in my rages. They were long days and longer nights. The bed became my drug – comforting, warm, addictive. Whenever Mum tried to drag me out, the only thing I wanted to do was sink into its bliss.

She nursed me through my insomnia and pain, battling through the emotions knowing that they would end at some point if she just believed. Focusing on the future which I couldn't see.

What was my purpose?

I was making rich people richer and bedding women. Empty vessels to me, zero emotion, another notch on the bedpost or pound in the bank.

What if I wasn't here?

Would there be any difference to this world if I disappeared?

The rich people will find someone else to make them rich, the women would bed some other chancer, the drugs will be snorted by someone else.

Mum and I spent a few nights just crying onto each other's shoulders, eventually taking walks out around the playing fields, each walk getting longer and then vegging out in front of daytime TV, talking about Chloe and our childhoods: Where we had gone wrong. Where we had gone right. I don't know where I would be without her. Probably not on this green Earth.

The shakes started to go, the vomiting and sweats subsided, the headaches eventually cooled. Jeez, it sounds easy but when you are in it your head wants to burst open and you want to claw out your eyeballs.

I must have apologised to mum a thousand times.

"It's OK. You just need to heal," she kept saying. "It's like your leg is broken. You rest it to make it heal. You give it time. Only it's just your brain this time. Your brain is broken. It needs to heal, away from feeding it the bad stuff. Give it time. Ride it out."

And that's what I did. I rode it out.

On the twenty-eighth day I woke up after the best night's sleep I had in a long time. My head was clear and I could smell the freshness outside. It was like someone had switched me off and on. Mum brought in a cup of tea and noticed the difference. She even commented on the clearness of my skin, like I had had a transplant overnight. She beamed from ear to ear, a twinkle in her eye – perhaps knowing that she had brought her son back and everything was going to be ok. I had my first thought of the office and guilt washed over me that I'd been absent and missed out on a deal or two for my clients. I called the boss, and he said, if I was ready, to come back to prepare a proposal for a client meeting in Singapore.

Maybe it would help take my mind off things.

On her porch, I said goodbye to Mum and we hugged longer than I ever remember. She stood in the doorframe of the house, her dressing gown hanging off her body, a few pounds shed in the last few weeks. I had ordered her an Ocado delivery to stick in her fridge with meals-for-one so she had enough food to keep her strength up. Then I slipped back into the warm, cosy leather seats of the Cayenne with the Armani jacket hanging in the back and ran my hand over the gearstick. I saw Mum standing by the door in the rear-view mirror as I drove off, leaving her alone once more.

Chapter Seven

On the way back from the redhead's flat I stopped by WH Smiths. Traffic was heavy and it took me ages to wind through the South Circular, over Kew Bridge and into Brentford. The pulsating music kept my brain active and I was thinking constantly about the redhead: What her story was? Did she have a boyfriend? What her name was? I ran through a list in my head, picking out randoms and matching them to her face, her demeanour and her personality. It's one of my favourite parts of The Challenge: dreaming and visualising. How would the research sculpt my approach? How would I adapt to their personality, the conversations I might have with them?

In Smiths the place was higgledy-piggledy with newspapers, books, cards, chocolate and stationery. I picked out a box file which matched the others at home and took it to the self-service, scanned and swiped my Amex over the card reader. I got home and connected my phone to the wireless HP printer. I printed out the photos of the redhead taken today and watched the paper spit her out. There she was, looking up at me, her hair blowing across her forehead, her loose jumper tight against her chest as she walked into the wind. Two small, round lumps protruded out from the tightened top. The HP ejected a few more sheets and I held them out, the paper damp from the ink. When they dried, I placed them in the new box file and looked at the shelves, full of the other successful challenges. I looked along the names, remembering their faces, memories of the research and the preparation that went into them, all in alphabetical order. I looked past the H's, I's, J's and K's. My memory jolted me back to JFK and looking down at her boarding pass. *L.* I distinctly remembered seeing an L. I looked up at the wall and found Katie and Maya. I couldn't believe it.

No L.

It must be a sign. I moved Katie's folder to the left and Maya's to the right, remembering her soft brown skin and dark brown eyes. I placed the new folder between them, the label blank. For now. Stepping back the shelves were full of all the successful challenges. The ones where I considered I had done a good job – morphed into a person that they desired and carried out the operation without them knowing and getting them into bed – the finish line. Looking at the shelves, perhaps it was time for the redhead to be the last one, and then move on to something else. Maybe Bitcoin, I thought.

I stood back and admired my handiwork over the last few years. I pulled down Maya's folder and opened it up. The menu from the Indian restaurant she took me to on our first date, the colourful cotton bracelet I wore around my wrist and a few leaflets from the galleries we went to sat at the bottom of the file. Her brown eyes and straight brown hair, parted in the centre, peeked at me. I took the photo out and remembered taking it from the mezzanine of the club I was in. She had been drinking a vodka red bull with her mates, dancing to the beats on the dance floor, her ponytail whipping back and forth as she moved in time with the music. She was a feisty one, a harder challenge which I relished. She was worried about going out with a white guy, and what her family would think, which of course I had planned all along. I begged her for me to meet her parents. She declined of course and offered instead to sleep with me. A compromise.

The next day I dumped her on the pretence that I was looking for a serious relationship and if she wasn't willing to let me into her life then it wasn't going to work. Of course, it did the trick. I knew I wasn't going to go and meet her parents but I got her into the sack, nonetheless. A risk but one that I had researched a lot. A success. I closed the boxed file back up and slid it next to the new file, the white blank label off-balance with the rest of the wall.

Back to the present, I needed to do more research on the redhead, so early the next day I dropped another text to the boss.

It's getting worse mate; I've been on the loo the whole day and night. Must be a dodgy curry I had.

He responded immediately. Told me not to worry and stay off the foreign muck and eat a kebab next time. I jumped in the Cayenne and drove off, traffic heavy with commuters on their journey to work. I pulled up outside her place at 8:15am. It had taken longer than I anticipated and hoped I hadn't missed her, if she even had a job to go to. Her curtains were still shut, a good sign, so I settled down for the long one. I had popped into Tescos on the way over and grabbed sandwiches, chocolate and a couple of packs of Kettle Chips. I felt like an undercover police officer on a stakeout. I switched on the radio and listened to Talksport, them blathering on about another lucky Manchester United win.

Just after ten, her front door opened and she stepped out. I sat up to attention. There she was. Her red curly hair was neat and bounced above her shoulders as she skipped down the front path. She was wearing a black blazer over a white blouse, the top two buttons undone. She had on a short black skirt and black tights, covering the pale legs I had been dreaming of. She was holding a black handbag in one hand and a portfolio case in the other. Classic interview look. She had a spring in her step and she seemed happy. The two dimples either side of her lips were creased. I let her walk past the Cayenne then I jumped out. I fed a fair few coins into the meter and waited for the ticket to be printed. I turned and watched her go down the street, her arse swinging left and right.

Hmm, good proportions.

I forced the ticket out of the machine and put it on the dashboard, slammed the door shut and pressed the fob. The indicator lights flashed twice as I jogged past them, running to catch up so I didn't lose sight. I turned the corner and she had joined the growing stream of people walking down the high street. She looked a bit out of place amongst the casually dressed, non-workers of the morning, her black slender clothes jutting against the colour of jumpers, cardigans and light coats. She was walking towards the train station.

Bingo, perfect for me.

She waited on the platform looking at her phone. The train trundled along and she got on and took a seat next to the glass partition of the vestibule. I stood by the glass next to her, behind and with my back to the double doors so out of her eyeline but giving me the full view of her hands and lap, the portfolio rested on her knees, her bag by her feet. She didn't notice me when I boarded which was great. I peered through the glass and watched her. She got her phone out of her bag and fired up Facebook.

Perfect.

A memory came up on her feed. Two years ago and there was a selfie of her in New York, the Brooklyn Bridge in the background. I thought back to when I must have seen her. Two years, that sounds about right.

Blimey. Another coincidence, another sign.

She flicked through her feed and stopped momentarily on photos of couples beaming up at the camera, before swiping onwards. She also stopped on a few pictures of babies, cats, landscapes and inspiration quotes. She ignored the adverts and the self-help videos. She got bored and closed down Facebook and brought up Insta. She did a quick search and a sunset caught her eye. She clicked on it and it filled the screen. It was of the Grand Canyon, the famous red stones catching the orange rays of the setting sun. She scrolled back up, clicked on the search box and typed in 'American Sunsets'. Square images of palm trees, mountains, the ocean, Santa Monica Pier and the Rockies appeared. She scrolled through them, occasionally tapping on a photo which filled the screen. She scrolled further, picking places I was familiar with: Route 66, the Washington Obelisk, Monument Valley, Niagara Falls. I made a note in my Galaxy.

The train rumbled into Waterloo and she gathered her things. The platform was on the other side to me, so she stood looking out, her back to me. I took a couple of steps closer, seeing her hair, her neck and the collar of her blazer. It was just like two years ago in the queue at the airport. Coincidence. I inhaled. The sweet smell of candyfloss. The doors opened and she stepped down with the other passengers.

I let her get some distance on me and followed her through the ticket barriers. She turned left and walked along the concourse to the end of the station. A guy raced up to her and tapped her on the shoulder. She spun round.

What did he want?

He offered her a pink glove.

How did I not spot a glove fall from her bag?

She took it then grimaced, mouth some words at him and he went on his way.

What was that about?

She went down the steps and hopped up the steps next to the Royal Festival Hall. I raced up the stairs too, being careful not to lose her. As I climbed them, the big black sculpture of Nelson Mandala's head rose to my right. I spotted her moving between the tourists, the white spires of Hungerford Bridge in front, the curved building of Charing Cross station on the other side of the river. She moved up the steps of the bridge and walked across. I had been along this bridge many times, so knew how to keep my distance. She kept glancing out to her right, taking in the view of St. Paul's and the skyscrapers I called home during the day. She stopped halfway and I slowed my pace. She whipped out her phone and took a selfie, London's skyline in the background. I considered going up to her and offering to take a photo. I dismissed it.

Too soon Nath.

I have made that mistake before, jumping the gun and ruining it.

She carried on, headed down the steps and through Embankment station. At the other side, she stopped, took out her phone and put her head down over it. I cautiously moved next to her to see what she was doing. She had Google Maps up and was typing in an address. The screen changed to a map view and she looked up. She walked forward, her phone out in front of her, following the directions. After she crossed the busy Strand, she checked the phone again, before slipping it into her bag. She went over to a Starbucks, pushed the door and went in.

I waited on the other side of the street and leaned against the white-fronted Itsu. Buses, motorcycles and taxis fleetingly obstructed my view. Then I saw her sitting at the bench at the front, looking out of the window. I consciously moved over to MacDonald's and stood outside, so she didn't spot me. I could see the door of Starbucks but not her. I checked my Breitling. 10:45am. The lads in the office were probably starting to think about a boozy lunch.

Five minutes later the door opened and the redhead came out. She turned left, walked a bit then left again up Bedford Street. I followed her. She stopped, smoothed her skirt down, adjusted her blazer and tucked a lock of hair behind her ear. She walked on and turned into a large glass-fronted office building. I noticed a small café opposite so I headed in, ordered a coffee and a panini and sat by the window looking out over the street. I saw her sitting by a small wooden table by the window, a lampshade arcing over the table, shining a spotlight over her head, her red curls seemed to glisten in the light. She flicked through a newspaper on the table and turned her head abruptly as a tall, older brunette came into the reception area. She stood up, gathered her things, walked over and shook the brunette's hand. She disappeared behind a double door with a circular window in the middle of it. I sat back and crossed my fingers she would get the job.

About an hour later I saw the door open and she walked out. The other woman followed and enthusiastically shook her hand. It looked like a good sign. She waved to the lad behind the desk and she stepped out into the cool air. She had a wide smile on her face; her eyes glinted. I was struck by her smile, her beauty. It seemed familiar again. She turned on her heels and headed back towards the Strand. I got up and followed her, back over Hungerford Bridge. If she headed home, I would leave her to it. But she didn't. She turned left and wandered along the Thames. She stopped every now and then to watch the street performers and the human statues. She walked slowly, without a care in the world. Occasionally her hair whipped up and danced over her head. It was quite difficult to keep a distance behind her as she stopped so often. I decided to hang back further to allow a larger gap. A food van was conveniently nearby, so I ordered a hot chocolate and a muffin. The guy was chatty and commented on the weather. When I turned to spot her, she was gone, lost among the crowds of tourists.

I didn't panic, this usually happened when I was tailing a challenge. I walked briskly on, holding my drink in front of me so not to spill it over my Ted Bakers and munched on the muffin. I meandered through the rucksacks and the groups that followed a disembodied umbrella in front. I spotted her through the arches beneath the Oxo Tower. Quickening my step, I reached her as she entered Blackfriars tunnel. A violinist screeched her bow on the strings, the sound bounced off the tiles. I waited for her to exit the tunnel before I went through. In front of her as I left the tunnel was St. Paul's Cathedral, standing tall and strong on the other side of the river, the wobbly bridge stretched over the Thames. I saw the mop of red hair moving towards it but she took a right, through a courtyard, a gigantic, bricked chimney rose tall above her. She went through the doors of the Tate Modern and the security guard checked her bag and portfolio. She went in and I followed her.

She walked into the gargantuan Turbine Hall, empty of exhibits, a faint murmur of people talking and shifting about. I went up the escalators and stood on the bridge that ran through the vast space to the new wing. I looked down and I spotted her moving across the large floor. Black legs striding out beyond bright red curly hair. A bird's eye view, the perfect position. She sat cross-legged on the floor and placed the black portfolio and her bag next to her. She sat upright for a moment then laid down, resting on her elbows. Her body was straight, pointing at me, her eyes staring at the ceiling. At one point her eyes flicked towards the bridge. Our eyes met fleetingly and I took a quick step back and I was gone from her view. My heart quickened and I felt a rush of adrenaline. The chase was on.

Chapter Eight

Lucy. Her name was Lucy. I rolled the name around on my tongue. I hadn't had a Lucy before. The serendipity of finding this final challenge excited me with how well it fitted into everything. Short and sweet. L. L for Lucy. I was glad at how simple it was. And how very English. I'd been hanging around outside Itsu every morning since she got her new job and like clockwork, she went into Starbucks at 8:45am. Today I took the next step and went inside. I was sitting in the café wearing a beanie over my head and heavy, black-rimmed glasses, trying to look inconspicuous and anonymous. I was wearing my Canada Goose jacket done up to the top and sat amongst tourists, near the counter. When she came in, I dropped my eyes down towards the table, pretending to read a trashy thriller. The Indian behind the counter greeted her like an old friend.

Ah, Ms Lucy!

Lucy. I liked the name. It suited her, matched her even. I had been running girl's names through my head like a pub quiz, trying to guess what it might be: Lisa, Leanne, Lara? I thought Lily might be appropriate. But when I heard the Indian say Lucy, it immediately fitted. I liked it. I heard her order a flat white with an extra shot and swipe her contactless. When her name was called out, she grabbed the white mug with the famous green logo: A mermaid encased inside a circle. How appropriate. She looked around and I averted my eyes, looking busy. She wandered off to the opposite side, and grabbed a seat with her back to the wall.

Great. A perfect view of her perfect face.

She rummaged in her bag and pulled out a cheap romance book, but she wasn't going to read it. Valuable information. She removed it to see more inside her bag. She pulled out her phone and placed the book back inside. She scrolled and tapped a while as she sipped her coffee. I couldn't take my eyes off her. It was like looking at a Da Vinci masterpiece – every inch of her was perfection – and not just her features but her mannerisms and the way she conducted herself. An intangible aura. It was like looking into the soul of a painting and knowing everything about the subject's personality. She was captivating me. She finished the last of her drink, got up and left the café. I quickly went over to her table, sat down on the vacated warm seat, and took her mug in my hands. It was still warm. I held it whilst looking around the café, seeing what she saw. In that moment I felt like I was her.

Two weeks into my research, I was convinced she was in love with America. Whenever I looked over her shoulder on the train journeys to work, she was always searching for holidays, images and videos of the US of A. She followed mostly American travel writers and bloggers and I knew that she had been to New York. I decided that for her to fall for me I needed to be an American. I needed to pick a place that the British had heard of but knew nothing about, unless they happened by chance to have visited there. It was a gamble but I picked Colorado, close to the Rockies but not on the hot list of destinations. I pulled up Google Earth and typed in 'Colorado' into the search box. The Earth span as Google located the state and zoomed into a big red pin. I zoomed out and swiped around. Colorado Springs was the biggest city and at the foot of the Rockies. Even I had heard of the place but had no idea about anything there. I concluded Lucy would be the same. That's ok, the less detail the better and I could always blag it to move on the conversation.

I started to concoct a back story. Knowing she had been to New York already, I thought I'd play it simple and pretend to be from there. From my travel trips I had a working knowledge of the layout, the names, the sights. But for it to be believable, it couldn't be Manhattan though, but upstate. All the romcom films had well-to-do families who lived upstate, although I had no idea what 'upstate' meant. I needed a reason to get from New York to Colorado and made up a few sketchy details of meeting someone and following them there. Following people; I guess every story has a small element of truth to it. It couldn't be a girlfriend as that would put her right off. It needed to be plausible so I thought of a loved one, but obviously something tragic would have to happen to them to get the sympathy and doe-eyes. I thought back to Mr. Honky Honk who beeped at me the night I first saw Lucy and that dream I had.

With a nick nack paddy whack give a dog a bone.

I shook it out of my head and thought a sudden car crash would do it. "Boo-hoo, poor me. Lonely and in need of love. Give me a hug please."

My heart beat faster.

I started to picture the American that I would embody. What would his style be? Classic frat boy, it had to be – I imagined all the romcoms she would watch and reruns of Friends. So, I took the tube to Westfield and walked among the shopfronts to get inspiration. The huge atrium housed an ice rink, kids pushing plastic penguins to keep them upright. I saw the prices and whistled loudly; no way was I ever having kids. I stopped myself going into The Village, the luxury part of the shopping centre, with its curved angles and central Champagne Bar. Maybe later. I checked the touchscreen map and found Hollister.

The two-storey, faux house front jutted out onto the concourse, a fake balcony protruded from the top floor. I walked into the dark store, a muscled guy welcomed me and pointed me in the direction of the men's section. Music thumped and cologne churned around the air. I browsed the clothes, all cheap cotton and American fashion. I could just imagine the frat boys going mental in this store. I picked up a frat boy-style shirt in a medium and a couple of hoodies. I went to the changing room, stripped off and pulled the shirt on. The fabric prickled my skin.

Ugh. Cheap cotton.

I didn't try the hoodies on so dumped them on the side, picked up a dark blue t-shirt to wear underneath and headed to the tills. A hot young girl behind the wooden counter greeted me, barely sixteen with pouting lips and a tight Hollister patterned crop top that exposed her midriff, the detail of the lace of her bra pushing through. The blue bird logo sat just above her left breast which I eyeballed. She pointed to the colognes and asked if I wanted one, shining her pearly whites.

If she was a bit older….

As I took the brown paper bag from her, I had a good look at her chest before heading out the door. The muscly guy said goodbye to me and I wondered if he had tried it on with till-girl yet.

I wandered around the shops looking for more American wares. I spotted Vans and tried a couple of pairs on. They cut into the back of my ankle – bloody cheap footwear – and considered heading to a proper shoe shop, like Church's in The Village. I remembered seeing Nike on the map so slipped off the Vans, left them on the floor and headed there. The bright lights welcomed me in and I pulled down a pair of blight blue running shoes, the ones with the air bubble in the heel, and told the assistant to get me a size nine. He came back and I slipped them on.

Yeah, they will do.

He boxed them up and took them to the till. I passed a Tommy Hilfiger and figured I've got enough chinos to do the trick – standard fayre for meetings in the US. I walked past shops looking for a suitable-looking hoodie to complete the look. Jack Wills had some on faceless mannequins in the window, so headed in to check them out. The brand was British but that didn't matter. I found a light grey hoodie which would do the job, paid and headed to the Champagne Bar in The Village. I downed a couple of flutes then headed back on the tube. Job done.

I dumped the bags back at home and switched on Netflix. I watched a couple of episodes of Friends and tried to copy Ross' accent, intonation and idioms to get the accent right. After a couple of hours, I noted the time and headed back to the tube. I got off at Covent Garden and zigzagged through the throng of people, dodging tourists and commuters who had knocked off early. Walking quickly through the arched covered piazza, I heard opera being sung on the lower atrium and thought that was something Lucy might like. Proper romantic stuff. I came out the other side and walked down the street where she worked. I ducked into the café opposite, ordered a coffee and sat at my regular table by the window to wait. It was 4:55pm. A few minutes past five, Lucy wandered out. She looked left and right as if determining where to go and decided on right and walked towards the Strand. I got up and left a couple of coins on the plastic table and headed out. It was a mild day and the short sleeves were out. She walked down to the Embankment and I expected her to climb up the steps along the Hungerford Bridge and home as usual. Instead, she snuck a left and walked along the river, past the Egyptian obelisk with its two Lions facing towards it, a mistake by the builders – the Lions were supposed to be facing out, looking for attackers.

Idiots.

Couples sat on the raised benches looking out to the Thames. She glanced at them as she walked past. She eventually stopped at the first empty bench, climbed up the small steps and sat, gazing towards the grey low buildings of the South Bank. She delved into her bag and pulled out the trashy romance again. She sat and read, occasionally glanced up, her eyes following a sightseeing boat. The evening was bright and dry. She was totally lonely and I sensed she was desperate looking for company. I considered ditching the act and be completely normal, myself. Just walk up, say hi and sit down next to her. In fact, I very nearly did but a last-minute panic stopped me. What if she thought I was a tosser? Didn't like me as Nathan? My personality, my job, my past.

Nah, I needed to get into character for her to like me. Still too early for me to make my move.

Chapter Nine

A month went by on my Lucy challenge. I had jetted off on some short trips to a few places to secure deals. I had been east, west and south. Each time I returned to the office I got a cheer and a slap on the back. Another bonus came my way and I blew £10k on a night out with the three W's: women, whiskey and weed. That was a heavy night and took me two days to recover. Except I didn't really enjoy it. I kept thinking of Lucy, even when I was sleeping with the women. I checked in on her whenever I was in London. She was like a human clock; I could set my Breitling to her. 8:45am Starbucks; 5pm leave office. A handful of times she left a few minutes later, when she went off to meet a client with her boss, the tall brunette I had seen her shaking hands with at the interview. Lucy was always the first to leave. I never saw her with anyone socially. She was a loner although I could tell she was desperate, judging by the paperbacks she was getting through and the tins of cat food in her bin bags.

She looked longingly at other couples sitting together or walking hand-in-hand. Sometimes I had to duck behind a tree when she looked back at a couple in love, their hands intertwined. In the meantime, I was working on my American accent and testing it when I went stateside. I was nearly ready, I just had to bide my time. My long lunches and fake trips that I engineered gave me ample time to follow her and get my research right. I wasn't going to mess this one up.

One Friday I was sitting in the café opposite her work. It was just after 5pm and she hadn't come out. I wondered if there was a client dinner tonight. The dipstick receptionist had already left for the weekend. Eventually I saw the wooden doors separating the reception and the office open and clocked Lucy walking out. She was chatting to a blonde colleague with legs that seemed to go on forever; she was wearing heels, making her calves all slender. Her white blouse was open at the neck and plunged down. The wind pushed the silk against her breasts as they stepped out into the street, revealing a nice large couple of mounds. She brushed her hair back as the door closed. She was well fit and she knew it. For some reason I hadn't seen her before – maybe she got to the office before Lucy and left after. She flicked her hair round the other way and I glanced at her face.

It looked familiar.

Perhaps all bleached blondes looked the same to me now, all blurring into one. Her nose was the thing that made me question myself. Even from where I was sat, I could see it had a dent vertically down the centre, like someone had pressed a small iron bar into it. Her philtrum was skewed, as if she had once had a cleft lip, so it was not so aligned with the symmetry of her face. I remembered this but I couldn't place it. They split and went their separate ways. Lucy toward the Strand, the blonde towards Covent Garden. I decided that I would follow the blonde tonight, to see if I could work out the nagging feeling of familiarity rattling around in my mind. It could be important.

She was easy to follow, her bright blonde hair swinging back and forth. Her high heels clacked against the cobbled stones of the piazza. She reached up and put both hands to her head, scrapped her hair back into a ponytail and threaded a hairband around it. Her hair now bounced and swung around in time with her steps. She walked straight past the tube station, crossed the road, past M&S and headed down Neal Street, past all the chuggers and the shoe shops which vied for her attention. She crossed over the middle of the road, dodging a tooting taxi as she went. The driver leered at her and checked out her arse as she walked quickly on. To be fair it was a lovely arse, one which I hadn't hesitated to stare at as I followed her. She passed a few clothes stalls packing up for the day and came out onto Shaftesbury Avenue. She dived into a black-fronted pub off Greek Street, regulars spilling out, smoking and holding half-empty pint glasses. I entered and took up a spot by the bar, ordered an IPA, gave a tenner and took the scant change. I turned around looking for the blonde. I saw her at a table with an athletic-looking brunette who already had a glass of red. She was hugging the blonde so her face was obscured but I could tell by her body she was fit. I waited and watched, peering over the rim of my pint glass. They separated from the hug and I saw the friend's face. I recognised it immediately.

Kaz.

The swimwear model. I had dined off that story for weeks. Proper legend status. That's why I remembered the blonde. Her mate.

They had both come into some poncy bar in the city one night and were all over us. Confident, gorgeous, fit, drunk and well up for it. My mate Roger, his nickname not his real one, was gagging for the blonde. I said I'd be his wingman and take the brunette off his hands. I was chuffed as she looked like she was a model – high cheekbones and pouts – and as it turned out, was. We chatted them up all night, they were loving the attention but more so the Cristal, and Kaz was loving the white lines. I remembered the blonde sitting in between Rog and I whilst Kaz was off doing a line.

What was her name?

I was teasing Rog, egging her on to come back to our place for a threesome. He wasn't happy but played along, knowing I was joking. I reckoned part of him was letting me do it to see how far she might go. When I left them to it, he shouted my name to piss off. I shouted back for him to get a room, looked at him, looked at her, and said something like 'he's harmless'. She wasn't listening and probably couldn't hear over the din of the music. She looked well out of it anyway, her eyes rolling and trying to keep her head upright. I saw Rog slip a roofie into her Cristal, the dirty little rascal, and I went off to find Kaz.

I found her stumbling out of the ladies, her finger rubbing her nostrils, white powder on the tip of her nose. When she saw me, she put her arms around my neck and shoved her tongue into my mouth. It was like a fight, who could fit their tongue furthest into each other's mouth. I led her away out of the entrance, slipping a blue pill onto my tongue to help me out later, hailed a taxi and we went back to hers.

As usual I left at the crack of dawn, sneaking out so it wasn't awkward. The next morning in the office when we all saw each other we greeted each other like caveman. Grunting, high fiving on the previous night's activities, swapping sex stories. I pulled Rog aside giving him the 'you owe me one' line for splitting up the prey. I asked how his night went. He grinned and flashed his pearly white and said *the usual*. He wasn't his usual boastful self though.

I switched back to the present and realised I was staring at the two of them. Suddenly self-conscious I took a slug of the ale, put it down and left the pub, passing the media-types standing outside. I walked down the road to get a safe distance, turned a corner and stood in a shop doorway. I pulled out my Galaxy and searched for Rog, pressed the green call button and he answered within two rings.

"Nathstar!" he screamed down the phone. I pulled the phone from my ear.

"Roger you dirty bastard!" I replied. He hooted with laughter.

"How you doing buddy?" I enquired.

"Yeah, good mate, still in the office. Got to finish a report tonight so Beijing can have it first thing. Where are you?"

"Um, Soho mate," I said looking around. "Hey Rog, you'd never guess who I just bumped into."

"No idea mate, tell me."

"Remember we went to that bar, uh, ages ago, probably last summer. We met a couple of birds that were well up for it. You went for the blonde and I took the brunette."

"That don't narrow it down mate," he chuckled.

"It was in some poncy new wine bar. The blonde was sitting between us and I was trying to get her to have a threesome with us whilst the brunette was off doing a line."

"Yeah, come to think of it yeah, I do," he faltered. "You went off with the brunette if I remember."

"Yeah, that's right. Kaz was her name. Swimwear model. Off her tits on coke. Great shag. Well, you'll never guess. Just saw them in a pub in Soho."

The line went quiet.

"Rog, you there mate?"

"Yeah, yeah I'm here mate. Sorry just got distracted," I could hear the hum of computers and screens in the background. I pictured him at his desk.

"Er, that's great. Did you speak to them?" He seemed defensive. I was suddenly curious. I tested him.

"Yeah mate I did. Said I recognised them from the bar, asked them how they are getting on."

"Oh, right" he responded. "Did she mention me?"

"Who, the blonde? Yeah, god what was her name, she just told it to me and it's completely gone."

"Jess mate. It was Jess." I heard him swallow and could almost hear him squirm in his seat. I prodded some more.

"Oh yeah, that's right. She said you were the perfect gentleman."

"Did she?" he responded a bit too quickly, surprised, a slight sigh of relief in his voice. I changed tack.

"No mate, course she didn't." He took a breath. This was unexpected fun. "In fact, she asked if she could see you, wants to have a word about that night. She seemed keen mate! Why don't you come down? It's a pub on Greek Street. I'll tell her you're on your way so she doesn't scarper before you get here. Maybe you can get a second bite," I suppressed a giggle.

"Nah, you're alright mate. I'm snowed under with this report," he said quickly.

"Well, after mate. I'll keep them busy until you get here."

"Seriously Nath, I can't tonight. Look, speak to you tomorrow alright?"

"OK, OK, take a chill pill. I'll give her your number alright?"

"NO!" he shouted down the phone. This was the best call I had in ages.

"I mean no Nath. Leave it eh? I had a bit of fun, move on. Never go back to the same bird, right? Otherwise the ring will slip on your finger before you know it."

"Yeah, yeah. Alright Rog. Don't worry. I'm going back in. See you tomorrow mate."

And I rang off, almost skipping down Greek Street. I was feeling good. I pictured Rog sat at his desk thinking about our conversation and what he thought I was doing right now with the girls, losing focus on his big presentation. He would be there past midnight easy. I considered dropping him a WhatsApp about half eleven, saying I'm having a grand old time with the girls and Jess was getting feisty, desperate to see him again, and to come quickly. That might add another couple of hours on to his night shift. I chuckled to myself. What did Rog do to her, the dirty old geezer?

Chapter Ten

Today was the day. I had decided to make my first move on Lucy.

A few days ago, I finalised a deal in Frankfurt, and they signed on the dotted line. It made me and my bosses enough of a bonus to buy a Ferrari *and* a Spanish villa. I was peer-pressured into celebrating with some German tarts, a couple of lines and a few Jägerbombs; we almost missed the early morning flight home. I got two weeks off for doing a good job, so thought that I had done enough research, practised the American accent and prepped my backstory that I was ready and confident to go for it. I got in a couple of days of beauty sleep, hardly left my bed, only popped out to grab a takeaway, a haircut and a massage at the Thai place around the corner, the lady walking over my back.

Not many people get to walk all over Nath, I mused.

I slipped into my chinos and eased into the blue Nikes. The Hollister t-shirt-and-shirt-combo worked well with the look I was going for, plus it bulked me out a bit. The JW hoodie completed the look and I had suddenly morphed into "Joe" – having been inspired by next-door-neighbour Margaret's GI husband and her yapping dog. I put my MacBook into a rucksack and headed out the house. The sky looked threatening so I pulled up the hood, tucked my hands into my pockets and headed towards the tube. I got to Starbucks in plenty of time, ordered a cappuccino and chose a table out of the way. I opened up the Mac and put my rucksack on the spare chair opposite, to stop anyone else sitting there. I glanced at the clock in the top right corner of the screen, 07:43. Lots of time to go.

By 8:43, the café was pretty much full. A flustered-looking woman came over, her phone in one hand, a takeaway coffee cup in the other, and motioned for me to move the rucksack so she could sit on the spare chair. I made my apologies and said I was waiting for someone. She tutted and moved on. She mooched around, gave up and headed out the door. She struggled to open it and as she did Lucy came in.

This was it.

Her curly hair was slightly damp from the drizzle outside, and it was starting to frizz. She was greeted by the Indian at the counter and she ordered her usual. She moved over to the collection counter and I removed the rucksack from the spare chair and looked busy. I pictured her eyes looking around the café and then felt a presence. My heart was going a million to the dozen.

Silence.

I kept my head down, keeping up the act.

Then a banging noise behind the counter forced my hand.

"Hey," I said, laying on the American accent as much as I could.

"Hi" she responded.

Silence. Awkward.

"Erm, can I help you?" I said, trying not to look like a rabbit in the headlights, genuinely amazed by her beauty. Lucy, here, literally, stood in front of me, looking at *me* for the very first time.

"Um, oh. Er, can I sit here? Please?"

Her voice was soft, rich and delicate, like angels playing on a harp.

Her face was so familiar, like I had known her for years. I must have taken over a hundred photos of her and printed them all out. The 2D photos, however, did not do her justice.

"Oh, yeah, sure," I said, giving it the full American drawl.

And so it began.

We arranged to meet later that day after she finished work. She toddled off and she eyeballed me as she left the café. I called that a successful start. I'm in no rush, I knew where she was going and knew where she'll be for the day. I finished the dregs of my coffee and popped open the MacBook screen. Microsoft Word was open and lines of gobbledegook scrawled across the white screen, results of my nonsense typing; acting was what I think they called it. I moved the cursor over to the little red round circle, pressed it and no, I didn't 'want to keep this new document "Untitled"?' I snapped the lid shut, walked out and headed home.

As I got off the tube, I felt a bit horny after meeting Lucy. I glanced into the little Thai masseuse shopfront and my regular was scrolling on her phone looking bored. She looked up and saw me, gave a friendly wave, beckoning me in. I got a one-hour deep tissue massage letting her soft, soft hands go over my skin – all the time thinking of Lucy. I went home, mooched around, watched a bit of Netflix and around 2pm got back on the tube and made my way to Covent Garden. I went into the café opposite Lucy's office, ordered a coffee and watched the glass front. I saw the receptionist staring blankly at his screen, occasionally lifting up and putting down the landline.

At 4:45 I left the café and went into Starbucks and ordered a couple of flat whites to take away. Even though I know she had an extra shot, I skipped that part of the order. That would have been too perfect and suspicious. Whilst waiting, I ran through various scenarios, what to say, what to do, thinking about the backstory. I thought about how the evening would end, how I was tempted to book a hotel room to keep the tourist story going. I hypothesised that she would probably be up for it if I played the game right, but it didn't really fit into the character I had created. Also, it would leave her gagging for more. I decided tonight wasn't going to be the night and worked out in my head how I would let her down. I spotted her mop of red curls bouncing down the road just after five. I was taken by her beauty again, knowing she was coming to me, rather than me watching her from afar. I seemed to have impressed her with getting her coffee, using my initiative to get her order.

She led me over Hungerford Bridge. I laid on the tourist act, pretending to be in awe at all the sights, drinking in her facts. After I gave her the sob story and made my eyes water, she was genuinely touched. I felt a connection, an emotional connection, as if there wasn't a deceitful barrier between us. Yet a lie was tying us together, guilt tugging at the strings.

She led me to the Tate and we laid next to each other: her head by my feet, my head by her feet – top to tail. It felt completely natural and I enjoyed it – being in her presence and with her. I let the silence wash over us, nice to be in our own thoughts, calm and collected. As I closed my eyes, I almost forgot my act.

Almost.

I sat up on my elbows and looked over to her, her head flat on the floor, her curls falling by her ears, interlacing together. From this angle I could see the underside of her face, the profile of a cleft chin, the dark nostrils and the point of her nose. She shifted, perhaps feeling her eyes on her and sat up on her elbows. We eyeballed each other for a few moments, I felt myself fall into her eyes, into her soul. This felt different. She broke the trance, we got up and headed out; all a bit polite and first-datey so far.

We dived into a restaurant. I was gagging for a stiff drink but kept up the pretence that alcohol was bad and should be avoided. The last time I had a meal without alcohol was at Mum's. My mind flashed back to Chloe and Mum, the bender and the recovery. Being clean, honest and myself. The real me. A guilt washed over me. I let her drink and she was opening up. My clear head allowed me to focus on my character, my words, the accent and my story. We were there for a while. Usually, I would have stopped the evening after dessert, a nightcap and moved onto the next base. Tonight, I was actually enjoying myself. The conversation flowed as she got tipsier. Occasionally I caught myself slipping out of the American accent and into my natural English. When I did, I glanced up to see if she had noticed, but relieved when she hadn't battered an eyelid. She was sinking into me. I felt great – it didn't seem like I had only spoken to this woman for the first time this morning; I wished I wasn't putting on the act, playing this game, that it was Nathan sitting opposite this stunning woman, instead of Joe. Being myself and letting her fall for me, the real me. I pushed that thought quickly out of my mind, we wouldn't be here if it wasn't for the American and I needed to focus.

She asked a few personal questions and I was ready for them. I gave enough information to whet her appetite and not enough detail that I might stumble or cause her to question. When she probed, I did the 'I don't really want to talk about it' line and it worked. She was shy enough not to confront me for more and I was relieved that she didn't push it. By the time we left the restaurant it was dark outside. I wondered if she was going to invite me to hers, prepared for the response. Instead, she led me on further down the river. I felt her fingers brush mine, and a tingle shot through my body. I forced my brain to get back into character and I prepared myself for the reaction I had earlier thought about if she went further. She did. Her little finger curled around mine as our arms swung next to each other. When I felt it – going against every urge in my body – I jerked my hand back. She reacted and I gave her the rehearsed apologises. It worked a charm. She was getting deeper into me and thought this was far too easy, my research was doing its magic. It felt like I knew everything about her – and everything she said confirmed it.

We turned a corner and Tower Bridge shone out, sitting regal and majestic over the Thames. It was an impressive sight and reminded me of the beauty of London. I whipped out an iPhone 4 I brought a couple of days ago. I had typed in a few fake numbers in the contacts and used it to take photos around London and close-ups of my face, in case she got hold of it. I took a selfie, pulling her in to me. Then she whipped out her phone and she surprised me when she pulled her face into me and planted her lips on mine. I was taken aback and shocked.

A sober kiss.

It felt wonderful, natural. I seriously couldn't remember the last time I had had a sober kiss. I could feel every sensation. Her lips were soft and a light breeze caused her curls to tickle my cheek. I was conscious of all the feelings cascading through my body, the tingle in my lips, the goosebumps across my skin. I was lost in the moment when she pulled away. She looked at me, her dark eyes penetrating me, her soft breath intermingling with the cool air breeze. I went back in wanting more. We kissed in front of the bridge, the lapping of the water beneath us. I didn't want it to end. She rested her hand on my chest, pushing me away slightly. I slowly opened my eyes, drinking in her face. Clearly, I had won this challenge, after just a few hours. I wanted to go further, perhaps beyond the scope of my brief. Maybe I ditch the plan and let things take its natural course.

I was about to say something when my conscience reminded me of my character. Instead, I snapped back and took a selfie, this time pulling us close together. She took my hand and we walked together along the river, onto the bridge and stood astride the gap in the middle where the bridge lifted. I held her round her waist and it felt good. I considered going back to hers – stuff holding out and waiting. I wanted more. As we walked to the tube station, the evening drawing to an end, I had a word to myself and decided to stick to the plan. We raced down the steps at Tower Hill, giggling and laughing and collapsed onto the checked seats of a waiting tube. I looked at her and gave her the rehearsed spiel: 'I've had a great evening, let's not go too fast'. She looked disappointed, as was I, but it kept her keen and wanting more. Or was it me that was keeping myself keen? She rested her head in the crook of my shoulder as the tube rumbled through the stations. A few drunks got on, wasted men in suits and a few short skirts. I pictured myself doing the same and cringed. She stood up as we arrived into Embankment, gave me a peck and jumped off. I watched her walk down the platform as the tube carried on. I got off at my stop and I walked home, hands in my pocket, almost skipping. I passed the wine bar, a smattering of locals still in, a night bus went past and deposited a couple of dazed, drunk lads at the bus stop.

I laid down on my bed and went to sleep with a smile on my face.

Chapter Eleven

I was standing outside Itsu, leaning against the glass, the morning after the night before. Which had been fantastic. I was reeling from both the amazing evening with Lucy and the great night's sleep I had had. I was wearing my usual Pradas and Guccis so she wouldn't recognise the clothes, and me. Right on time, she appeared. I swear she had a spring in her step, her curls bounced more than yesterday. A lovely bright white dress with what looked like tiny flowers dotted all over it that allowed easy access. I watched her sip her coffee sitting on the table next to the one we had sat at the day before. She pushed the heavy door and skipped along the Strand to her office. We'd arranged to meet at 5pm, like yesterday so I had a whole day to kill. I turned and headed down to the tube, got a massage and changed my clothes. Despite the best efforts of the masseuse, I couldn't relax into it. I was getting itchy feet and wanted to get back to Lucy.

So, by 11:30am I was back sitting in the café across the road from her office in my JW hoodie, hoping to catch a glimpse of her when she went for a lunchbreak. I was waiting, full of anticipation, butterflies in my tummy. It wasn't my usual nervousness of fear of whether I would be found out, but something entirely different. I willed the clock to hurry up. I got out the iPhone and scrolled through the pictures from last night, not for the first time. Her eyes sparkled, matching the twinkling lights of the bridge behind her. I zoomed into her face, her eyes large and staring back at me.

A bit of movement in front of the office caught my eye. I saw the long blonde hair of her colleague Jess come out of the office, followed closely by Lucy. There she was, looking radiant. I sipped my cappuccino and kept watch.

A silver Prius pulled up outside a moment later and they got in. I sensed something was wrong, so I stood up and moved quickly out of the café. The car moved off and I panicked. I looked left and right for a taxi. My best chance was the Strand but then I would lose them. I saw a black cab crawl out of a side street and waved urgently at him.

Fate.

He spotted me and pulled up. I jumped in and saw the Prius turn in front of the large arch of Covent Garden. I told the cabbie to catch up, and he looked back at me. I slapped a fifty under the glass and he slammed his foot down. We caught up immediately, the Prius stuck in a queue of traffic behind a delivery van stopped in the middle of the road. He looked back at me quizzically and I said I was a PI, my client's got suspicions that his wife was cheating. He looked at me conspiratorially, with a wink.

"Right you are gov. It's all spies and mystery today ain't it." He leaned forward and turned up the radio, James O'Brien blathering on again. I sensed he relished the prospect of a covert operation, all that Tory bashing rubbish he listens to. To be fair, he kept his distance from the cab like a pro, never letting it leave our sight.

It eventually pulled up outside the massive St Pancras Hotel. The girls got out and darted inside. The cabbie pulled up behind a row of taxis parked up waiting for fares. I thanked the cabbie and he winked at me. I slipped him a twenty and told him to keep the change.

"Nice one fella. Good luck," he said, surprised.

Maybe it was his biggest tip today.

I kept a wary distance from the glass-fronted doors before sneaking carefully into the lobby. They must have either gone into the restaurant at the front or the brasserie at the back – the one that backs onto the new concourse. I backed out onto the street and raced around to the station, up the stairs and passed the giant statue of lovers embracing. Making sure I wasn't spotted (I was wearing my "Joe" attire after all), I peered through the glass door of the brasserie and tried my best to spot them. Not seeing them, I went through the restaurant and into the hotel lobby, checking they weren't in a corner.

Nope.

I stepped across the threshold of the other restaurant, the long, white-topped bar running along its entire side. I had been there many times, ploughing clients with champagne and mussels. Apparently, they were to die for but I never did like seafood.

I spied them chatting to a couple, their backs to me. Lucy's hair was unmistakable, let alone Jess' straight blonde next to her. The people they were chatting to were older and totally not trendy, the man's cheap blazer was definitely high street. I chose a table out of the way and hid behind a menu, watching.

The amount of times Lucy threw her head back, it was clear she was having a grand old time. Jess was constantly filling glasses up with a steady flow of wine. Occasionally their laughter echoed around the vaulted ceiling. I hoped Lucy wouldn't forget about our little rendezvous. At one point, Lucy picked up her phone and swizzled her head around. In panic I lifted my glass up to cover my face, spilling water on to the white tablecloth. I stared through the glass. She was waving at someone to my right. A bit close for comfort. I looked over.

Bloody hell.

It was the tosser from that bar where I had first spotted her in London. The one drooling all over her.

What was he doing here?

She went over to him and he gave her a big hug. Judging by her reaction it was a coincidence. For a split second I considered if he had engineered this. I shook it from my head.

Don't be ridiculous.

Was that jealousy rearing its head?

She went back to her table just as the couple were getting up to go. I checked my watch. Good timing. She would be back in plenty of time.

I watched the couple leaving, trying to suss out who they were. By the time I looked back, the tosser was gathering his things, looking up at Lucy and Jess.

Uh-oh.

He was walking over, a nice bit of swagger in his step like he had won the lottery. He slid along the white leather seat and made himself comfortable and put on some ridiculous

Harry Potter glasses that made him look like a twat. Jess waved for another bottle of wine. I settled back and watched.

Time was ticking along. I nervously checked my watch, creeping towards 5pm.

Was she going to stand me up for this tosser?

The wine was flowing and Jess kept topping up all the glasses. They were clearly enjoying themselves, having a jolly old time. But to leave me out in the cold? 4:30 and no sign of them leaving. If she wanted to get back in time to meet me, she was pushing it. I thought about doing something, jerking them out of their fun. A text would have done it, if I had her number. Could I walk over and surprise them? Nah, that would be too bizarre.

Ugh, it was so frustrating.

That tosser was getting all of Lucy's attention and I was fuming. I could imagine his cheap aftershave tickling her senses and her getting turned on, particularly with all the alcohol that was going down her throat. The urge to go over there and slap him silly was overpowering.

Then all of sudden there was a flurry of activity. Panic from them. Jess and Lucy were fussing. They remembered but too bloody late. No way would they get to the Strand at this time of day. The tosser was dithering, not wanting the date to end. His face was a picture when they hurried out. It looked like he was going to cry such was the disappointment. I watched them leave the restaurant as I busied myself in the menu.

Tentatively, I crept out of the lobby and into the cool air, being careful to see if they were still there. They weren't. I looked around and saw Lucy's red curls bouncing and Jess' blonde hair swaying as they stumbled across the cobbled road. Lucy reached out and grabbed her hand to help her steady herself. I followed at a distance.

They went inside a pub, a smattering of noise emanated out as the door opened. I left it a few minutes and when a couple of lads went in I followed, pretending to be part of their group, eyes alert. They headed straight to the bar and I stood next to them arm resting on the bar behind them, trying to locate the girls. Crossing my arms to hide the hoodie, I spotted them sitting on a table in the corner, deep in conversation, a glass of wine each.

Dumped. Stood up. Rejected.

The two lads I was next to saw them too, one of them nudging the other and grinning. I ordered a pint and went and sat at a table far enough away. The two lads moved on to a table between us, giving me a good enough shield that Lucy wouldn't spot me. They talked for most of the night. Or to be more accurate, Jess talked for most of the night. I knew those types, the world revolved around them. I would be even richer if I had a pound for the number of times I sat opposite a tart who gave a monologue for most of the night.

They took it in turns to get a round in, and I nursed my one pint the whole night, being careful not to get up and draw attention to myself. At closing time they got up and left, a few of the guys in the pub eyeing them up as they walked out, sniggering. I gave them a couple of seconds then followed them out. I spotted them in the distance, arms locked together, stumbling and wavering along the road. Jess hailed a taxi and they both got in. Maybe they were going back to hers for a bit of a snog. *Nice*, I thought as I pictured it. Then shook it from my head – Lucy definitely wasn't queer. I left them to it. Nothing more for me to see here and set about thinking about what my next move would be.

Next morning, I stood outside Itsu at 8:45 wondering if Lucy would get her usual flat white and shot. I waited until 9:15 and there was no sign so I wandered off to her office. As I turned the corner, Jess and Lucy were coming the other way. I darted back around the corner and waited a minute. I peered around the corner and the coast was clear. Just a few commuters and office workers hurrying around, looking at their phones, headphones in their ears. I walked across the road and sat in the café opposite the office. I picked up a Metro and finished it within ten minutes. I got up, went around the corner and bought the Financial Times. I went back to the café, my cappuccino still on the table, sat down and opened the pink sheets, killing time. About half past eleven I walked into the office. The guy receptionist looked me up and down as I strode over to the big wooden desk he was half-hidden behind. He waited for me to speak first.

"Erm, hey man," I drawled in an American accent. "I'm looking for a woman called Lucy. Red curly hair, about yay high."

I put my hand up to my shoulder, palm flat facing down. Without a word, he typed on his keyboard. Then he picked up the landline, punched a few numbers and lazily held the retriever to his ear. He stared at me and I feigned disinterest, looking around the empty space. He replaced the receiver and with a nod of his head and a flick of his eyes to the table and chair, motioned me to take a seat.

"I'll wait right here," I said, creasing my eyebrows in disbelief.

Bloody hell mate, with that attitude the world would stop turning.

He shrugged his shoulders, got up, buzzed his pass through the double doors and walked in, leaving me alone in the big space. I saw him through the circular glass idly wandering around an open-plan office, speaking to a few people. He was walking about when I saw Lucy come out of a side office. They almost bumped into each other. They had a short conversation and I saw her eyes flick through the round porthole to me. I returned her wave. She bounded out and stopped abruptly in front me, hesitating from touching, conscious that office eyes might be on her. Apologies spilled out. I told her not to worry and motioned her to sit at the table. She sat on the same chair she had for her interview. I told her I had been waiting outside Starbucks that morning in case she swung by for her flat white. She kept apologising and then questioned how I had found her. I gave the prepared speech, making out I have been busy all morning searching. Her prince on a quest to find his princess. She seemed more than satisfied, believing every word.

Bingo.

We agreed to go out and get some lunch. She grabbed my hand and it felt natural and comfortable. We ate a sandwich in the Piazza and watched some loser entertain the tourists, no doubt thinking how many people were going to desert him when he whipped out his hat. We set a date for that evening, and I said I'd love to see the real London, pushing the agenda to her comfort zone, her place of safety and familiarity. It was easier, psychologically, for her to invite me back to hers, not that it would be difficult. She agreed, and my stomach did a flip. We set a time and place, same as before.

I sat in the café, holding the FT as wide as I could, covering my face. My eyes peered up over the top of the pink pages looking over the road to Lucy's office. It was 4:55pm, nearly time. I wanted to wait for her to leave so she stood outside Starbucks like I supposedly had for a few minutes, thinking I'd stood her up this time, and just as she was giving up hope, run up to her, out of breath, apologising. The old 'keep 'em keen' tactic. 5:10pm and she was still not out. I tapped my feet impatiently, my knees bounced up and down almost hitting the plastic table. My tactic wouldn't work, in fact it was the other way around: I was feeling a bit too keen.

I spotted her red hair through the portholes in the internal doors. She was coming. I bolted off the chair, threw the paper on the table and ran out before she came out on the street. I raced through the throng of people snaking their way to the stations, stopped outside Starbucks and looked left and right in anticipation, as if I was panicking. I spotted her and gave her a wave. She gave a cute wave back. I'm on.

Chapter Twelve

The night went exactly as I imagined.

We headed to her part of town, and I pretended to be wide-eyed with fascination at somewhere so new. In reality I had been there at least a couple of dozen times. I let her lead, pulling me by the hand. We kissed and touched, held hands and nuzzled into each other's faces. It felt so natural and safe. We went into a pub to grease the wheels, and after a few drinks in her she started to get dizzy and handsy. As if on cue, she invited me back to hers. Perfect. She led me to her flat and we went in. It was pretty much exactly as I pictured. A few girly throws and cushions, photos of her and her mum, Ikea furniture and a few dog-eared paperbacks on the table – books I had seen her read over the last few weeks.

A rush of adrenaline kicked in; it was like seeing a movie set in real life after seeing it countless times on the big screen. I gave her a double-entendre compliment about how nice and perfectly formed it was and she was on to me, sticking her tongue in my mouth, rubbing herself on me. It was a bit aggressive and she was stronger than I had anticipated but I liked that. But before we got too far down the road, she stopped, spinning the old line of taking it slowly. I was fine with that, in fact more than fine. It gave her even more of an allure. And it meant I would see her for longer.

The next morning, she got up and headed to the bathroom. What a night. I felt triumphant and satisfied, not just knowing how successful this challenge was becoming but also another feeling I rarely had the morning after the night before.

Contentment.

It was the embodiment of perfection. Everything had worked like clockwork. All that research and prep paid off with a ten-point-o. We had snuggled up pretty much the whole night, her purring and me scooping her up if I woke and she had moved away. I enjoyed feeling her soft breath against my chest, gently tickling my fingers up and down her upper arms, and of course smoothing her hair with my palms. Like stroking a dog or a cat.

When I heard the shower taps turn on, I jumped out of the bed and started looking through her things. The cupboard was full to bursting with bras, dresses, shirts and trousers hanging up, shoes strewn on the bottom shelf. I opened the drawers underneath a desk with a mirror on top: a couple of make-up items, hair-bobbles, paper clips, a few passport photos.

No sign of a fella.

On top of the desk was just a hairbrush with red curls jutting from the spokes and more romantic paperbacks. Nothing exciting. I walked out and saw the bathroom door. I imagined her in the shower on the other side, her beautiful pale skin caressed by the falling water wishing it was my fingers, the droplets following her curves.

Now, if we'd had sex, that would have been the end of a successful challenge. I'd dump them and move on to the next one. But Lucy was different, so different. The sex was just a pinch point. In fact, it didn't even feel important. I wanted to go further. I wanted to be with her, spend time with her and chat long into the night, staring into her eyes. I wanted to hold her hand.

My god, I sound like a bratty teenager.

I don't know if it was the extensive research that I had done or nailed the American character but something about Lucy was magnetic. With the travel in-between the reconnaissance trips, Lucy's research phase was the longest I had spent on a subject. Thinking about her and what she liked and didn't like all the time perhaps made me too involved, and I was finding it tricky to separate Joe from the real me. Or could it be that I was actually falling for her?

Nonsense.

This was a challenge not one of her trashy romantic books. And she would be my ultimate success. Nothing could top this. This would be my last one. I'd keep going, shag her and finish the job and then dump her from a greater height. Then that would be it, no more tricking or lying. I would dump the files in my spare room and start afresh, maybe even settle down and try to find someone for the real Nathan. Someone like Lucy.

Sitting around her small kitchen table, we were drinking tea and munching on toast. I was looking into her eyes, her hair damp from the shower. Some of the curls were dry and sprang out. She hadn't any make-up on and by God she was gorgeous. Proper girl-next-door: didn't know how pretty she was, plain and simple looks. She wasn't going to set the world alight, but it was humble and satisfying to look at her. I snapped out of it and got back into character. I gave her what I rehearsed in my head and what she wanted to hear: that I'm so smitten by her that I want to extend my stay, if that's ok by her that is. I'd have to fork out a fortune keeping a hotel room so I suggested moving in with her for a short time until I worked out what I would do. When she agreed I actually felt pretty happy, that I'd be near to her and see her up-close rather than through a lens or across the road. We agreed to meet up later, and she told me to let myself out. She sauntered out the door and I watched her walk away through the window. It was usually the other way around: me watching her from outside looking in. I mooched around her flat, knowing I'd been giving permission to be there. It was less of a thrill but nevertheless I opened cupboards, got down on my knees looking under the sofa, getting a fuller picture of who she was and what made her tick. I rifled through her underwear drawer, her clothes cupboard and picked up her shoes. I took her pillow, breathed in the candyfloss smell and cuddled it on her sofa, looking around at the view she would have reading one of her books. The cat ambled in and jumped up next to me, purring for a cuddle. I pushed it down off the sofa and it yelped. I sat there breathing in the air, her air, soaking up the ambience of another successful challenge. The last one.

I got back to my place just after 11 but got impatient pretty quickly. I had this weird gravitational sensation in my chest that was trying to pull me to her. I decided I'd surprise her and take her out for lunch. She'd love that. I thought I had better get a move on to catch her lunch break. I grabbed my Tumi, threw a few things in – some underwear and toiletries – and headed out the door. My legs felt like they were moving quicker than my body. I came out the house and pulled the gate to, almost slamming into the postman.

"Watch it mate!"

"Sorry mate, in a hurry."

"Here, these are for you," he said pushing a boring looking letter into my hand.

"Cheers fella," I said, ripping it up and shoving it in the front pocket of the Tumi, thinking to get rid of it later once I was off the tube. In the hurry I completely forgot about it and dumped the case at Left Luggage and made a dash to her office. I went in and spoke to the guy receptionist, 'remember me' face on as I went in. I was genuinely disappointed when the dipstick said I had just missed her. So, I stepped across the road and waited in the café. About 40 minutes later she came back. I breathed out. Just seeing her again made my heart skip.

I ordered a cappuccino and sipped it slowly, trying to play it cool and give some distance from her lunch break. My hands were shaking and my feet were unconsciously tapping against the café's floor. I tried to read some of the headlines of The Times but the words bounced off the pages, missing my brain altogether. I could only think of Lucy. I drained the coffee, got up and took a walk outside to calm my nerves. I headed up to Covent Garden and tried to distract my attention with the street entertainers, shop fronts and cafes. A clown with a bright orange wig, a red plastic nose and oversized dungarees was working hard to entertain the crowd. His white-powdered face had painted black tears under his eyes and down-turned red lips. How much would he make? A couple of hundred?

Hardly worth the effort mate.

A group of school kids were sitting cross-legged in the front row, all dressed in matching navy-blue blazers, laughing and giggling at the clown. He was pulling out the tricks and pretending they were going wrong, much to the delight of the children.

My mind wandered back to school, being surrounded by a braying and laughing crowd.

With a nick nack paddy whack.

A boy appeared in my imaginary crowd, wearing a bright orange wig, with painted black tears and a down-turned red lips, just like the clown but superimposed on a child. He just stared at me, silent and unwavering, as the rest of the crowd were screaming, braying and shouting.

This old man, he played three,
Sitting on a tree.
K-I-S-S-I-N-G.

He blew me a kiss and a hooter sounded as he pursed his lips. It jolted me out of my trance. The clown was preparing his grand finale by squeezing his claxon to get the crowd going. I moved away from the throng and went to the nearest café.

I had three coffees, a pastry and a Twix, each purchased in different shops, trying to waste time and get rid of that weird daydream. By mid-afternoon I said to myself the time was right, took a deep breath and headed back. My heart beat faster with every step I took towards the office. I went in and casually started speaking to the receptionist, over-friendly in the American way, my heart felt like it could burst out of my Hollister shirt it was beating so hard. Only a door separated her from me. He picked up the phone and dialled the number. It rang and rang. He looked up at me, rolling his eyes up, as if to say: 'typical woman'. I saw a flash out the corner of my eye at the porthole window, and saw Lucy approaching, looking at the bottom of the door. I turned my body, and saw the receptionist look up over his computer screen to the door, the phone receiver still at his ear. Lucy's head popped up and she gave me the 'one-minute finger' signal through the glass and disappeared again.

It felt like a lifetime when I spied her through the porthole window again. There was only so much conversation I could get out of the receptionist and the silences were long and awkward. He swung his hips round on his chair, his knees dancing back and forth whilst his cheap, scuffed black shoes were anchored to the ground. Lucy was walking fast with her head down; I was glad she was hurrying. She burst out of the door, and when she looked up it looked like her eyes were about to burst a dam. The left side of her face was starting to redden. Without saying a word, she grabbed my hand and pulled me out of the reception and onto the street. We sat in the café and the tears were flowing. She was telling me everyone in the office was stressed and someone just snapped at her for no reason. She wasn't fooling me – that was a slap if ever I saw one. I told her to skive off work, thinking I could treat her and make her feel better. I was concerned for her and wanted to protect her, make her feel safe. We headed down the Strand and she pointed out The Savoy. I had been there many a times schmoozing my clients, some of whom stayed there. There was a very posh afternoon tearoom inside, which I knew Lucy would love. I suggested going in to forget about what just happened and she eagerly agreed. We grabbed hands and walked into the lobby; her eyes wide open looking around.

We sat at a table and the waiters fussed about. We ordered and some posh chump came up behind me and reckoned that he knew me.

Shit.

I turned and immediately recognised him. He was a partner at a legal firm I had to work with when there were some irregularity issues with a deal I put through a few years back. Big guy with an imposing pinstripe suit. No wonder he was here, the invoices that he put through for a fortnight's work was almost as big as my bonus. I remembered bricking it when he was laying it all out for me: prison, bail, bankruptcy. Laid it on thick. I was fresh out of Oxford and taking a few liberties with the accounts. I was probably high. All of the bluster he made me sweat through didn't happen of course. He got me off, but the smoke was well and truly up my arse. I had done it by the book since. Well mostly.

He was looking older now, his hair completely grey. He approached the table extending his arm for me to shake his wrinkled and liver-spotted hands. When I didn't take it, his wife's face started to panic, her botoxed forehead betrayed worry lines. I slipped back into character, my heart racing. I felt a trickle of sweat behind my hoodie. When he heard the American accent, he jolted his hand back in surprise. His wife fussed and apologised, saying he was losing his marbles, or something to that effect and they disappeared.

Thank fuck for that.

I was so relieved that I wanted to gulp some of the champagne from the next table down my neck. I looked over to Lucy and she was enjoying the show. She believed the mistaken identity hook, line and sinker. The adrenaline subsided.

That was a bloody close one.

Next morning, I took a shower in Lucy's flat. After the incident at the Savoy, I realised I needed to be more careful, although it was impossible to factor in cases like that one. It was part of the thrill, and I'm glad that my character was American. I turned the taps off and headed into the bedroom. Lucy seemed different; my touch made her shy away, rather than sinking into it like last night. I pulled on the Hollister shirt but decided to leave the hoodie – it seemed quite warm out, a spring day, so I rolled the sleeves. She took ages in the shower and I banged on the door. She was dazed and confused, her mind elsewhere. A little red flag went up in my head but I dismissed it pretty quickly as the previous night had been brilliant. She must be thinking about going back into the office and confronting whatever it was that caused the ruckus. I hoped she would deal with it. Bullying has no place in the office, unless you can get away with it of course. We got dressed and sat around her table having some breakfast. I feigned that I'd go and do some tourist crap this morning, already planning to surprise her at her office for lunch. A knot formed in my stomach when I realised I wouldn't see her for a few hours. I shook my head. I wanted to give myself a slap to snap myself out of it but that wouldn't go down well at the breakfast table.

We headed out on the train and got off at Waterloo, walking through the arches to Hungerford Bridge, her usual route. I went to tail off along the riverbank whilst she went up the stairs. I gave her a kiss and we split up. I walked along the South Bank where we strolled just a couple of days ago and stopped to look up at her, waiting for her to be far enough along the bridge so I could retrace my steps back. Instead, she stopped and looked back at me. I was quite surprised but gave a wave. I liked to think she is looking back at me, a final glimpse of her man before we met again.

I continued walking to carry on the act and stopped behind a tree. I peered out to check if she was still watching. She wasn't. She was halfway across the bridge, quickening her pace. I stayed put to give some distance and thought I saw her red hair bobbing down the stairs on the other side. I turned back and headed to Waterloo to catch the tube home to Ealing.

Chapter Thirteen

I got to Waterloo and it was busy with commuters blocking my way. I wasn't rushed but wanted to get home, reset, and back for twelve so I didn't miss her again. I popped into Costa and grabbed a BLT and a cappuccino and sat down at a table. My decision that Lucy would be the last challenge felt like a huge weight had lifted off my shoulders. Unwittingly, Lucy had shown me a longer game, one where I actually felt I needed to be with someone, to share things together and get through the world. Maybe it was my age and an automatic lever clicked in my head to settle down. Friends? Pah! I didn't have anyone that I could rely on. All my so-called mates were work-colleagues who would only be with you if you were drunk or high after work. I had pretty much lost contact with my school friends after I was excluded. I beat most of them up.

Jeez, I was a dickhead at school.

The ginger boy in the clown wig entered my mind, his eyes staring, his face painted white, his mouth agog, his navy-blue blazer too big for him. I pictured my Mum standing in her oversized dressing gown at the door of her house as I drove off. I pictured Chloe with paramedics around her, blue lights flashing. Jess hugging Lucy when she was supposed to be with me and feeling the red mist form.

Jeez, I was a dickhead out of school too.

A few months after Chloe died, I had a call from Mum. She just wanted a chat but she was weirdly quiet on the phone. After several minutes of standard conversation – how are you? What have you been doing? - her voice broke and she started crying. I let the sobs wash over us as she took a few moments to compose herself. I didn't know what to say to my Mum whose daughter had died except *it's ok*. It sounded so hollow coming out of my mouth. She took a breath.

"Your Dad. He's been in touch."

The words hung in the air. I felt my blood pressure increase, my heart thumped through my chest. Images spun through my mind.

"What did the bastard want?" I asked, trying to keep my voice level.

"He wanted to offer his condolences," she said.

"And did you tell him to piss off? Slam the phone down?"

"No of course not Nathaniel. I spoke to him. He was sorry."

"Sorry? That's it? *Sorry?* He left you in the shit Mum and all he could say was he was sorry?" I blurted out.

"I know love, I know. But you know. It was good to hear a familiar voice." She trailed off leaving a void behind. A void I should have filled with visits and phone calls. I'd left her alone.

"And…," she continued, "he wants to meet up with you."

"Not a chance," I said, quickly. "I don't want to be anywhere near him."

"I know, that's what I said. But I said I would ask you. He is your Dad. He left you a lot of money. Paid this house off for us. Even after everything."

I stayed silent on the line, not being able to think of anything. Images just flashed across my mind – Mum, Dad, Chloe, plates smashed against the wall, Dad shaking Chloe, alcohol, Dad's angry mouth contorted in front of Mum's scared face. My hair being ruffled by his mates down the pub when I was barely a teenager, playing football in the park, Dad in goal, sparring with him in the living room – the boxing gloves too big for my hands. The good and the bad all mixed together.

"Money doesn't buy you everything," I said, thinking of my lifestyle and Lucy at the same time.

"He's old now Nathaniel," Mum said, bringing me back to the present. "Remorseful, you know?"

"Why does he think that he can come back into our lives huh? It's been, what, ten years? More? A lot has happened in those years Mum. When we needed him, he buggered off!"

"I know, I know," Mum pleaded. "But sometimes people deserve a second chance. Sometimes you don't think you've done something wrong until you realise it and you're sorry. For the hurt. You don't realise how much you've hurt someone. You can either keep silent or face the truth."

"Yeah, sometimes. Or sometimes you can get on with your life and never look back. It's his conscience not mine Mum."

"Will you at least think about it Nathaniel?"

"Yeah, sure. Done. I've thought about it," I replied, sarcastically.

"OK, I understand. There's a lot of pain there, I know. I hope that when you need someone to forgive you, they'll be there for you."

And she gently put the phone down.

Sitting in Costa nursing my cappuccino I thought Lucy was the one to get me out of this mess. I *needed* her to get me out of this mess. She would forgive me if she knew the truth. If she knew the effort I went to get her to like me she would stay with me, forever. I wouldn't be alone in a crappy dressing gown standing in a doorway waiting for a visit. The look she gave me in the Tate: that was real. Those were Nathan's eyes, not Joe's. I would come clean that evening. I would get rid of all the box files this afternoon when I got home. I would ditch the American accent, the fake clothes and be honest with her. She would be shocked at first, maybe a bit disgusted, but she would come around. She would gaze into my eyes like she had in the Tate and her heart would melt. I would tell her about Chloe and Mum, and my past mistakes.

The truth.

She would empathise and coo and envelope me in her arms, soothing me, wipe away the tears and tell me it was going to be ok. Yes, I was sure of it. I knew it. She was that kind of person. I knew everything about her.

Down on the platform I let two Jubilee line tubes go past as I considered my new future and took my time through the long tunnel that connected it to the Piccadilly line. It was like the world had lifted off of my shoulders. I was a new man. I even threw a few pound coins into a busker's hat along the way. The Heathrow train was so packed with suitcases and oversized rucksacks that I had to squeeze in between two Japanese tourists and a pretty blonde with a NYC baseball cap pulled down covering her eyes. I walked down the high street and I saw Margaret coming the other way with her yappy dog on the lead. I stopped to chat and she made a comment about the weather and how it was affecting Joe's behaviour. Then went off on one about her ailments again. I eventually made my excuses when there was a gap in conversation and walked away. She called me back.

"Oh Nath, er, your lady just popped round. She seems lovely Nath!" I stopped, turned and asked her which lady that was.

"The lady you said to come and pick up your DVDs. You weren't in so I gave her the spare key and I told her to drop it through my letterbox when she was done." I looked at her full on, a look of confusion across my face. My mind was racing, thinking of all the different women I knew – my mind was mentally going along the names of the box files. None would have known my address. I fleetingly thought of Chloe as she was the only woman who had ever been to my house.

Margaret sensed my confusion. A look of a horror on her face.

"I haven't asked anyone to pick up DVDs. In fact, I don't own any," I said, still trying to work it out.

"Well, she showed me a photo of the two of you on her phone. It was in front of Tower Bridge. Ah she's lovely Nath. In fact, you're wearing the same sweater as you are now."

My heart stopped.

"What did she look like?" I asked, a panic in my voice, already knowing the answer. Margaret looked surprised. Her faced dropped, thinking of the key she had just given to a perfect stranger when perhaps she shouldn't have.

"Redhead, curly hair," she said flatly, the colour leaving her face. I felt my eyes widen, picturing the spare room, all those box files. All the evidence.

"She's probably still there Nath," she said hopefully.

I had never run so fast before in my life.

Chapter Fourteen

I turned the key very slowly. My heart was racing, sweat was pouring from my head and under my arms. A prickle went through my body as I stepped slowly in, listening.

Listening.

Everything was silent. The Nikes cushioned my feet as I walked on the wooden floors. I took a few steps and strained to look into the kitchen and living room. Empty. I glanced up the stairs looking for clues, hoping. Just hoping. Creeping up the stairs, ever so slowly, I peered through the bannisters.

She was there.

In the spare room, lying on the floor, arms outstretched towards the wall of box files, like she was praying to them. I could see a gap in the shelves, where she had taken one of them out, disturbing the uniformity of the files.

Her file.

The one with all the printouts of her.

She wasn't moving. I reached up and closed my hand around the wooden bannister, firstly for support and then to aid lifting myself up a few millimetres so the weight of my body didn't go on my feet onto the wooden stairs. As if by magic, I felt a long, thin piece of wood loosen from the bannisters.

Coincidence?

Fate?

I wasn't entirely sure why those feelings coursed through my body. I lifted it up, ever so gently, and the bottom slid out. I moved it down and it came out completely. I held it tight and took the last few steps up the stairs. My trainers sank into the carpet, sound now completely dampened. Walking slowly into the spare room, the rows of the box files loomed large in front of me. Her head twitched ever so slightly, as if she sensed a presence in the room, and I closed the door. The clicking of the lock made her sit up abruptly. She didn't look around, her body stayed frozen looking ahead. She must have known it was me. Waiting. Guilt flowed through my veins. Adrenaline pumped through my body. Anger at myself for being found out. Fury at my failure. It was like I was someone else. Someone completely different.

My dad.

At last, she made a movement. As she swivelled her head around, I swung my arm down and the wooden stick cracked against her beautiful, red curls.

Her head jerked forward, blood splatted on the carpet, sinking into the fibres. I dropped the stick, bright red blood at the end. I stared down at her, blood pumping through my veins, my heart beating like a bass drum.

Boom, boom, boom.

I pictured the lawyer at the Savoy, his face grave and serious. His lips in a grin, moving silently

With a nick nack paddy whack.

Then my dad, looking disappointingly at me like he used to at Chloe, his mouth moved

Give a dog a bone.

I paced around Lucy, not knowing what to do, her body motionless on the carpet, her eyes shut. I ran out the room, slamming the door behind me, trying to give myself time to calm down. To think.

I downed a pint of water. Paced around the kitchen. Opening and closing cupboards, not knowing what to do. A packet of cable ties spoke to me out of one of the drawers. I raced back up the stairs, taking them two at a time, stopping in front of the closed door. Deep breathe in, deep breathe out, composing myself.

I let myself back in but seeing her lying there, motionless, set me off again. She was moving, groaning, mumbling. I used the cable ties to lock her wrists and ankles together, so she wouldn't attempt to run away before I have the chance to explain. To set things right. Let her love me for who I really was.

But my brain wasn't controlling my mouth. I was properly bricking it, blaming her, words spilled out of my mouth, saying I'm sorry, what was she doing here, how did she find out? The act had gone, the ruse was up, the challenge was over, the accent was irrelevant now. I had a bleeding head and vomit on the floor of my house, in front of my secret.

Lucy. Luce. Poor Lucy.

I bent down and cradled her head in my hands. Her eyes were rolling back, in and out of consciousness. She still looked beautiful, the colour drained from her face, her red curls covered her pale skin. She was saying something, whispering. I couldn't work it out. I thought she was babbling. This couldn't be good. Her voice was barely audible so I leaned in. She muttered something about not being called Lucy, or how I knew her by another name. She was gabbing about, not making any sense. Then she fell silent. Her eyes closed. Her breathing stopped. The blood drained from my face and I collapsed in a heap on the floor. As my mind shut down, the last thing that went through my head was that infuriating rhyme

This old man came rolling home.

Part Three

'Nathan'

Chapter One

Lucy heard footsteps coming up the wooden stairs. Her head was pounding and she felt her hair stuck against the side of her head, matted down. She slowly opened her eyes as her head lolled around on her shoulders, realising she was sitting upright, her hands tied behind her back. The sunlight spiked her pupils and she flinched. She closed them tightly, willing the hammering in her head to subside.

How much time has passed?

She tried to remember. The bright blue Nike trainer, the wall of box files, the blow to her head. She opened her eyes again and in front of her the shelves of box files filled the wall. It wasn't a dream. She was sitting on a hard, wooden chair, plastic cutting into her wrists behind her back. She tried to move them and a sharp pain of burning shot into her skin, like a Chinese burn from school. Her legs felt weak, bloodless and she tried to move them. Her feet, too, were tied together. She felt the pain like a papercut above her ankles. A body moved in front of her. It was Joe. Or was it Nathan? Or even Nathaniel. She struggled to remember the events before she blacked out. He squatted in front of her, the wall behind framing him, the box files in perfect alignment with each other – it was almost like a trendy wallpaper. He looked into her eyes and swept her hair behind her ears.

"Joe?" she asked.

"Take a sip of this," the English accent was unmistakable. He held up a glass of water to her lips and rested the edge on her bottom lip. She turned away, not trusting him. He grabbed her chin and flicked it forward, holding tightly on to it. Skin crumpled in his hand. He put the edge of the glass back onto her lower lip and tipped the water into her mouth. It was cool and nice. She took a tiny sip and let it run down her throat, spreading into her chest. He put the glass back up and tilted it again, more water entered her mouth. She held it in, the back of her tongue blocking it going down her throat. She spat it back at him, light red mixed with transparent liquid landing over his face and dribbled down his white top. He jumped back in surprise, cursed and wiped the water away. He set the glass down and gave her a slap, full across the cheek, the same side that Jess had hit. That her dad hit too. The force made her head turn towards the window.

She pictured Jess' red eyes in the toilet of the office, pleading to her that Joe wasn't who he said he was. She felt stupid and immature. And naïve. This was London, the big city: you can't trust anyone here. She turned her head back. He was pacing up and down in front of the box files. She looked across them and saw her file back on the shelf, neatly tucked between Katie and Maya. There was a red smudge on the white label, a half fingerprint. She caught his eye; it was wild but not panicked. He stood by the window, his hands on his hips. He took a deep breath in.

Starring casually out of the window he murmured "What did you mean when you said, 'Lucy is not the name you used to know me by'?" She didn't say anything back. He had given up on the American accent. Her mind was humming and throbbing at the same time.

"What did you mean?" he repeated, this time a bit louder and more forcibly, but not angry. She maintained her silence. He rushed over and gave her another slap, this time on the other side. It stung. Blood trickled onto her tongue. She shook her head to will the pain to disperse. He was back looking out of the window. He took his index finger and gently wiped dust off the ledge.

"Is your name Joe?" she asked. "Or is it Nathan. Or Nathaniel?" He turned and stared at her. She felt the power on her side.

"What did you mean?" he repeated, taking an aggressive step towards her. She flinched, turning her head waiting for the sting to come.

"You don't recognise me, do you?" she said with a hint of knowing, a veil of a secret that tantalised him. He walked over to her, squatted down so that their eyes were level, their eyeballs meeting. He looked deep into her eyes as if searching for an answer. He got up and went back to his spot at the window. He was probably mentally scanning all of the images he had taken of her, all the places he had followed her, trying to find a clue. He turned to face her again.

"New York, two years ago. I saw you at JFK boarding my plane," he said absent-mindedly, staring out of the window. Lucy thought back to her New York trip.

How weird.

She didn't remember, but then again, an American-looking guy in New York was not a rarity. She pictured all of the photos in her file.

Is that how long he's been following me?

The thought sent a shiver down her spine.

"Before that," she teased and shifted in her seat. He spun round.

"Before that?" he asked, surprised.

"Way before that," Lucy said matter-of-factly, her lips curling up to a smile causing the dimples to deepen. He looked through her, trying to decipher the riddle.

"When?" he asked, a nervousness in his voice.

"I didn't realise who you were, who you *really* were, until I saw you in those boxes," she nodded up. "When I saw you in Starbucks, I felt something in my stomach, a familiarity, but couldn't place you. When you started speaking in your accent, I realised it couldn't have been whoever I was thinking of. Just like that bloke in the Savoy."

He looked up to the ceiling as if piecing pieces of a jigsaw together.

"I put it behind me. I like you Joe. I like you a lot. Or I did. You were different to anyone else I met – you took me for who I was."

His eyes narrowed guilty, looking at her with those deep brown eyes. She felt the electricity flow between them, the same as when they had been sitting opposite each other in that pizza restaurant; it's menu now sat in the box in front of her.

"I enjoyed myself when I was with you. It felt right, natural," she saw him turn, a small smile crept on his face, a smile of victory. She continued with his back to her.

"It was only when I saw the photos of you with the other women, a younger you, with different hair, that I started to realise. The N on that letter in your bag. The surname 'Clyne'. The name 'Nathan', the word 'Nathaniel'. When I thought your accent could be fake it all clicked together."

The realisation she had had, on the floor before he struck her, had hit her hard. A punch to the stomach that was harder than the blow to her head that was to come. She noticed the hair on her head tightening, the blood drying.

"Nathaniel Clyne," she said, matter-of-factly. "Class 4D, St. David's Secondary School."

He spun round and looked at her in the face, his eyes darted around, trying to understand, to get some familiarity with this new piece of information. He came over right in front of her, bent down on his knees with his back straight. They were eyeball-to-eyeball again, their noses almost touching. He was looking deep into her eyes, trying to find the answer, at the back of her irises, in her soul.

"I, I don't understand," he stammered. His eyes were glazing over, his mind going back 10, maybe 15 years.

"Nathaniel Clyne. Class 4D, St. David's Secondary School," she repeated. "The school bully."

She sneered as she said this, feeling like she had the power back, despite her hands and feet tied together. He continued to search in his mind, his eyes darting left and right, his brow furrowing.

"You were a dickhead then and you're a dickhead now," she spat.

She felt strength entering her body, she had him on the ropes. He was trying to understand. She suddenly knew more than him and he felt uncomfortable. The prey had become the predator. She let the silence envelop him, letting him stew. He reached down to the floor and picked up the glass of water and took a sip. The water seemed to flow in, giving him energy. He stood upright.

"I don't know what you're talking about. I didn't go to a secondary school called St. David's." She knew he was lying. She could see through him suddenly. He was bluffing.

"*Chloe Clyne, Chloe Clyne,*" she taunted. His eyes jerked up.

"*She ain't fine. She pooped her pants all the time,*" she continued, "*with a nick nack…*"

He took a step forward and slapped her face, much harder this time. She froze her face in its landing position, looking down at the shag pile carpet. She smiled to herself.

"*…Paddy whack give a dog a bone…*" she sang, softly, purposefully.

Joe couldn't take it, his tears filled with water.

"*CHLOE CLYNE WENT ROLLING HOME*" she shouted. He hit her with a right hook, smashing her cheek and causing her to topple over with a dull thud. He slammed the door, the room shuddering as he left.

Lucy closed her eyes.

Gotcha.

Chapter Two

I leant on the kitchen worktop and took a deep breath. I went over to the sink and washed my hands. A stream of blood mingled with the flowing water down the plughole. My right hand was aching after that punch. I pulled a pint glass from the cupboard, filled it to the top and downed it, wising I had something a bit stronger. I grabbed a cloth from the cupboard underneath the sink and wiped it down, capturing the stray splashes of water. I wrung it out, threw the cloth on the tabletop and stared out into the garden.

Think.

The garden looked peaceful and tranquil; a magpie sat on the lawn, another one joined it. It hopped over and cocked its head quizzically. It flew off leaving the other on its own.

One for sorrow.

I watched it for a second, scurrying over the lawn, pecking at the grass, trying to clear my head. I tried to comprehend what Lucy had just said. How did she know what school I went to? How did she know my name? Where I lived? And how did she know that fucking rhyme? It boiled my blood. No amount of research on her part could have unearthed that, unless she spoke to people I went to school with. I thought logically. Maybe she had been playing me, at my own game. I thought of the Michael Caine film, the one where he and another con try to deceive a woman and it turns out she is conning them. I tried to figure out how it might be possible.

Had she *let* me follow her?

I went through my mind, thinking of all the different locations and places she'd been. Had she known I was looking over her shoulder at her social media? Had she been playing me? If so, it would be an incredible double bluff. The question re-entered my mind but quickly shook it away.

Impossible.

I opened the Smeg and took the half-empty milk bottle out. I unscrewed the blue lid and downed the contents, wiping away the remnants from my top lip on the back of my arm. I opened the bin and stuffed the plastic bottle inside and went back to the window.

Think, Nath, think.

I went back to my childhood, the taunting of Chloe rang in my ears the first few days I went to St. David's, the big, secondary school. She had been surrounded by bigger boys and girls, in the middle of a circle, that rhyme leaving their lips, Chloe holding her hands over her ears, eyes shut tight willing them to disappear. I was small for my age and had been too scared to go over and help her. I watched from the side-lines and hadn't done anything.

I let her suffer.

I willed my memory back to those days, squeezed my eyes shut to try and remember the faces. The memories flooded back. I pictured some of the faces, older now, having been tagged in other friends' Facebook posts. I didn't recall any girl with curly red hair. I forced my brain to go back further. The teachers, the kids, the siblings. I screamed out, not getting an answer. The magpie flew away in fright.

Who was this woman?

I tried to calm myself down. I ran the tap and scooped up water and splashed it over my face. I grabbed the cloth and wiped away the spills.

My mind transported me back to my second year. The first day back at school I had seen a group of boys and girls in a tight circle. I heard the familiar singsong of the rhyme, her surname cutting through the playground. A fire lit inside my mind. I walked up and saw Chloe in the middle, her hands on her ears again, mentally willing it to all stop. As if she could magic them away. I couldn't face seeing her like this, a victim, a mouse in the paws of a cat. Several cats all braying and taunting. My dad had been trying to toughen me up all Summer, going to boxing classes and football courses. I ran over and started yelling at the group. I swung my arms around and landed a couple of punches on the back of heads. A couple of the bigger boys towered over me and started to shove me around.

I felt like the mouse now.

They were pushing me more forcefully and I tripped over. Laughter rang in my ears. A large crowd had gathered, spurring on the fight. I stood up and took a swing at one of the boys. It landed hard and he took a step back. The crowd ooohed. The other boy came up to me from behind and put his arms around me, trapping my hands to the side. I jiggled left and right, trying to shake him off. The other boy came up, visibly angry, his face reddening with every nanosecond. He came to me fast and I leaned back putting all my weight on the boy behind, jerked my leg upwards and it landed with a thump between his legs. The crowd stepped back, turning, feeling his pain. Even the girls. I came back to the present and tried to mentally scan the faces of the girls to see if they had a resemblance to Lucy. They were all blurry in my memory. Back to the fight, the boy behind let go when he heard the crack and I spun round. He had his legs crossed and his hands over his dick, protecting them in case I tried it again. He was in a defensive position so I threw my arm out straight and it landed on his nose. He stumbled back and blood started to flow, around his mouth and onto his shirt. I spun round wildly, addressing the group.

"Leave her alone," I yelled, "leave her the fuck alone." The crowd started to disperse, keeping their distance from my crazy eyes. Chloe sat on the floor, her pink backpack resting on the ground. I picked it up and put an arm around her, leading her away from the crowd.

"Leave her the fuck alone," I shouted back again, tears brimming in my eyes. "Leave my sister alone," I called to no one as we walked to the canteen to get her some chocolate.

I snapped back to the present, tears filled my eyes at the memories. I wiped them with the back of my hand and refocused on Lucy upstairs. I still didn't get it. Those words.
4D, St. David's Secondary School, the school bully.

The headmaster came to the canteen and told us to come to his office. I remember Chloe asking if she could keep the chocolate. I was given a telling off, threatened with expulsion. I fought my innocence and he was sympathetic, looking between me and Chloe, chocolate smudged around her mouth. Innocence shone through her face.

I got a week off school but the upside was that no-one bothered Chloe, not to my knowledge anyway, certainly not to her face. I saw a change in her attitude, happier, smiling. We seemed to have gotten closer. I got a name for myself in that school and I liked the respect and the supremacy it had afforded. I had landed a knock-out blow on some GCSE kids even though I was two years younger. I used this to my advantage, drunk on power, and messed with other kids, not really knowing where the line between too far and joking around was. Sometimes I went over the line, sometimes not far enough. Sometimes there were tears, sometimes there were visits to the headmaster, my mum sitting in front of his big desk, disappointed in me.

I tried to focus back to Year 4.

4D.

That was the name of the year class I had been in. I scanned through the kids in my class, pictured the classroom and children sitting on chairs, trying to recollect a connection with the redhead upstairs. I was failing. I took my MacBook Air out of a drawer and fired up Facebook. I scrolled through the names of 'friends' trying to jog my memory. I clicked on a few from school and looked through their profile, seeing if I could spot her, searching to see if her face popped up in any of their photos. This was impossible. A needle in a global haystack. I scratched my head, trying to figure out where I had gone wrong in my research with Lucy. Lucy, who was upstairs now, facing my big secret with blood clotting around her head. The place where I hit her. I was always so careful, never bringing girls back here. She found me. I don't know how but she did. The first time I had missed something, been careless somewhere along the line. I weighed up my options. She would go to the police, there was no doubt about that. Another option was to kill her. I shook it from my mind.

Don't be so bloody ridiculous Nath.

Too many cops shows on Netflix.

Idiot.

I decided to go back upstairs, look in her eyes again, to see if I could work it out. Maybe she would say a bit more, a word that would jolt a memory. Let me get to an answer.

I walked up the stairs, purposely being heavy with my feet to let her know I was coming. I swung the door open so it made a bang. Jolt her. Make her scared. She was still lying on the floor from when I had hit her. I could see her hands tied behind her. Those hands that I was caressing not too long ago. Her head was flopped forward, her bright red curls hanging over her face, her breath moved them millimetres back and forth. At least she wasn't dead. I walked round to face her. Her eyes were closed. I put my hand under her chin and lifted her face up. Her eyes rolled in their sockets and then they focused upon me. I felt a pang in my stomach. Those eyes. The locks of her curly hair fell over them in a cute spring, covering half of an eye. I tucked them behind her ear, a small gold round earring piercing the lobe. I liked the feel of her hair. The smell of candyfloss hit my nose. I must remember to cut another bit off. She swallowed and opened her mouth to speak. I swear I saw a small smile.

"I'm hungry Joe," she said, her eyes penetrating mine. I mentally scanned the cupboards downstairs and the Smeg, knowing they were all empty. I heaved the chair upright with an effort and looked her in the eye.

"Who are you?"

"I'm hungry," she repeated. I got angry at the insolence. I took a step forward and she winced, expecting another slap. *Good, behave* I thought in my head. Instead, I put my hands on her shoulders and shook them, yelling in her face, spittle shooting out and landing on her nose.

"WHO ARE YOU?" I screamed over and over again. She smirked, thinking she was winning the battle.

"You haven't worked it out yet have you?" she said mockingly, softly, almost too quiet to hear. She was still playing with me. The shouting didn't seem to bother her. I landed another slap on her face, hoping she would submit. Her face froze looking down again. She slowly lifted her head up and shook her head, the curls dancing over her shoulders. Her eyes flashed a defiance, an evil look appeared.

"*Chloe Clyne, Chloe Clyne...*" she started to sing and I gave her another full hander. This time my palm stung.

"Joe," she said, power rising in her voice. "Or Nath, or Nathaniel, or Nathan. Or whatever other name you go by. Even if I told you, what are you going to do with me, huh? Have you thought about that? I know your dirty little secret," She glanced at the files behind me.

"I'm sure the police would be very interested in your little room. It'll be all over Facebook and all your chums will see what a conniving little shit you are. You think your employers are going to let that go? A local stalker will definitely make the front pages."

The word 'stalker' struck me like a strange word.

"I'm not a stalker," I said slowly, deliberately. There was a pause, she looked at me disbelievingly, her eyes burned through as if I was the biggest dickhead in the world.

"I'm not sure how else the police will classify you Joe. Hundreds of photos of women in your house, all filed and sorted? By alpha-flipping-betical order. Do you think these women know you took these photos? I'm sure if they asked them it will all unravel. You're a fraud Joe. A shitty little criminal. What's the going jail term for stalking and beating up a woman?"

She tutted loudly and rolled her eyes. I saw how it looked from her perspective. From the police's perspective. I turned to the window again, looked out across the backs of rows of terraced houses, close enough to almost see into each other's rooms. I looked down and saw my lawn. The two magpies were back, making a merry dance around each other. I mulled what Lucy had just said and I had an idea.

Two for joy.

Chapter Three

Joe abruptly left the room. He had been looking out of the window when she was laying out the impossible situation he was in. All those photos, all those mementos, all that *evidence*. There was no way out for him. He was busted. She heard the front door slam shut and the place went quiet. She heard a couple of birds cooing outside, saw white fluffy clouds rolling over the rooftops against a bright blue sky. It must be getting to late afternoon. The sun was starting to come around to this side of the house, shadows glanced on the walls, the cross in the window creeping across her chest, like the crosshairs of a gunsight.

She took a deep breath.

Her hair was plastered against her head, the throbbing sensation had faded replaced by the hot sting across her face. She looked up at all the box files, her mind racing with all the women he had manipulated. What other acts had he performed, personas he had created, lies he had told. How many have there been before her? These may just be the successful ones, what about the unsuccessful ones, or even the practice ones? She thought about what she would do when she got out of the room. She would go straight to the police of course. She would run through the accusations and tell them to come to this room and find all the evidence they needed. They could find the women in the files and interview them. It would all unravel and he would be banged up.

Good, he deserved it.

She thought about prison, what it would be like to be locked up, confined and lonely. How you wanted to burst out, tell the world, but you were trapped. Like her right now. Like her before she even met Joe.

She heard the yapping of a dog in the next-door garden.

Margaret.

She yelled, she screamed, she hollered. She jumped up and down on the chair, banging the legs on the carpet but all they made was a muffled sound. She screamed until her throat hurt, screeching for help. She heard a noise and she turned her head, listening for a sound. She craned her neck round, trying to get her ear closer to the door, alert, straining for a rescuing noise of some sort. She heard a key scrape in the lock. She thought it might be Margaret coming to investigate but realised she still had her key. She heard Joe's voice; no, it was Nathaniel's. English. He was talking cheerfully, apologising, saying he must have left the radio on. He said he would go and turn it down and apologised again for disturbing her. She imagined Margaret peering around the door into the hallway, seeing if she could see any signs of a disturbance, looking for her.

She heard Joe clattering about downstairs. Metal on metal. She heard the bi-folding doors slide open and then silence. Then she heard him coming in and out the garden, that metallic sound again. Through the window she could hear him pottering about outside, things being thrown in a metal container. He came back into the house and heard his footsteps on the wooden stairs. He came into the room and went to the wall with all the files on, not looking at Lucy.

"I'm hungry," she pleaded, but he ignored her. He grabbed two of the first box files on the top shelf - Abi and Anna and took them away, running down the stairs two at a time. She noticed he still had the blood-stained t-shirt on and hoped Margaret had noticed it. He disappeared and she heard the clang of the metal container again. He came back up and took two more – Beth and Briony – and left the room again. Her mind tried to figure out what he was doing. This time it took longer for him to bound up the stairs. He took two more off the shelf, turned, then looked out the window. He put the files down, moved toward it and opened it in one quick sweep. The fresh air rushed into the room, a warm feel on her face. She smelt burning. She looked out and saw white smoke rising outside the window, coming from his garden. He picked up the two box files and threw them out the window. Then he took three at a time and threw them out the window. Every single one bar one. The one in the middle.

The one with *Lucy* written on the side.

It was staring at her, taunting. He left the room and Lucy watched the smoke. It grew in intensity every now and then, sometimes singed paper flew through the window. All the evidence was going up in flames. She was stuck in this room, arms and legs tied, her name staring out at her from the white label.

Except it wasn't her name.

Not really.

Chapter Four

I watched the flames lick up the metal dustbin I had just bought from the hardware shop along the high street, along with firelighters, lighter fluid and matches. The aluminium bin was light so it was easy to carry home, bouncing on my legs as I hurried back. As I approached the house, I saw Margaret moseying outside.

Christ, what did she want?

She was peering through my front windows.

Nosy cow.

I called after her and she jolted around to face me. I waved cheerfully, a look of concern growing on her face to match mine.

"Everything ok Margaret? I asked. She eyed the metal bin and my blood-spotted shirt.

"Yes dear. I thought I heard shouting from your place, just making sure you were alright. No burglars or anything like that."

"Oh, I hope not!" I chuckled nervously, her face showing a touch of terror in case there were. Any burglar would have the fright of their life seeing Lucy in the room all tied up.

"Don't worry Margaret, I'll go and investigate."

I pushed the key into the lock and turned it. I spun round.

"Oh, I left the radio on. I'm so sorry. I had it turned up whilst I was doing some painting. I'm so sorry, I'll go and turn it down. Thanks for checking!"

I went in quickly, seeing her eyes peering around the door, saying *"did you see that lady, she's still got my key"* as I slammed the door shut. I took the bin out the back, piled in some paper and wood lying around the garden and threw in firelighters, spraying lighter fluid on it to get it going. Flames licked up but there wasn't enough fuel to burn. I raced upstairs and grabbed two of the box files, flew down the stairs and chucked them on the fire. Again, I squirted lighter fluid over them and they burst into flames, orange and red danced around the edges of the cardboard and reflected in the shiny metal. I ran back upstairs and seized two more and threw them on the fire. They caught after a few seconds to the other one's flames. The new ones collapsed down on the other files, eyes looking up at me, beautiful eyes and memories of nice nights and conquests. A smell of singed hair rose up too. I watched them for a second then raced back up the stairs. Lucy turned around as far she could to catch my eye. I could see panic in her eyes, her plan – *the evidence* – literally going up in smoke. I took two more files from the shelf but realised it was quicker to throw them out the window. I took all the box files and flung them out the window. I left Lucy's one as that was not quite finished yet.

Back in the garden I tossed each file into the burning bin when there was space. Whilst I waited, I opened the files and flicked through the papers and touched the locks of hair. They brought back happy memories. These were the ones I worked hard for. Weeks of patience, meticulous planning followed by thinking on the spur of the moment. You never knew what was going to happen until you took the plunge. There was only so much preparation you could do before you realised you were ready, went out and put your plan into action. A bit like preparing for an exam. The first interaction was always the most nerve-wracking. Had I got the clothes right, the look correct, the backstory believable? After the first hour or so I could gauge if I had hooked them. Then I could start to relax and riff a bit more. There were so many facts I needed to memorise so they didn't trip me up later down the line and I got found out. So, I kept the details sketchy and if they probed for more info, I was flaky and said I didn't want to talk about it. Bizarrely it gave off an emotional vibe, an endearing, sensitive quality that the women purred over.

I remembered all the dinners and lunches I had had, holding hands and kissing, cuddling and the sex. I watched all those physical memories burn up in front me. I kept adding the files to the fire, the flames reached up past my head. By the time

I had chucked on the last one, the fading light of the day was disappearing over the rooftops. I let the last one burn and went upstairs. My clothes stank of smoke and the few drops of blood Lucy had spat at me were dry.

I went into the spare room. Lucy's head was slumped forward again, her curls hanging in front of her forehead. A look of defeat. I pulled the locks back and stroked her hair. Dried blood clumped strands together. She opened her eyes and looked at me. They were red raw. I noticed streaks down her cheeks. I forcibly turned her face towards the window, smoke still rising up from the garden. Her eyes drifted open. My fingers gripped her skin tightly to hold her and looked at her square in the eyes. A shadow came across her, where I blocked out a last ray of sunlight. She looked crushed, down. I grinned a big grin. I was feeling victorious, a success. Her eyes slowly looked up to mine and, squeezed between my hands, her lips creased into a smile.

Chapter Five

Lucy must have fallen asleep as the next time she woke up it was almost dark outside. Joe had his hand on her chin and cheek squeezing them together, forcing her to look out the window. She saw the line of smoke from all the burning he had done. That's all the evidence gone then. He was grinning a stupid grin, thinking he had won, that he had got one over on her. In retaliation, she squeezed a smile through his hand on her chin, taunting him. He started calling her derogatory names. Playground names. Her mind wandered back to school, of him in his navy-blue blazer, ruling the roost in the playground, his disabled sister moved to a different school. He swaggered around the chair, calling out vile names to see if he got a reaction. She gave him one.

"3A," she said. He stopped still.

"What?" he asked.

"3A," she repeated. "That's what class I was in. At St. David's." He went over to the bookshelf, empty except for one, and rested his elbow on a vacant shelf, his hand rubbing his chin and mouth, pondering.

"What year?" he asked at last.

"The same year you were in 4D," she replied. His eyes widened. His eyes were flickering back to his past. He looked at her, still blank.

"So, what about it?" he sniffed.

"You still don't remember me, do you?" He looked at her incredulously.

"No, Lucy, I fucking don't. Do you mind telling me what the fuck you are on about?" he yelled. A bird fluttered away past the open window. He walked over and shut it with a slam. She sighed and took a breath.

"I was in 3A. I had moved down from Nottingham, from a school I liked. My dad got a job down here so we followed." He stopped her.

"You didn't tell me you went to school down here. You never said you lived in London," he pointed at her accusingly.

"I'm not sure you are the one to tell me about telling the truth. *Joe.*" He stepped back and rested his arm back on the shelf, allowing her to continue.

"I was only down here for a year. It was a shit time. No thanks in part to you." His eyes furrowed, looking confused. He still had no idea.

"My dad got a job but hated it and they didn't like him. It wasn't what it was billed to be. Long hours. I was causing him stress too, going through my own teenage issues. He started to drink more. Got a bit violent towards my mum, sometimes me. I was forced to go to this new school, away from all my friends. I was pretty shy and homesick so I found it difficult to make friends. Especially with this hair." She glanced up with her eyes, her hands and feet still tied.

"It didn't help that my body was changing, from a child to an adult. I was getting confused and angry, things were growing bigger and hair was sprouting out from places, my voice changed. It was awkward, I was an awkward shape. I didn't know who I was turning into and I didn't like it. I had to go to school and I got taunted because of my red hair. Kids pulled it and mocked me." She looked up at him, boring her eyes into him.

"But your hair is gorgeous!" he said, surprising himself.

"Well, you didn't think so then," she replied back curtly.

He looked embarrassed. It wouldn't have been unusual, any excuse to give a kid a kicking.

"Look, my arms are hurting Joe. Loosen me," she pleaded, trying to take advantage of his guilt. He shook his head.

"I don't remember any red headed girl at school called Lucy," he said, still trying to piece it altogether. "I think you are lying."

He turned and looked at the empty shelves.

"That's because at school my name wasn't Lucy," she replied. "It was Lee."

Chapter Six

My legs buckled underneath me. I fell to the floor and looked up at Lucy. Lee. Lucy. Her deep dark eyes were penetrating me, her gorgeous red curls flopping over her eyes. I searched around her face, trying to understand. I tried to find clues, the cleft chin, the cheekbones, the jawline. They all said 'Lucy' to me. I forced my mind to go back to school. A redhead called Lee. I searched my memory. A flash zipped into my brain. I said it before I realised.

"Gay Lee," I blurted out.

Lucy nodded.

She slowly sing-songed, "Gay Lee, Gay Lee sitting in a tree. K.I.S.S.I.N.G."

My mind soared back to school, that rhyme. That rhyme with my sisters' one. It rang and rang around in my head.

"You're Gay Lee?!" I spluttered. She nodded.

"But… but… WHAT?" I shouted, perplexity etched over my entire face.

"Around that time, I was confused who I was. My body was changing and things were getting more, erm, manly. I didn't feel comfortable in my skin. I fancied boys. I fancied you Nathan." I stepped back in shock, banging against the shelves.

"When I saw you in Starbucks, I thought you looked, well, familiar. I couldn't place you, and when you spoke with that accent it went from my mind. It was only when I saw all these things, the lies, the younger photos of you." She nodded up at the bare walls. The file 'Lucy' looked out of place on its own.

"I thought you might have fancied me too. I thought all your bravado was an act. Bullying the gay boy when you in fact were gay too. I thought you were suppressing it and being nasty to me was your way of bottling it up. My dad reacted the same way as you just did and it just wouldn't sink in. I went to a few self-help groups and saw a therapist. Being gay was a lot less common up north than it is nowadays. I tried to manage it, deal with it, but I just wasn't comfortable with my body. I knew it had to change. It took me five years: five years of therapy, self-help, doubt and questions before I was finally allowed to have the hormones and then the operations. I came down to London to visit doctors and therapists: this is where all the best ones are apparently, and so many support groups. But my dad couldn't understand. Five years of arguments, shouting and tears.

"My dad tried to change my mind, beating it out of me. As part of the process, they force you to live in your preferred gender for two years and one time I came home in a red dress. I didn't realise quite how much he had drunk that day and he flew into a rage. He beat me with a belt. My mum didn't know how to handle having a gay son either. In the end he just couldn't handle it but Mum eventually came around. I was always Lee to them – always was, always will be. Dad left in such a rage that day the door fell off the hinges. I haven't seen him since."

My mind shot back to my dad, abandoning Mum and Chloe to fend for themselves. *What if Chloe had come out 'normal'.*

"Then I had the operations. After it happened, I felt new, alive, who I was supposed to be."

The thought of an operation focused me back to the reality. I looked at her disbelievingly. Him. Her. I started to feel sick. What had I done? No wonder she didn't want to have sex – I had no idea what would be *down there*. Bile built up in my stomach. I ran to the bathroom and vomited into the toilet basin. Lucy was a man. She had had operations. Wait, he had an operation to change him into a her. And I had fallen for her. Kissed her, caressed her. More bile came to the surface. I flushed the loo and leant back against the wall. I was starting to get a headache, a dull thump at the back of my head. My brain was full, trying to understand everything I had just been told. Lucy was Lee. I had bullied Lee at school, years ago, taunting him for being gay *and* a ginger. He became Lucy, and I followed her around, trying to get her to sleep with me.

No, him.

And I fell in love with him.

A trans.

I reached over to the basin and puked more. My head was ready to explode.

I wiped my mouth with water and went back into the room. Lucy's back was towards me, her red curls brushing against her pale neck. I still couldn't see it. Even her legs were slender, girl-like. I went around and faced her. She looked so innocent, so *feminine*. The person that I had fallen in love with. The idea that she used to be a man evaporated seeing her so vulnerable and so beautiful. I sank into her eyes once more. She had been crying again. Instinctively I wrapped my arms around her and tightly held her close to me. She let out a small cry of pain, her arms strained behind her. I smelled her hair and rubbed her cheek against mine. She responded and rubbed her head back and forth, caressing her cheek against mine, turning her head so her lips were closer to mine. I let her kiss my lips.

So tender.

Tears flowed down my cheeks. I suddenly jerked away and punched her in the mouth. I didn't even mean it. It was like I was outside of my body watching me do it. Again and again and again. She toppled over on the chair and I sat astride her, pummelling her face. Tears were streaking down my face, rivers flowing, red mist was covering my face.

Anger, rage, fury, fire.

Her face transformed into my father's. I was shouting. *WHY DID YOU LEAVE US DAD?*

It was all coming out.

YOU BASTARD!

He was screaming, begging me to stop. Then his face morphed into Chloe's and I fell off her, disgusted. Apologising.

I curled up into a ball in the corner looking out of the side of my eyes at the bloodied face on my carpet, her head at an odd angle. There was Chloe, all alone, rocking back and forth. I crawled over to her and moved her bloodied, wet hair from her cut-up face, her heavy breaths cutting the silence, her chest rising and falling.

"I love you Lucy, I love you," I sobbed. "Forgive me and I'll forgive you."

Tears dropped onto her cheek and I wiped them away with the back of my hand, blood smudging across her pale skin. She let out a groan and one eye slowly opened, the other swollen shut. I laid down next to her, our noses almost touching.

"It's ok Lucy. I'm sorry, I'm so sorry Lucy." I kissed her on her lips, on her cheeks and her wet eyes, smoothing down her hair.

"I want to be with you. I love you. I'll do anything. I'll be honest with you forever." The words spilled out from my mouth, like I didn't have any control of what I was saying.

"Please Lucy, please. Say something."

As her eye shut, I put my forehead on carpet and began thumping the floor with my fists, like a petulant child not getting their way.

BANG BANG BANG

I stopped but the thumping seemed to continue.

BANG BANG BANG

I sat up straight and listened.

BANG BANG BANG

It was the front door. I froze. The thudding continued.

BANG BANG BANG

Lucy groaned and moved her head. I got up and shook my hand, my knuckles cut and raw from her teeth. I tiptoed down the stairs and opened the door a couple of inches. A tall broad policeman stood in the doorway.

He looked familiar.

My eyes were still wet, blurry. A policewoman was on the street by a parked squad car, blue lights flashing in the dark street. Curtains twitched. My mind started swirling, images and shapes came in front of me. A Margaret-shaped figure was peering over the wall between us. They both looked in, down the hall, looking for anything suspicious. My brain was going crazy, going in and out of focus. Everyone looked familiar, yet not at all.

School?

The policeman's eyes dropped, spying the flecks of dried blood on my white shirt and saw my cut and bloodied hand hanging loosely by my side. He looked back up to my eyes.

Yep, I recognise you. Where from?
He removed his helmet.
"We've had reports of a disturbance," he said.
My eyes started to focus.
May we come in Sir?" he said.
I felt my eyes widen in recognition.
That tosser from the bar.

Part Four

'Josh'

Call it intuition. If you want, call it luck. But for me it was gut instinct from being on the force for over ten years. And it was my first case of being completely right. I still couldn't stop grinning.

My partner came over and squeezed my shoulder as I finished up the paperwork after the arrest of Nathaniel Clyne.

"Great work you," she said as she plonked a chipped mug of strong coffee down next to my antiquated police-issued computer. "You're rising quicker than Tesla stock."

"And it'll come down quicker than Blockbuster if I don't dot the I's and cross the T's," I said. For a not-yet-thirty-year-old police officer, Tricia Thomas was hot on the stock exchange, choosing to manage her pension pot into her own multi-varied investment portfolio. She was a smart cookie and shunned the corporate dog-eat-dog world for public service instead. The first in her family to join the force.

"Nah, you were born to do this Nicholson. I wish I had your instinct. I wouldn't even have looked twice at him."

She was referring to my first suspicions of the perpetrator the night I had met Lucy in the new bar on the South Bank. I had spotted a man who seemed to be watching Lucy from afar, hiding in dark corners. Decked out in a very nice suit and a flashy watch. He reminded me of a stereotypical young banker. Like Charlie Sheen in Wall Street, minus the red braces. Actually, I wouldn't have been surprised if he had been wearing red braces underneath that very snazzy jacket.

I had been slightly the worse for wear that night, being off-duty and trying to relax with a night off with the lads. So, I couldn't be certain if he was dodgy or if I was imaging it due to the amount of drink I had imbibed. When she went to the toilets my eyes followed her. Not sure if it was the drink but I seriously couldn't tell. I mean, my sober brain knew it was Lee walking over to the bathrooms, almost accidentally going into the men's instead of the women's, but my impaired brain was getting the testosterone flowing. From behind you just wouldn't have known. The man hovered outside the bathrooms, watching like a hawk, and when Lee emerged, his demeanour changed. His back straightened and his eyes focused. Alert. Ready to pounce. My stomach did a flip. I remembered back to university – the fights, the name-calling, the venom lads used to direct at the gays and lesbians. The times I had bowled over to break them up. Adrenalin flowing. That had been my first inkling that I wanted to become a police officer. Restoring the status quo, calming hot heads, attempting to show reason. Except this man didn't do anything. Just watched.

When Lee came back from the toilet, he was all over the place. Sorry, I should say Lucy. It's still quite confusing for me. Like calling your new girlfriend by your ex's name. So, Lucy came back from the bathrooms, looking wasted. I did wonder if she'd taken something in the toilets. Other women at this party were definitely taking something. I had seen the effects of drugs and alcohol on well-to-do posh boys right through to the homeless and addicts. Crime scene photos are not a pretty picture. Worse in the flesh. She made her excuses to go home and to be honest I was disappointed. I had enjoyed her company and the night was still young. I suspected she wasn't using: Free champagne in a new bar, plus moving to the big smoke, plus everything else that was going on would have been huge for her. We came together for a goodbye hug and I saw the man agitatedly dancing from one foot to the other, looking in our direction. I told her to be careful and to call me anytime.

Genuinely, I really wished she would.

As she left the bar, I looked around for the man, but it was a busy place, with so many blokes in dark suits I couldn't spot him. My mates called me over, and I gave them the toilet-break signal, which I used to take a lap of the bar. He had disappeared so I helped myself to a passing champagne flute and joined up with the gang just as the music notched up another gear. In what seemed a matter of minutes I spotted him with a group of other expensive-looking suits. It must have been my imagination, I thought. These things happen after a few free drinks.

***

"Can you describe him please?" Tricia said, moving uncomfortably in her seat in the interview room at the police station. It was her code for another time waster. It had been a few months since I had seen Lucy at the bar. I had put in a good word with an old uni mate of mine to help her out with some work. It sounded like she had got it.

"Yeah, easily. About six foot, maybe a little shorter. Shaved brown hair and a little goatee." Tricia glanced at me. I could read her eyes.

"Was he white? Black? Asian?

"Oh, I see. White."

"And remind me again why you think he stalked you?"

"I don't know really. I just have this feeling. You know sometimes you are being watched?"

"Unfortunately, it's difficult to uphold a feeling in a court of law." I could feel the prickliness in her voice. The number of timewasters we have had to interview over the years can be overpowering at times. Trish never seemed to hide her frustrations.

"What PC Thomas means," I interrupted, "is that we need hard evidence. From what you have told us, everything was consensual." I flicked my notebook pages over.

"You willingly had dinner with him. Twice. You invited him back to your house. You had consensual sex. Twice. The only thing he didn't do was text you back." I could see Tricia suppress a giggle. Tears formed in the eyes of the woman sitting opposite. Blonde hair, high cheekbones, piercing green eyes.

"I know. But I saw him again a few weeks later. Except he wasn't, erm, him. He was different. Like he was an actor who had changed his costume."

"Are you sure it was him?"

"Definitely. It was in a bar in Canary Wharf. I went over to him. He claimed he didn't know who I was. But I could see it in his eyes. His eyes, they were the same. You can tell. But he was different. Different clothes, different haircut. I know it was him."

"The bit I don't understand," Tricia said, "is how did you conclude he was a stalker." The blonde bit her lip.

"Well...." She suddenly looked sheepish. "I read an article on Buzzfeed. It was about this guy that changed into a woman's perfect man. Changed everything. He follows them, goes through their bins, looks at their social media. And then...."

"Yes?"

"Well, sleeps with them." Tricia rolled her eyes up at the strip lighting.

"PC Nicholson here will take your details and a statement, write it up for our files. If something comes up, I promise I'll let you know." She stood up. Her eyes told me this was for me and left the interview room. I took a deep breath and readied myself to do my public service.

"Can you please describe this man again for me. To make sure I have everything correct."

Yeah, yeah," she said, looking at the door Tricia had walked through. "She doesn't believe me, does she?"

"Well, she doesn't *not* believe you. We need a lot of evidence to convict anyone. And that's difficult with the details you have given us so far. So, you said he had a shaved head."

"Yes. Yeah, he did. Although when I caught him in the restaurant it wasn't shaven. And he didn't have a goatee. He was clean shaven. Side-parting, light brown hair. Had this really expensive suit on and a watch that probably cost more than my flat. Slicked back hair. If I could have guessed, I would have said he was a banker."

A pulse flicked through me. Enough to pique my subconscious but not enough to join the dots. Yet.

"I see. Please go on."

An hour later, I dropped her statement on Tricia's desk.

"Flipping heck Nicholson, you've been gone a wh ... Ah." She put the end of her pen in her mouth and swivelled round. "Well, that's a long statement you've taken for a delusional story. But I guess pretty blondes love a man in uniform. Especially one that gives them all the attention they want. Did you get her number?"

"Haha," I replied, feeling my face go warm. "Very funny. And that wouldn't be at all appropriate."

Regardless of Tricia's comments, something festered in my mind and suddenly I had an overwhelming concern for Lucy. I called my mate Jonathan and asked how she was settling in at his firm. Apparently, all good. A few snarky comments from some of the people who had been able to tell but he had nipped it in the bud. Her direct line manager, Emma, was keeping a very close eye on her.

"It does wonders for our diversity and equality policy," he tried to joke but I could feel the crassness of the comment down the phone line. I could only imagine what Lee had been through after uni, and then during the change to becoming a female. Over the last few years, the odd post had come up on Facebook, showing her transformation. And when I had seen her in the flesh, I had been amazed at the effectiveness of it. Obviously, I could still tell, and my mates said afterwards that they could see it a mile off. But after a few drinks... well, it would be difficult to know....

Immediately after his cringe worthy comment, Jonathan suggested we met up for an after-work drink. It would give me an opportunity to check up on Lucy. See her again. Make sure she was alright. I said I'd come over to his office on my next day off.

It was a bright sunny day as I navigated through Covent Garden. My shifts on the beat in this part of town were usually at night, when extra officers were needed as the pubs and theatre-goers spilled out onto the streets. Trouble always seems to arise when people converge in small spaces. And the usual types of trouble were caused by alcohol and pickpockets. So, it was different to see the grimy buildings in daylight, the shopfronts devoid of neon and in their natural state. It felt like they were having a fag around the back, in their dressing gown with no make-up on. Which is why the sight of a very smartly dressed man, leaning against a fast-food restaurant window holding the Financial Times stood out like a sore thumb.

Perhaps it was the confluence of the memory of the blonde's statement, a glimmer of recognition of the man at the bar eyeing up Lucy or the fact that he was absolutely, definitely not reading the newspaper – just holding it out and peering over its top. Like a spy in that Hitchcock film.

I crossed the road and watched him from afar. Waiting, like he was.

A few moments later, the man straightened his back, craned his neck and folded his newspaper. I looked to see what he had been looking at. And then I saw her. Red curls bouncing around her shoulders in time with her steps as she walked. Her curves. Her conservative dress. Her look.

It felt like I was in riot gear, watching a fight kick off and knowing the signal to get stuck in was imminent. Every hair stood to attention. A pulsation coursed through my veins. Things started to narrow into focus.

I followed them across Hungerford Bridge. As I did, I texted Jonathan to ditch our drink, telling him something had come up. Well, something had come up.

An instinct.

A gut feel.

The man was a few paces behind Lucy, ducking and weaving in the flow of commuters going home. Reaching the station, I was a few paces behind him, although I could clearly see Lucy's red curls ahead of us. She got on a train, and the man jumped on too. I walked past them and got on at the next set of doors. I could see them both. He was stood directly behind her, looking over her shoulder as she nonchalantly flicked through her phone. I swear I saw him take a big sniff of her hair, closing his eyes as he did so. A sudden rush of passengers squeezed into our carriage, squashing up against each other. I almost lost my footing as I strained my neck to keep an eye on them. He was almost on top of her now, a smile on his face as other passengers pushed him onto her. She was oblivious.

At the third stop, when the doors opened, the crowd heaved out, spilling half the carriage onto the platform. The man followed Lucy off the train and I struggled to exit with people blocking me. By the time I got to the ticket barriers, the crowd was too thick as they bottlenecked at the turnstiles. I looked through the busy throngs but I was too late.

They were gone.

"Don't scoff," I said to Tricia the next day. "But you remember that blonde woman who said she was being stalked…?"

Tricia scoffed.

"I don't remember the details, Nicholson, as much as you surely do." She busied herself at her workstation.

"Yeah well. It might be nothing but check this out." I relayed what I had seen the evening before. She sighed. A pause. "Well?"

She pondered for a second. "What have you seen? A guy that walked in the same direction as someone. Who got on the same train. Who got off at the same station."

"Yeah but,"

"No buts, Josh." She rolled her eyes. "I think the blonde is playing on your mind. I understand that you know this man – sorry, woman. Probably have concerns for her safety. You're a good man Nicholson. But right now, there isn't anything there except some very loose connections. Connections that are in your mind. You may be seeing what you want to see. My advice? Keep an eye on it if you want. In your spare time. We don't have the resource. Or the time." She turned back to her computer screen.

"Have you finished the report on the Green Man estate from last week?"

I sighed. "No not yet."

"I suggest you make that your priority. There's a lot to do to get a conviction. We need to be meticulous."

"I hate paperwork," I sulked. "I'd rather be out on the streets than sat in front of the computer. I swear they've dumped it all on us."

"Yeah, I know. Turn your frustrations into opportunities. This is a biggie for us."

And it was a biggie too. Tricia and I were seconded as SOCOs to be part of an early morning drugs bust to collect forensic evidence. It was a big deal so we wanted everything to be just right. And that meant filling out the mountains of paperwork. It wasn't just crossing and dotting the 'I's and 'T's. It was re-reading, fine-tooth comb stuff, reassess-every-action-and-word paperwork. It consumed me, and Lucy disappeared from my mind.

It wasn't until a few weeks later that, by sheer coincidence, I was in Westfield Shopping Centre on a day off that I swear I spotted the man that had followed Lucy. If I was a witness giving a statement, I would have described his attire as 'expensive'. It was just a plain white t-shirt, jeans and brown shoes, but they screamed designer. Yet he was in the Vans shoe store which seemed out of place for a man wearing very high-end clothes.

The tingling sensation in my stomach couldn't be ignored. My heartbeat quickened and I felt my cheeks warm.

So, I followed him as he went into Nike, then Jack Wills, keeping my distance. As I waited, the hairs on my arm stood on end. Alert. It felt like a stakeout. He exited carrying shopping bags and I followed him to the up-scale part of the shopping centre where I watched him drink two flutes of champagne in quick succession. Then I trailed him all the way to a house in Ealing.

Nathaniel Clyne.

I had managed to work a favour in order to get the name of the homeowner of the Ealing house. Information is pretty easy to get when you know who to ask. He works for a high-end financial institution in the City. He has no priors, just an alleged fraud and a couple of cautions for fighting. He had a sister who had died a few years ago after a car accident. Nothing suspicious in the notes. The database didn't spit out anything of relevance when cross-checked to stalking cases, or reports. Nothing came up matching his description. In between long shifts, and when I got the chance, I went to the house to check up on him. Either his lights were out or there was no movement. I was hesitant to speak to Tricia about it just yet. Let's get some hard evidence first.

It was on my eighth visit to Clyne's house, early one morning, that I spotted him leaving. I had just finished my shift, changed into my civvies and had an inkling that I ought to check up on him. Just something in my body told me I should.

When he emerged, Clyne was dressed exceptionally casually including a rucksack, Nike trainers, a Jack Wills hoodie. My mind raced back to Westfield and a buzz trickled down my spine.

It felt like something was going to happen.

As I followed him down the street, I paid for parking on my phone, hoping I wouldn't need to extend my mortgage for the bill. He got on the tube and eventually settled in a Starbucks on the Strand. As he took out a silver MacBook from his bag and busied himself by tapping away on the keys, I ordered a drink and settled down at a table on the other side of the café, keeping my face hidden under a baseball cap.

A full hour later, a woman tried to sit on the chair that was occupied by his rucksack. Clyne flustered her away just as Lucy entered the doors. He looked up quickly at her and then busied himself on his laptop.

This was interesting.

A bolt of energy seemed to shoot through the air. After she got her drink, she looked around the café, approached Clyne's table and he offered the empty chair.

Honey to the bee.

They started chatting. His demeanour changed to what I had previously seen: shy, humble, reserved. He looked like a completely different person to the one who had been going in and out of his Ealing house, with the reputation of a bank: to someone who seemed shy, humble and reserved.

This was the act.

This must have been their first encounter. It was strange – there was an awkwardness to them – a lot of looking at each other, not a lot of words seemed to be spoken.

All of a sudden, Lucy seemed to panic and left the café.

I wondered if she'd rumbled him. Clyne then gathered his things and left in the opposite direction. I thought about running after Lucy, to see what was going on but dismissed it. What would I say? I needed to wait a little longer. I followed Clyne back to Ealing, where he spent an hour in a massage parlour and then returned to his house. Nothing happened. Time ticked on. The previous night's shift weighed down on me and I fell asleep.

It was close to midnight when I woke, in a daze, not knowing where I was. I saw Clyne walking up his front path, then the lights going on, him drawing the upstairs curtains and then the lights going off. I yawned, switched on the ignition and pulled out to go home, trying not to think about how much money I'd put in the meter.

The next morning, I again sat in Starbucks, in the same seat as the previous day, wearing a different coloured baseball cap. I was channelling American cop shows. Lucy breezed in at 08:45, a spring in her step wearing a pretty white dress. Clyne was not present yet something seemed off. Again, I resisted the urge to speak to Lucy. She sat down at a vacant table and I waited a few minutes to see if Clyne turned up. He didn't so I left the café, crossed the road and took up a spot opposite. My instincts were that Clyne was here, watching her. I surveyed the street, looking for anything unusual. There was so much motion, cars and buses, people, mopeds that it was a blur. I shook my head. Clyne wouldn't be moving. I scanned the environment for still people. A homeless person was lying along a wall, a man stood by a stack of newspapers and a smartly dressed man was leaning against a shop window. I glanced back at him.

Bingo.

There was Clyne. I quickly moved out of his line of sight, hoping that he hadn't spotted me. Suddenly, Clyne half turned away, shielding himself. Lucy was leaving Starbucks. She disappeared around the corner, then Clyne turned, watched her go and then headed off down the steps to the tube. I too, hurried down the stairs almost falling over him as I turned the corner.

Literally.

He was bending down, tying up his shoelace. My heart jumped up into my mouth. I muttered an apology, hearing a *"watch it prick"* as I darted away. I was in front of him now, so pressed a few buttons on the ticket machines, trying to look at the reflection in the screen, half-turning my head. But I didn't see him. I'd lost him. I couldn't tail Clyne, but I could follow Lucy. I just needed to know her movements. And I knew who to ask.

Right on cue, at 11:30am that morning, Lucy and her colleague Jessica exited their office. An Uber scooped them up, ready to take them to St Pancras for a client lunch. Jonathan had been kind enough to give the details, even swapping a few things around for me. When the car sped off, I saw Clyne leave a café in a panic on the opposite side of the road.

So that's where he was hiding.

Again, on cue, a black cab peeped its bonnet around the corner and Clyne waved it down.

Clockwork.

I had them all where I wanted. The chase was on. I walked briskly to the Strand to jump on the Northern line – I had some time to catch them up, plus I was still on my own expense –the taxis drivers had already been briefed to take their time.

When I arrived at the restaurant in the St Pancras hotel, I saw that their clients – a male and a female – were sitting at the table I had instructed the maître d' to use after I had called ahead. He sat me at a table that gave a perfect view of the entire room. Several minutes later, Lucy and Jessica arrived and sat with their clients. A full ten minutes later, Clyne entered the restaurant looking flustered. I cautiously observed him scanning the scene and then sitting at a table that gave him a good eyeline to the foursome – the one I had instructed the maître d' to give him – and for me to observe him. As far as I could tell, Clyne had not spotted me.

A good hour into the lunch meeting, it looked like they were finishing up. So, I sent a message to Lucy. She spun around immediately and waved enthusiastically. It was hard to resist taking a peek at Clyne to gauge his reaction. Especially when she bounded over and gave me a big hug.

When the two clients left, I was invited over and took up a seat opposite the two women with Clyne in my sights over Lucy's shoulder. I had heard that wearing glasses helped to disguise where people were looking, such was the reflection from the glass. So, I slipped on some black-rimmed specs I had bought from a charity shop. Clyne was perfectly visible over Lucy's shoulder. She was between the two of us.

The wine flowed. Jessica was very easy on the eye and easy to chat with. She wasn't shy about topping up my glass either and to be frank I was enjoying myself. We laughed, told stories, got lost in the moment. Did I imagine that Jessica was flirting with me? More bottles arrived. I had to be careful. I wasn't on duty, but I had to keep my wits about me. Clyne was getting agitated, particularly the way he kept dismissing the waiter. He had been sitting there for some time without ordering a thing. The two women were charming, and as the drink flowed, Lee became more feminine after every sip.

"Oh shit!"

It was Lucy, checking the time. "I've got to go!"

Jessica grabbed her phone.

"Lucy's got a date," Jess smirked as she called up the Uber app.

This must be it. I noticed a change in Clyne's demeanour. He perked up when both ladies readied to go. I checked my watch – just before 5pm. Was Lucy supposed to meet Clyne soon? I let both women leave, not before Jess gave me a peck on the cheek. Then I thought why the hell not and asked for her number. *It would have been strange not to*, I justified to myself. And a lovely perk. For a moment I completely forgot about Lucy.

Then I saw Clyne get up and I clicked back in. I followed him out of the restaurant but stopped in my tracks when I saw him peering through the glass door out into the street. Beyond, Lucy and Jess were hunched over their phones. I took a seat in the lobby, far enough away to see what was happening. A few minutes later, Clyne slithered out of the door.

The cool air hit me when I exited the building, rubbing my eyes as I slipped the glasses back into my pocket. I hadn't eaten anything since breakfast and the unexpected alcohol had knocked my senses. A horn aggressively honked in the near distance, catching my attention. I noticed Clyne jogging across a pedestrian crossing, and, squinting further, I spotted Lucy and Jess dart into a pub. Clyne stopped dead still, waiting, contemplating his next move. A few minutes ticked by. A couple of lads sauntered by and ducked into the pub. Clyne followed them in before the door had a chance to shut. This was getting interesting.

***

"Well, well, well," said Tricia, blowing into a steaming takeaway coffee cup as we sat in the squad car on the high street. "It's certainly a very interesting story. Remind me, what did her colleague, Jessica, look like? I mean, you've mentioned her quite a bit." I could see the sides of her mouth curl up.

"Irrelevant," I sniffed. "The point is, it's all very dodgy, don't you think?"

"Did a crime take place?"

"No. Of course not. But…"

"Of course not," she repeated.

A car drove by and beeped its horn. We tensed ourselves for a bit of verbal. Nothing.

"Yet."

"Look, I know the history of this man." I shot her a look. "Woman. You obviously care for her. But there's nothing we can take to the Super. It's all incidental. Conjecture. Clyne would deny it."

"At least he would know we were onto him. Stop it."

My concerns for Lucy were growing. Not just with what I had seen but also the memories of university, the amount of ABH and GBHs I had had to deal with. I hadn't dealt with any stalkers but I assumed that when things don't go their way, they would turn to violence. Stalkers want to control everything. And if that control slips, panic sets in. Add into the equation Lucy's past and it could get messy.

Had Lucy told him about her past?

She had kept it a secret and probably for a very good reason. It would be hard for anyone to guess her past just by seeing her on the street and peering over her shoulder at her social media feed. Or even by going through their bins.

I had witnessed it so many times on the high streets and behind closed doors, when homosexuals were picked on for no good reason except choosing to love the same sex. Judging by Lucy's Facebook posts and demeanour, she was still hiding her past. I couldn't blame her. Many transgenders want to start their life anew as their new identity – to be accepted for who they are, not who they were – and kept it secret for as long as possible. An alpha-male banker like Nathaniel Clyne would go crazy if he found out. Or when he found out.

"Look. Why don't we swing by every now and then, huh? We aren't a million miles away and we can always blag it. I'll cover for you."

"Really?"

"Yeah, come on. Let's go in that direction and see if we spot anything suspicious."

"Thanks. It means a lot."

"You big softie."

I reached over and playfully punched her arm.

"Watch it Nicholson, I'll have you arrested for assault," she said smiling, pushing her empty coffee cup into my hand. "Here get rid of this and let's get going. Breaks over."

We cruised around the area, bypassed Clyne's house a couple of times and stopped for another cup of coffee. It was a slow day. The only person of note was an elderly woman that came out of the house next door with a scruffy terrier. The suburban high street was quiet at this time of day. We were lost in our thoughts. The radio crackled, coming into life, breaking the silence. An accident on the North Circular. Tricia switched on the blues and twos and we made a beeline to it. Traffic was snarled up as we weaved through stationary cars, vans and lorries. A cyclist had been knocked over and was receiving treatment from paramedics.

"She came out of nowhere. Stupid bloody woman." An angry man, frothing at the mouth, ran over to us before we had even stepped out of the police car.

"What was she doing coming up my blind side like that? It's not my fault."

"Ok sir calm down. We'll get to the bottom of it." Tricia was always better at dealing with the angry mob. That was our usual routine. I headed over to the paramedics, to get a view on the situation. The cyclist looked bad. Blood on the road, the bike's back tyre completely mangled, a skid mark towards the rear of the car. The paramedics had a neck brace on the victim. This was going to take some time.

When we both finished taking statements and the motorist had gone, we slipped back into the patrol car. The sky was getting darker as the sun made its pilgrimage to the west. Tricia rubbed her eyes. Wisps of hair from her tight bun had escaped, tickling her neck.

"Dinner?" she said, eyeing up my stomach.

"You heard it too?"

"I think half of London heard it, Nicholson."

"Haven't had lunch yet."

"Standard day. I saw a creperie on the high street. Let's see if it's still open."

She switched on the engine as I reached into the glove compartment where I had stored my phone. For obvious reasons you are not allowed to carry your own phone when out on the job. Apparently, it's unprofessional to be distracted by your mum ringing you to remind you that it's Auntie Val's birthday next week, and don't forget to send a card. Especially when you're trying to make an arrest.

A couple of missed calls, a few jokes going around on the lads' WhatsApp group and a text message. From Lucy.

I need your help, it read, followed by an address. *Meet me there asap.*

I recognised it immediately. I glanced at my partner. She must have noticed something. The colour draining from my face perhaps. That was enough for her. She switched on the blues and twos and put her foot down.

I stepped into the room. It took me a split second to assess the situation.

The light was off, a shadow crossed the room. The shelves in front of me were bare, except for one box file with a name on it.

Lucy.

Burnt paper and lighter fluid filled my nostrils. And the unmistakable smell of blood. I knew that smell. It's not something I can describe but when it's in the air, my nostrils detect it. The walls were white, bright white. The carpet a light colour, with splatters of blood soaking into the fibres. Her wrists and ankles had red ligature marks. Lucy's head was bent forward, like she was sleeping. Dead bodies are like that. People peacefully sleeping. Except those that had been there a while. Bloated, discoloured, stiff. Or had suffered a violent episode. Cuts, lacerations, abrasions. Like Lucy's face.

I dropped down on my knees, pulled out my knife and sliced the plastic ties off. Then I checked for a pulse. I felt it. Tricia was dealing with Clyne so I radioed for an ambulance.

Hurry.

I could see Tricia's face in my mind cringe at the unprofessional word at the end of my call-out. Lucy's face had been battered but other than that she was ok. She would heal. On the outside anyway. Internal scars take time, rarely heal. Memories, smells, people, words – they all open them up again.

When you least expect it. Lucy's gash had been ripped open, a chasm which would take years to close.

Trust is a fragile thing.

I scooped her head into my palm and squeezed her hand. Her eye winced. I wasn't sure if it was the pain or distrust.

"It's ok Lucy. Everything will be fine. Help is on its way." I kept talking, soothing, reassuring. She opened her eyes, just a crack. I think she recognised me. Her lips parted as she took a small breath.

"Shh, it's ok. Don't speak. An ambulance is coming. You're safe."

She closed her eyes. A soft smile flickered on her lips and I felt a warmth envelope us.

"Thank you," she said, in barely a whisper.

Author's Note

Thank you for reading my debut novel. We all need a bit of escapism in this crazy world and I hope that *The Opposite Sides of a Coin* gave you just that. Your time and attention are precious so I am exceptionally grateful that you've come this far.

I ask one small further favour, and that is to submit a review and help me spread the word.

Even if it's one sentence on Amazon or Goodreads or to other people in your social network, anything you do will be greatly appreciated.

As an independent and first-time author, I thrive on reviews and people sharing my work so others can find escapism and joy in reading too.

Thank you in advance.

Dominic Wong
May 2021

Acknowledgements

And then lockdown happened.

In times of uncertainty and fear grows opportunity and belief. A chance to recalibrate and understand what is important. When the world stops, you cannot help but slow down too. It afforded me the headspace to be creative again – away from the daily grind of commuting, chasing and being busy – spending time building relationships and helping others.

This novel has been in the works for a couple of years. The kernel of the idea came when I was writing on long plane journeys to Los Angeles – twelve hours of clouds, landscapes and in-flight movies drifting by. Telling a story from two points of view has interested me for a long time and I love narratives with twists: *The Sixth Sense*, *The Shawshank Redemption*, anything from Agatha Christie to name a few inspirations. Boredom with being trapped in a metal tube allowed my brain to whirr into action and I wrote many dead-end ideas, many being deleted as soon as the plane's wheels touched the ground. But the process had begun.

It was a few years after I chose to become self-employed that I started to have an idea for a story. This story. As many writers do, I struggled for a while to put all of my thoughts and strands into a cohesive narrative. And then one evening I watched the movie *Beast*, starring the impressive Jessie Buckley, and it was her character that was the key to finding Lucy and unlocking everything. I woke up at 6am the next morning with a vision for the whole plot and character development in my head. Seventy-two thousand words spilled out of me over the next eight days. I just didn't want to stop writing. Energy flowed through me and onto my laptop screen. Then when I finished, I rewrote the first part, Lucy's story, in the third person. I wanted the reader to feel as if Lucy was being watched whilst Joe's story, in the first person, makes the reader feel they are watching her. Ditto with Josh – the stalker being followed.

I am grateful to Alastair Hoare, Laura Noakes and Kathleen Whyman (read her brilliant book – *Wife Support System!*) in these early days of a first draft and being so encouraging. Your kind words and feedback inspired me to keep going.

They say after spending an intense amount of time on one novel you should leave it to rest. So, I did. But Nathan stayed in my mind and when lockdown happened, and with inspiration coming to me from volunteering at the local foodbank, I got excited again and I wrote the sequel – *The Same Sides of a Coin* – which focuses on Nathan's redemption. An extract is included in the following pages.

This impetus brought me back to The Opposite Sides of a Coin and a great deal of labour and love ensued. It probably wouldn't have seen the light of day if it wasn't for the positivity of Debbie Faulkner, Nicky Hornsby and Rachel Allen who read my subsequent drafts. I am eternally indebted to Sue Thomas (her book, *Nature and Wellbeing in the Digital Age*, will change your life!) for line editing and discussing character and plot development. Thanks also to Jamie Higham for his incessant positivity, Leanne Warren, Bernard Davis and Julie Shaw for final checks, to Karen Lloyd for designing the cover and Owen Vachell for the photo.

Words cannot do justice to the amount of thanks I need to give to my mum and dad for their unwavering love, support and guidance – through the bad times and the good – over the past forty years. I don't say it enough, but I love you both.

To Ollie and Milo – my two boys growing up to be strong-minded and creative men – you inspire me in ways I cannot express and make me proud in every little thing you both do.

And to the wonderful mother of my children. Erin is an inspiration to not just me and our kids but also to our friends and the thousands of women she works with on a daily basis. Every day for the past twenty years I have known you, I have adored you.

Let's keep dreaming.

Keep reading for an exclusive extract of the thrilling sequel

The Same Sides of a Coin

The past holds them back.
The future lies uncertain.
Only the present can set them free.

When tragedy strikes, 21-year-old Rachel travels to Tsunami-hit Thailand to find herself – whatever that means. She meets Nathan, a repented stalker on his own journey of redemption, escaping from the shackles of his past.

Jasmine, a middle-aged alcoholic, journeys to Bali as she struggles with her addiction and the death of her estranged and abusive father. She meets Pierre and Sommy, two altruistic foreigners with their own tragic histories.

As they battle with their pasts, they must decide whether their hope, fate and future lie in the hands of strangers, or themselves.

"Fast paced, believable characters and a real page turner. Absolutely loved it. Bravo!"

The Same Sides of a Coin

By Dominic Wong

Half of Rachel's face was resting on soft white sand. She could hear the calm lapping of waves in the near distance. Sunlight seemed to dance into her eyes, causing her to squint and blink. She turned her head slightly, as much as she could, looking up to the bright light. Palm tree fronds breezed in the gentle wind, like fingers waving, scattering the sun's rays. Their trunks seemed to bend over, bowing their green heads at her. Or perhaps leaning over to take a closer look. Heavy green coconuts clustered at the top, threatening to fall down on top of her.

The humidity was high, even for this time in the morning. She felt sand on her cheek, inside her ear and speckled through her light brown hair. It covered her peeling shoulders and tanned legs as well as dusting the pretty red dress with the printed yellow butterflies.

The events from the previous night still echoed around her head. She could still smell the musty odours of the fire. In front of her was the makeshift camp, where they sat every evening watching the sun set over the horizon. In a parallel universe she would be sunbathing in this paradise, letting the rays soak in her skin. Her belly would be full of fresh, tropical fruit and a handsome man would be by her side.

Just like yesterday.

It was the metal handcuffs cutting into her wrists behind her back that ruined the illusion. And the dirty blue handkerchief stuck in her mouth. She could taste the salty sweat of its owner. Her shoulders were strained back by the tightness of the cuffs and her red dress had ridden up to her thighs.

Beyond the campfire sat Nathan, on the dry soil against the base of a thin-trunked palm. He was looking intently at her, as if his eyes were trying to burrow into her head; his face twisted in horror and fright. He wanted to say something but words seemed to get caught in his throat.

It was all her fault, of course. She was the reason she was in this predicament. This was what He had in store for her. It was her punishment for her own stupidity. The vicar's face came into her mind. She thought she had passed enough of His tests but maybe this was one more. Her body relaxed into surrender.

Let's get this over with and move on. Like everything else.

Another scar to heal.

Nathan shifted, as if sensing her change.

Tears started to cascade from her eyes on to the sand. She stifled a sob. She didn't want a sound to escape her lips.

Then Nathan looked up and started speaking. Strength grew with every word.

At last. Here it was.

God's Will.

Chapter One

"God I'm bored," Rachel complained out loud to no-one in particular as she picked her way through overgrown vines and centuries-old sandstone bricks. Behind her, a thin girl with straggly blonde hair and dark roots, not much younger thn her, stopped in surprise. Rachel looked back at the stranger, letting the tour guide carry on through the dense trees.

"How can you be bored?" She scoffed in a clipped English accent. "This is one of THE hidden treasures in Cambodia – in the World even. I mean it's a UNESCO World Heritage Site!" Rachel glanced around at the dilapidated temple, undergrowth and leaves; as far as she could see, thick creepers snaked their way up into the dark green canopy. It seemed like they were enveloping the ancient carvings and structures to keep it a secret away from prying eyes. Rachel guessed the girl hadn't even heard of UNESCO before she had picked up a guidebook. The girl huffed past, almost nudging her shoulder on the tight path. Rachel turned and followed her, sighing.

Trudging along the single file track she watched the girl's pink sarong dance around her legs. Rachel could see her toned slender legs through the light material reaching up to exceptionally tight shorts. An orange and blue pashmina draped over her shoulders and torso, attempting to hide a tiny vest-top hugging her slim waist.

No love-handles on her, Rachel thought. No lumps, bumps or scars. A magnet for her fellow, horny backpackers.

"Where are you from?" Rachel called after her, trying to make conversation and appear friendly. The girl turned her head slightly.

"England."

Rachel sighed.

"Yeah, I know that. I mean whereabouts."

"Oh," she replied, taken aback at the spikiness of the comment. "Guildford. In Surrey." She turned her head back, hiding her grimace and quickened her pace. Rachel took the cue, held back and passed another ruined shrine trying to hide from the outside world. She wasn't bothered about carrying on the conversation either.

Besides, she had already made a decision.

By now she had met so many gap year teenagers from the home counties, visited more temples than she could count, sat on enough cramped and uncomfortable buses for hours on end and encountered so many pristine beaches and picture-postcard sunsets that they had all become monotonous.

It was time for a change.

Just over two months ago, she had packed her brand-new backpack and set off for the Banana Pancake Trail which stretched across most of South-East Asia. Scores of backpackers had helped guide her through the popular and well-trodden routes, swapping stories, routes and places to avoid. Starting in the bustling high-rises of Hong Kong which she quickly left to avoid the scammers and the uncomfortable heat to travel along the 55-kilometre sea bridge to Macau. There, she stayed a couple of nights and ticked off the sights – even being persuaded to jump off the Macau Tower on a bungee by a charming South African lad. But its gaudy buildings and neon casino lights made the countryside even more enticing.

Wanting to get out of the city as quickly as possible, she woke up early on the third day and made a beeline to the train station. Using a combination of clean trains and cramped buses she snaked her way to Vietnam through lush rainforest scenery, past paddy fields as far as the eye could see and over numerous bridges; the sludgy and polluted rivers underneath emptying out into the South China Sea. The further she got from Hong Kong, the poorer the countries became. Hostels became dirtier, her appetite diminished and the air seemed heavier.

Homesickness was creeping in.

She took a five-day escorted 'jungle safari' with a bunch of young, eager backpackers to Laos to tick another country off the list before heading down the east coast of Vietnam, mixing scooters and rickety buses to Ho Chi Minh City. Again, to get away from the concrete, noise and con artists, she escaped the bustling city as soon as she could, catching a bus north west into Cambodia.

The journeys, landscapes and people she met blurred into one. Not one for adventure that was *too* extreme or isolating, she sought out the major tourist points along the way to snap a photo to prove she had been there, found internet cafes to update her blog, shacked up in unclean, hot hostels and ate in restaurants that sold local delicacies catered to western tastes. She kept reminding herself she was away from the pain of home and out in the raw world – even if that world consisted of mainly talking to European and American travellers; the occasional Asian when the need for local services transpired.

She had met a lot of backpackers like her – young women with braided, unwashed hair and tie-dyed tops; guys with fabric wristbands and long, unkempt hair – seeking new experiences and diverse friends, hearing of and discovering new places to explore and parties to find. All the while smoking pot. Lots of pot. Their names and faces became indistinct from each other. Sometimes it took a few hours for her to realise that she had actually met them before in some other God-awful bed and breakfast or on some other rip-off excursion.

Approaching people came easy to her and she had encountered many people along the way. She wasn't shy or afraid to start speaking to a total stranger – as long as they didn't look too threatening, drunk or high. In fact, pretty much every step of her journey she had had a companion – either joining in a group or someone else that was travelling alone. The thought of eating alone in a café terrified her. She would latch on to other people as soon as she could and went with their flow, allowing them to direct her route and to comfort her when tears flowed. Even on the long flight from Heathrow she had chatted to a businessman sitting next to her. She had enjoyed his company – not so much the connection but the feeling of belonging and safety. A common ground.

It was in some dead-end, backpacker's hostel in Cambodia, twenty-odd miles from Angkor Wat, where her journey took a turn of direction. The sun had just dropped over the green tree-tops, casting purple and dark reds on to whispery clouds above, as she arrived in a rattly bus from Ho Chi Minh City. Exhausted from the eight-hour journey, she went to the back of her allotted room, in between three rows of bunkbeds and slung her backpack on to the top bunk furthest away. She climbed up and rested her head on the paper-thin pillow, stretching out as much as the bed would allow. Bright, florescent lights hummed overhead.

Before long, young groups of travellers noisily entered the room, chatting loudly about the ancient temple they had just returned from. Rachel turned and faced the wall, feigning sleep.

"It was just so spiritual," a female voice said. American. Rachel imagined from her voice what she looked like from the dozens of young women she had met.

"Yeah man. So enlightening," said a male voice.

She heard the squeaking metal of the bedframes as the group sat down. Then the pops of the top of beer bottles being opened, followed by the clicking of lighters. A waft of weed danced over her.

Yo, Harry, where you going next dude?" A South African voice.

"Gonna head down to Tonle Sap, check out the fish market." Rachel assumed that was Harry's voice. It was from the North of England.

"Oh, I went there just before here." The American girl again; something about the sound of her voice was familiar. "Check out the floating village. It's awesome."

"Better than the one in Bangkok?" said the Harry voice; young and innocent.

"Are you kidding me? That one is *so* touristy." Rachel could picture her face screwing up. "This one is *so* authentic. *All* the locals go there."

Rachel was sick of backpacker's thinking they've stumbled on something untouched. Every path had been beaten, trodden, written about and a t-shirt made. In fact, one Swedish girl had said to her as she twirled her blonde hair with one hand and held a can of Angkor beer in the other: *if it isn't in the guidebooks, then it probably isn't worth seeing.* It made Rachel's blood boil.

"Where you heading to anyway," the American girl said.

"Gonna head up the East coast, get up to Hong Kong." That was the route Rachel had just been along.

"Nice. Honkers is bonkers man. We've just come down that way."

"Sweet," he replied. "Any tips?"

"Yeah, go to that fish market in 'Nam. Hey, babes, what's the name of that fish market?"

Rachel heard the bed creak again as someone sat up.

"Which one? We've been to so many," a male Aussie voice replied.

"You know, the one where that girl cried when the fisherman whacked the fish on its head."

"Oh yeah. Haha! She vomited on a woman's foot and ran away."

Rachel stiffened.

"She was bloody fuming!"

Rachel remembered the fish market in central Vietnam: a blood-stained trader battered the head of a barracuda, wiping out its life in one swift blow that caused Rachel to chunder and tremble in anguish. Were they talking about her?

"Poor girl!"

"Poor girl? Poor nothing. She wanted to go there. In fact, she hung around us all the time. Couldn't get rid of her. Robbie thought she had the hots for him."

Robbie? She remembered that name. South African. He had a girlfriend called Madison; an American. A tightness came across her chest.

"Yeah, couldn't get rid of her. You remember when she just started crying at the Bon Om Touk?"

"Yeah. Just, like, uncontrollably crying. Outta nowhere," she sniggered. "She's got some serious issues."

The Bon Om Touk festival was only a few days ago. A legless toddler had been swaddled in the arms of his rocking mother, hand outstretched for spare coins as hordes of people ignored them. Rachel couldn't stop staring at them. Robbie and Madison were shouting at her as the crowds got thicker. She could feel the tears filling up in her eyes. Jules was so kind, sitting with her, soothing.

"We managed to lose her though," Robbie said. "Maddy —

Shit, it is them.

" – told her to go back to the hostel, bloody cry-baby. We had a great time after that. Those boat races were incredible."

Rachel felt her eyes redden. It was like being back at school, people slagging her off behind her back. But this time she was there, in the same room, hearing every word.

Her mind went back to that poor woman begging within the crowds. She thought back to other events along her journey that had made her cry.

Was she that bad?

The time at some crappy hostel in Ho Chi Minh she had witnessed a girl fall off the top bunk and land on her neck on the tiled floor, her body convulsed whilst her boyfriend screamed at her to get help; but Rachel had been paralysed with fear and rooted to the spot.

She had been in shock.

And on a junk boat tour of Halong Bay, she had seen a drunk guy noisily dive off one of the hundreds of jagged limestone islands towering above the blue-green sea on to a snorkeler below, cracking the unsuspecting swimmer's spine in three places. Her screams had bounced against the rainforest-topped islands, whilst fisherman dived in to help.

That crunching sound was horrific.

Bad luck seemed to follow her wherever she went.

It's all part of life's experience, Rachel kept telling herself when bad things happened. *God's Will.*

It was true. She did cry a lot. Sometimes spontaneously, sometimes triggered by something she had seen, jolting her memory back.

On every step of the journey there had been someone there to put an arm around her, to sit with her until the shakes subsided. To comfort and digest every moment. The way Madison and Robbie were talking though, it was tedious – ruining their enjoyment. They obviously didn't want to hang out with someone with so much emotional baggage.

It was taking its toll on her enjoyment too. The colours seemed less vibrant; the food no longer appealed. She would've murdered a McDonalds if she found one. Besides, the opening conversations were starting to tire her now – Where are you from? Where have you been? Where are you going? Did you go to such-a-such a place?

Traveller's fatigue, a friendly Australian girl said to her one evening over a steaming plate of noodles.

"Oh yeah, and do you know what else?" Madison said, bringing Rachel back to the present.

"This made me cringe every time I saw it. She had one of those stupid plastic braid things in her hair." The group all tittered. Rachel could feel their eyes roll as she fingered the cheap plastic at the back of her head. Her ears were red hot in embarrassment. She tried to pull it, hoping it would slip out.

"Sounds like a bloody a nightmare." It was Harry again.

"And she's always fucking moaning. It's too hot, it's too cold, it smells," Madison said, mimicking her with a fake, high voice.

"If she hates it so much, go home, "Robbie sniffed, nonchalantly. "The silly little bitch." His comment elicited laughter among the group.

Tears formed in Rachel's eyes. Maybe she should go home. Get away from these idiots and get her mojo back.

No.

To go back now meant she would never return. She would slip onto the conveyor belt of normality. Besides, a nagging feeling kept rising in her chest that wouldn't go away.

The feeling that she was traversing a well-worn road. Crappy hostels and bed & breakfasts (all with WIFI and English-translated menus) filled with middle-class youngsters pretending to be slumming it on a budget when safety, money and a consulate where never far away. Most of them had smart phones anyway. Even on the remotest of beaches or on a mountain top temple, a message alert would break the ethereal atmosphere.

A sanitised adventure.

It was far too safe. If she was to heal, she needed to get away from these clowns for a start. Madison was right though. The hair braid had been an impulse buy to blend into the backpacking tribe. She felt like a fraud. This look wasn't her. This whole experience wasn't her. She had merged into the backpacker status quo far too quickly and the fakery was pushing against her. Even though she was a couple of years older than these teenagers, she *felt* so much older than them.

"And what's with her clothes?" Jules started up again. Rachel tensed, waiting for another verbal hit.

"What do you mean?"

"Well, she's always covering herself up. It's so damn hot here."

"Not everyone's got a bod like you Maddy."

"It's not that," Madison said, brushing away the compliment. "Everyone, like literally everyone, wears shorts. And t-shirts."

"Yeah…" said Robbie. Rachel heard the bed frame shift again as the slap of feet hit the ceramic floor. She could picture him leaning forward.

"There was this time," he almost whispered. The rustle of the mattresses suggested the others were leaning in too. "We were all swimming in this lake. God, where was it? Anyway, doesn't matter. Beautiful place. Mountains all around us. Secluded. All of us were stripped down. Loving it. We were egging her on. Telling her to get in too. Then, she wades in. Fully clothed!"

Madison sniggered loudly.

Rachel swung her feet off the top bunk and landed with a thud.

"Sounds like a nutter to me," Harry retorted, as four faces turned towards her. Two looked in horror as Rachel ran past them, tears streaking down her face.

"Oh shit!" Madison said, her eyes wide open.

"Don't tell me that was her," Harry said leaning back, taking a drag of a spliff. "Classic!"

Rachel burst out of the hostel into the humid air. Sweat immediately prickled her skin. She ran down the road, into the darkness, away from the building. Madison was calling out to her as she ran off the road into the dense foliage, tripping and stumbling, before sitting on a fallen trunk, hidden in the undergrowth. She put her head in her hands and sobbed.

She needed to get away. Choose a different route. Away from the sanitised backpacking path. Forget who she was and define who she will be. To set her place in the world.

To find herself.

Whatever that meant.

She didn't want to be like them because she wasn't one of them. Madison was like every other eighteen-year-old girl she had met along the way; boob tubes showing off their tight tummies, or wearing skimpy two-piece bikinis splashing in the waves, getting the attention of the toned, hot guys. She couldn't compete with them. There was no way she'd be wearing a crop top any time soon, not with her stretchmarks. Although she wasn't that much older than them, she certainly was more mature in experience.

The death of her baby was always going to age her quicker than others.

About the Author

Dominic Wong is a multi-award-winning marketeer in the theme park and visitor attractions industry. He was the first marketing director at Warner Bros. Studio Tour London – The Making of Harry Potter, as well as Warner Bros. Studio Tour Hollywood and Warner Bros. World Abu Dhabi.

He has created and launched his own innovative tourism products, including a comedy dining theatre production, and advises a number of high-profile attractions with their marketing strategies across the globe.

He lives by the sea in Bournemouth, on the south coast of England, with his wife, two sons and cocker spaniel.

www.DominicWongBooks.co.uk

Printed in Great Britain
by Amazon

61467305R00172